SHE-DEVIL

SKYE CALLAHAN

VINCI
BOOKS

By Skye Callahan

Sins of Ashville

Irrevocable

Unbreakable

Insurmountable

She-Devil

Redline

Ignition

Torque

Brake

Exhaust

Clutch

p155 her
p249 'course'
p251 'you'
'stare'

p256 'step'
'reach'
p268 'beg'
p274 'as'
p283 'hail'

Vinci Books

vinci-books.com

Published by Vinci Books Ltd in 2025

1

A CIP catalogue record for this book is available from the British Library.
Paperback ISBN: 9781036701833

Printed and bound in Great Britain by Clays Ltd, Elcograf S.p.A.

Chapter One

GONNA GET MINE

Brooke

One day, when they least expect it, I'm going to make them all pay.

I barged into the loft office overlooking the biker hangout below, closing the door behind me with a resounding thud. Sawyer, the President of Devils of Ashville MC, stared down at the notebook on his oversized, engraved desk refusing to raise his head to acknowledge my ruckus.

I marched toward his desk, planting my hands on either side of the notebook full of his chicken scratches. "I want to go on the run."

Sawyer raised his left hand and waved me off, but I refused to move. "I've earned it. I'm as qualified as anyone here."

If not more. For the last ten years, I'd worked twice as hard as any man here to earn my place in the club for half the respect. And although I didn't really care about the run

1

up to Utica, if I didn't demand to be included in club business, Sawyer would happily leave me in my office downstairs, processing alcohol shipments and ordering pretzels. I'd fought for my position as Club Treasurer, and as a fucking officer, I insisted to be treated as such.

Sawyer expected this run to be pivotal in consolidating our power over the local drug networks since one of our biggest allies and rivals, the Gold Family recently destroyed themselves like a stressed-out snake turning to cannibalism. I didn't give a damn about the external politics of it all. Didn't give a damn what people chose to pollute their bodies with or the quantity or quality of said pollution, but as the only patch-wearing officer without a dick—I grew tired of being the last to know and least likely to be included in club business.

"Why can't you just settle down and become a good Ol' Lady?" That was Sawyer's only concern. We all knew he'd only been humoring me and trying to relieve the thorn I'd plunged in his side when he finally agreed to let me join the boy's club. There were two types of women in my world, Mamas or Ol' Ladies. As the daughter of the Club's President, I was expected to conform to those misogynistic ideologies, but neither of those revolting titles were the least bit appealing to me.

I held a growl deep in my chest. Men could get away with violence. They could yell. Throw things. Flip tables. Hell, it was expected of them, and it all sounded rather appealing, but female violence was "unhinged," "hormonal," and made me a liability. No one ever said making it in the boy's club would be easy. Where they relied on violence, I wielded restraint. Quiet, conniving, and well-hewn restraint.

Sawyer continued to write in his ledger, his personal

hall-of-fame for fucked up deeds. "Vin has been asking about you."

Gavin. I shuddered at the thought of him and tasted a rancid acid in the back of my mouth that reminded me of his cologne.

Spook, Vin, Dodger, Bull; they all asked about me because they saw me as a power move. Not because they liked me—most couldn't stand me, and I gave them a good reason for it. Gavin was the worst of the bunch, giving into entitlement and throwing his power around from the moment he became Sergeant-at-Arms. He and his crew only cared that by topping me, they might win Sawyer's favor and take my position as Treasurer.

I cleared my throat. When I wasn't doing exactly what Sawyer wanted, he preferred to ignore my existence, but I wasn't walking away from this.

Finally, he looked up. "I have a meeting at one. Caine is bringing in our new Prospect."

His eyes narrowed on me, knowing how much I hated hang-rounds and Prospects. I suspected part of him also hoped that some new guy would show up who could finally put me in my place for good.

"Maybe you've seen him around Bone Grinders the last several weeks. Cannon says he's been real useful."

The heat of anger climbed up in my throat as I studied Sawyer's expression. I plastered a sardonic smile on my face. "Is *he* going on the run?"

Sawyer didn't answer, but the deadpan look he gave me was answer enough.

"You're bringing in a fucking Prospect to do a run when you have someone perfectly capable standing right in front of you? I did earn this patch." I leaned over his desk, pointing at the Treasurer patch on my cut. Sure, I could run all of the club accounts above and below the table while managing our hangout, The Pit, but no one cared about that. No one cared about all the time I spent keeping the heat off our activities. The state of my genitals meant far more than my rank. They'd all prefer me to lie on my back and let a man with a quarter of the knowledge, an eighth of the intuition, a sixteenth of the experience, and one-hundred percent testosterone take my position.

Sawyer let out a long breath and picked up his pen again. Since I was fourteen, I'd been a cog in his master plan to expand his gang beyond the borders of Devil's Point. A bargaining chip. A distraction while he clawed his way into new deals and took out the competition. That was the only worth a daughter held in my world. Sawyer thought he could beat me down, steal my power and force me to comply, but he only taught me how to use sex to get what I wanted.

The urge to flip his desk over on top of him grew, but our private conversation was cut short when the door to the stairwell opened and two men stepped in. I straightened, standing next to Sawyer with my arms crossed over my chest. Caine glanced at me, the same quick, passing glance we always shared when trapped in the same room, before setting his gaze on Sawyer.

Caine had been around as long as I could remember. We'd grown up together. Me; Caine; his wife, Thea; and my brother, Dixon. My dead brother. Caine was a few years older than me, but at least six inches shorter—more when I wore heels. Of all the people here, he'd once been my friend. That changed shortly after we buried what was left of Dixon's body three years ago. Now, everything between us centered around these awkward and frequent encounters.

His companion's eyes lingered on me and I waited for

his initial reaction. Typically, they fell into two categories: the smirk at the laughable idea of a female officer, or a lusty-eyed stare that completely dismissed my rank. But he kept a straight face, letting nothing slip by.

"You're early," Sawyer said with a ragged, clipped tone. No, he wasn't a man of punctuality, but he'd use any tool available to make sure the person standing across from him remained at a disadvantage.

Caine fidgeted, looking at his watch. "We can wait until you're done. I had one and didn't want to be late."

"It's twelve fifty-seven," Sawyer said, eyeing me, but I didn't move. If he fought me and I dug in, I'd make him look the fool, and he knew it. Sure, he'd eventually win and get his way, but he wouldn't want to give the new guy any ideas that he had trouble controlling his officers. I had learned a few of his tricks.

With another glare, Sawyer pushed away the papers in front of him and sat back in his chair. "Trent, right?"

We got hang-arounds like other people got stray cats. Usually they came and went when things didn't happen on their timetable. But Trent had been working steady in the garage—on our above the board work—for a couple of months. Mainly a gopher, but I'd heard Cannon bragging about his work over drinks in the bar.

I tried not to pay more attention than that to any man who showed up—most of the wannabes were worse than the patches. A girl with a patch caught their eye and suddenly they thought, *one fuck and I'm in.*

But now this name on payroll became a real threat. Competition. It was a sad and pathetic statement on my position in life when a patch-wearing officer had to look at a Prospect as competition.

Prospect stepped forward with a nod but stayed silent.

Caine had obviously instructed him to answer questions and nothing more. His dirty blond hair was pulled back into a stub of a ponytail, and he held Sawyer's gaze with his golden-green eyes. He wore a thin black hoodie with the sleeves ripped off and my gaze moved down to his bare arms.

Bare wasn't a just description when nearly every inch of skin was covered in ink from his knuckles to his shoulders. Sharp lines. Patches of color. Smooth details that joined each image in utter perfection. I followed the designs back up to his shoulders and noticed fragments above the V-collar of his shirt, stretching up his neck.

So many details.

I wasn't a fan of men—or people in general—but I could stare at a good tattoo for hours. Apparently, some people do that in art galleries, but it's not the same. Tattoos are intimate, living manifestations of a person etched into their skin. Love. Lust. Desire. Our deepest yearnings and fears revealed, even if neither the wearer nor observer fully understood the meaning of every detail.

My largest piece of art was still in progress. Soon, it would cover my back and wrap around my ribs. I itched for more. Especially standing there staring at his pieces.

Tattoos are better than sex.

I wondered how many more tattoos he might have hidden away, but questions and thoughts like that were bound to be misunderstood, interpreted as an ulterior motive to inquire about other things. And if I didn't stop staring, someone would notice.

I wrestled my attention back to Sawyer. He'd been quiet far too long, leaving me to wonder what he was thinking. That was a doorway into lunacy I wanted to avoid.

Is he suspicious?

We were all suspicious of newcomers, but Sawyer... Some days I'd call him paranoid. Reckless the next. Careless the following. And sometimes it changed hour-by-hour or minute-by-minute. That was one of the ways he maintained his power and authority—always being unpredictable and turbulent.

What is he plotting?

Caine shifted his gaze, first to me, then to his friend before Sawyer finally relented. "Who have you ridden with?"

Trent's stare didn't waver. "My uncle taught me to ride before...." He glanced down. "He was with the Brothers of the Wheel until they dissolved."

"Dissolved?" Sawyer laughed. "What a political way of putting it." He lowered his tone. "They were slaughtered, worse yet, it was someone on the inside."

Trent grimaced. "I've been laying low. Hard to move on when there's no one to trust and no family to fall back on. My uncle always wanted me to join BOW, and working in the shop with Caine and Cannon has given me a piece of that brotherhood he always spoke of. Ignited my hunger for more."

He was good. So good, I almost puked. Somewhat believable, but no one around here said what they meant. Laying out all your cards was always a bad idea. If you didn't keep secrets close to the vest, first you lost your edge, then your life.

Always have a backup weapon. Never lie to a brother, but guard your secrets, and equally important, guard everyone else's. I excelled at the secrets game, after all, that's the only way I managed to get a patch in this male-dominated circus.

"Well, Trent, are you up for a run?" Sawyer asked. His voice lost that grating, barking tone.

My eyebrows shot upward. *Mother fucking incredulous jackass.* From the look on his face, I guessed he made the offer just to screw with me. But I couldn't believe the rat bastard would choose a Prospect over me for such an important run.

Then again, I could believe it. Not like it was anything new.

I had to bite my tongue. *Pick your battles*, I reminded myself. *Choose the situation and audience with care or the punishment will be far worse.* I had to carefully balance what I intended to gain with what I would certainly lose, and this battle wasn't worth it.

One day.

One day...

"Yes, sir." Trent smirked. "Anything you need."

Too eager. I would make this Prospect's life a living hell. Much as I enjoyed admiring his ink, I swore that one day I'd rip out his tongue and wipe that look off his face with it.

"Brooke," Sawyer barked my name, and I jumped, losing my thoughts. He turned to me, and I didn't trust a bit of that glint in his eye. Then, he glanced back to Trent. "Prospect, this is my daughter. You'll take a little trip up to the Salt Grove and follow her lead."

What? I straightened. *Just the two of us? What is he planning?*

Oh, I had a feeling I knew what he had planned, and my stomach turned over on itself.

"He can't be running around like that." Sawyer gestured toward Trent. "Get him a leather out of the storage room."

Sawyer flicked his wrist for Caine and the Prospect to leave, and after they stepped out, he turned to me. "Lonnie owes me. Make sure he hasn't forgotten. Either get me pictures or cash."

Pictures? "You want me to break his legs?"

"You want me to treat you like one of the boys, so I don't suggest complaining," he said flippantly. "None of them would have a problem with turning to violence. In fact—"

"Yeah, I know. Enjoy inflicting the pain, but I suspect there's more to this."

Sawyer cocked his head, turning one eyebrow up in apparent amusement. "Ah, yes. Initiate the Prospect. Get inside his head and find out his secrets."

He nonchalantly returned to his work as if I was his personal secretary and he'd just asked for a cup of coffee. But it all made sense. I stood there, shaking my head. No matter what I did or the number of times I bailed out my so-called father or so-called brothers, my usefulness in his eyes came down to one thing. "That's the reason you're not sending him with one of the boys? Of course, you wouldn't ask one of them to do that."

"We all have strengths and skills," he mumbled. "It just so happens that your unique contribution to this club is between your legs."

Damn you. It was the only thing I wanted to say, but even those words weren't strong enough. I bit the inside of my cheek as my breathing became more ragged with each passing second that I shared air with that rancid man.

"And besides...." he continued, but I already wanted to vomit on his face. "Even if I did ask one of the boys to fuck someone—and let's face it, I have—they don't complain."

My lips curled, but I fought down the retort begging to break free. *Right, because you're god in this twisted world.* He didn't have to mention that one of those times he'd asked the boys to fuck someone, that someone had been his own daughter. He and I knew that, for the most part, he gave the boys license to do exactly as they wanted.

"Lonnie's wife will be home from work in two hours, so you're running out of time. Deliver the wake-up call. Then, how you handle Trent is up to you."

"Want me to take a picture of that, too?" I snapped. It was a stupid move.

I heard the pen in Sawyer's hand creak with increased pressure and inwardly shrank back. I wouldn't let him see me cower though. He expected this club to break me, but I refused to bow down. Not after everything I'd risked getting this far. The first time I told him I wanted to join, he laughed. The second time, when I'd actually done my homework and brought him information I knew he'd been trying to get his hands on for months, he beat the shit out of me. The third time, when I dared to mention my demands in front of the other members of the club, he let them deal out the blows. He thought I'd crash and burn within the first year, but the thought of one day hurting them more than they could ever hurt me kept me going.

"You wanted this. You wanted to be a part of this world, and yet, every damn time"—he slammed his hands against the table and pushed his chair back with a skin-crawling screech—"maybe you're not cut out for this life, given your inability to follow orders."

One time Sawyer didn't treat me any differently from the boys was when angry fists were flying.

"Got it," I said dryly, choosing not to push my luck too far in one day. It wasn't the run I wanted, but damned if I could turn it down.

Fuck someone over, then fuck the new guy. It was simple enough. Or so I thought.

Chapter Two

DEVIL WITHOUT A CUT

Trent

I WAS in over my head. Over the head of anyone involved in this shanty operation, which was becoming larger and more complex at every turn.

We'd all dreamed of finally bringing justice to the rogue motorcycle gang, but my assignment didn't start out that ambitious. Over the last few months, a series of fentanyl overdoses linked to rape cases in Ashville had gotten a little too close to home, taking the life of a fellow detective who'd been investigating the case. Then, a tip led me to Bone Grinders, a repair shop on the outskirts of Ashville known as The Point, or more locally, Devil's Point. A place cops and well-informed citizens avoided at all costs because it was the territory of the Devils of Ashville Motorcycle Club. I didn't imagine their acronym was DOA by chance.

The Club was a rising threat to the area, a tight-knit community with a well-established foundation, and they didn't even try to hide their involvement in drugs, guns, murder, or robbery. They didn't have to. And despite all that, the authorities had yet to catch a break that would shake the club to its core.

The club navigated the legal minefield as if they had detailed maps of every plan the police in the district came up with, raising suspicions that they had hooks in someone on the inside. Someone who gave them enough info to change their plans at the last minute and outmaneuver officers at every turn. Chief Lewis and Captain Ainsley then decided to bring in someone from another district—me—to get eyes on the ground. Few enough of the local police would know me on sight, and it helped that I looked more like a biker than a detective. The list of those who knew about this rogue operation was short; the chief and Captain Ainsley, as well as my captain, my partner, and Officer Ryan Corell, who was acting in my place as James's partner during my temporary reassignment. Which left me with few options if I needed backup.

I had only intended to hang around the shop long enough to find out if someone from the group was involved in the overdoses and catch the cop who might be feeding them information. But I stumbled into something deeper when Cannon, the Club's VP, offered me a job at the shop. Half of the workers were heavy drinkers and addicts: meth, heroin, coke. And there was plenty to go around. Others had only the slightest competence in repairing a bike. They were only around to collect a paycheck. Cannon and his son-in-law, Caine, were the only ones who seemed to have the slightest clue what they were doing. And in truth, they were good mechanics, and with my lifetime of tinkering and rebuilding nearly every type of vehicle, they were eager for me to step in and help.

Chief Lewis agreed to let me continue and made the necessary arrangements for the infiltration. The opportunity was too good—even though we didn't have the resources for a full undercover investigation, that's what it had turned into. We were already in unprecedented territory with the club.

With the official job offer, came the necessity of cementing my undercover identity. A new ID, bank account, shitty apartment—whatever I could get my hands on. The connections that James and I had made when he was under at The Retreat helped, but we were still working with a skeletal framework.

I don't know what our knack for getting close with the bad guys says about me or James, but here I was, one run away from official Prospect with the Devils of Ashville Motorcycle Club. Everyone in this part of town would soon see me as a Devil. An unpredictable outlaw with the temper of lit pine pitch.

I trailed behind Caine as we descended the stairs from Sawyer's office to the bar below. The Devil's hangout was located in a refurbished opera house of all places. When the steel industry moved away from The Point, the area wealth took a nosedive. The void left the perfect opportunity for groups like the Devils to take hold, grow, and prosper.

From the bar, Caine led me through a side door marked **MEMBERS ONLY** and into a smoky room where the club usually gathered for church. The long wooden table in the center of the room was lined with guns and ammunition, so I assumed the men present were gearing up for something serious.

"Guys." Caine tipped his head to the crowd of men gathered around. "This is Trent from the shop."

One guy snorted. "Looks like you took a wrong turn."

Another stepped out of the corner, cracking his knuckles. He was round and bushy like a Biker Santa, and as I recalled his name was Fitch, Caine's father. Also known to the club as The Wise One. He and Sawyer would play a large role in my continued association with the club—or my demise if I fucked this up.

"Used to be with the Brotherhood, right?" Fitch asked.

"Nothing official. My uncle rode with them. I was too young to join up."

"Uncle have a name?" another asked. I knew him as Gavin—or "Vin" among his friends. He frequented the shop to do—well, fuck up would be a more appropriate term—his own repairs, and usually ignored my presence entirely. His black, curly hair was slicked back and clung to the sides of his head so tightly it looked like a tacky, faux mullet.

"Vic 'Hawg' Clevenger." A real member of the Brotherhood. Although he'd died about twenty years earlier when the members of the club turned against each other, leading to a string of murders and violence.

"Hawg?" Fitch's eyes narrowed. "Whatever happened to that Softail of his?"

A subtle and carefully laid trap. "Didn't know he ever had one. He loved his custom Wide Glide though."

Fitch didn't respond. He merely leaned back into his corner and took a long drag from his cigarette.

The others, however, weren't so easily appeased.

"You must've made some deal with the Devil to escape that mess," Gavin said.

"He's a brother looking for a new home," Caine interrupted. He sounded forceful but wore his tension in shifting his weight from foot to foot. I'd seen it enough times to know.

"Not our brother yet," Gavin said.

I had to walk a treacherous fine line. Too much of a pushover and they'd never respect me or take me seriously, bit if I overstepped the bounds too much, the results would be just as bad. I cocked my head. "Then, why am I doing a job for the club? Does Sawyer not trust you assholes any more than a stranger off the streets?"

I knew that comment would tick them all off, but I chose to get it over with. I had to be brash, cocky, and confident, goading them into making the first move.

A man to my right charged toward me, throwing a punch, but I ducked and elbowed him in the gut. In standing my ground, I chose each maneuver carefully to keep the damage minimal. "I'm not here to cause trouble in the club."

The next attacker's punch came at me low, so I stepped aside and kicked out his knees, bringing my elbow down against the back of his neck as he stumbled.

The first man swung at me again, his fist connected with my jaw, but I grabbed his forearm and twisted until he went to his knees as well. "Is this necessary?"

"The Wheel fell because they trusted the wrong person," Fitch said, still puffing his cigarette lazily in the corner. "You understand our concern."

"Concern?" I stepped back as both men who'd attacked me straightened. "Looks a lot like animosity to me."

An arm tightened around my neck blocking my airway while the first two threw an additional punch each.

"Boys." A female voice filled the room. "If you can stop playing, we have work to do."

"Well, get to it, Mama," the man with his arm around my neck said—I then recognized his voice as Gavin.

"You're holding up my—" I watched her jaw pulse.

"Trent is with me tonight. We have a long ride to the Grove. Not to mention, you have your own run to get ready for, so fuck off and don't hold me up."

The arm around my neck loosened, but they weren't about to take orders from a woman, even if she did outrank most of the men in the room. Their reluctance was written all over their condescending scowls and wide stances. Instead, everyone in the room looked to Gavin, who suddenly released me and shoved me forward.

Before I could regain my balance, Brooke punched me in the shoulder blade. "Move, Prospect."

No one ever said this experience would be pleasant.

She directed me to a large walk-in closet at the back of a room, jerked a coat off the wall, and chucked it at me.

"It's not going to fit," I said. It was far too straight and narrow and would never fit over my shoulders.

She gave me a flat look. "Slim pickens 'round here, it seems."

But from where I stood, there seemed to be several options. "You want me to rip the arms out?"

Her lips turned white and a deep growl rumbled in her chest. "Do it, and I'll rip yours off."

The other guys didn't seem to fear her, but from where I stood, she had more than an ounce of intimidation in that small frame. Her leather jacket and dark jeans were fitted to her tall, athletic figure, and her hair cascaded down her back with a slight wave as if she'd had it tied up. The right side of her head was shaved, a harshness mirrored in her choice of makeup.

I put my arm through the sleeve to demonstrate. "Ain't happenin,' honey."

She ripped it out of my hands and jerked me forward by

the collar of my shirt. "Get this, Prospect, I'm neither yours no anyone's honey, baby, Ol' woman, sugar, or darling. I'm the Club Treasurer and I didn't get my patch through some honorary bullshit. Try that shit on me again and you'll lose more than your manhood."

Goddamn. I held my hands in the air. "All I'm asking for is a leather that fits. I have to be able to move."

I reached past her for another coat that looked to be about my size, but Brooke knocked my hand away. "Not. That. One."

"You're damn fussy about a piece of dead cow skin."

With a growl, she ripped another off the hook and chucked it at me. This one looked like it'd fit Fitch if he gained forty pounds.

"Are you serious right now?" I had expected a hard time, but this was downright petty.

Caine opened the door, joining us in the tight space. He scratched the hair at his temple—another of his tells. "What's—?"

"Fuck off, Caine. I'm picking up where you obviously failed."

"Really?" He eyed the coat in my hand and groaned. Then, he yanked down the coat Brooke had gotten all fussy over and handed it to me.

Brooke huffed and stormed out.

"What the fuck?" I asked, keeping my voice low so only he could hear.

Caine stared at the door. "Looks like Sawyer has decided to throw you to the rabid wolf."

"Not exactly the answer I was looking for." I shrugged on the jacket, pulling the hood of my shirt over the collar.

He squinted at me over his shoulder. "That leather

17

belonged to her brother. He disrespected the club and was stripped of it three years ago."

My stomach flipped with the not-so-subtle affirmation that this was going to be a shit day.

Maybe I should've just accepted the over-sized throw-rug for a jacket.

Chapter Three

DEVIL IN BLUE JEANS

Brooke

I AVOIDED LOOKING at Trent for as long as possible while we prepped our bikes for the ride. The Salt Grove was a good two hours away—if you did the speed limit. Lonnie and Sawyer had been doing business for a long time, but after some prying from Lonnie's wife, he moved up north to get out. He failed to consider that once you do business with the Devil, he never lets go, and a two-hour drive wouldn't make a difference when reckoning came around.

I twisted my hair up and tucked it under my helmet. When I turned to adjust my tail bag, I noticed Trent watching.

"Can I ask what this run is about?" he asked.

I groaned. "Prospects don't ask questions. Just follow me and do what I say."

With everything I might need tucked away, I yanked the zipper closed, and fastened the buckles on the leather flap. *Just get it over with. Deal with Lonnie. Fuck the Prospect.*

Yeah, fucking right.

Oh, I knew it would happen. I had every intention of following orders, and I always packed enough preventative measures to ensure it all went according to plan. A gun, a knife, and condoms—what order I used them in was yet to be determined. One thing I had learned from the men in the club, we didn't have to be nice to fuck.

And no one ever said any of it had to be pleasant.

Trent zipped up his leather jacket and straddled his bike. I almost dropped my keys and the instant pang of hurt it sent through me. *He shouldn't be wearing Dix's jacket.* The leather had been stripped of patches and identifying marks, but that didn't make it any different.

Sawyer was wrong.

He'd set out to shame my brother's name by stripping him of his colors and leaving his jacket around for any damn Prospect to pick up. Sawyer was wrong about a lot of things, but he was also too stupid and arrogant to realize it. His stubborn ignorance was the key reason my brother was no longer around. But since our President couldn't be wrong, of course it was Dix who disgraced the club.

I revved my engine, feeling the vibrations consume my body, and without a word, hit the throttle. This was where we separated brothers from men on bikes. Anyone who had never ridden a hog for two hours straight shouldn't be setting foot in our clubhouse in the first place.

Part of me hoped this guy's balls were so big they'd be ready to fall off by the end of the night and he'd have no interest in fucking. But Sawyer would blame me for that, too.

Instead of thinking about it, I rode hard and fast, using the open road as the only catharsis I could get. Even though I set a break-neck speed, Trent kept up. Around every curve, through every intersection, and past the cop tucked behind the billboard where he always waited. I wondered how tempting it might be for him to pick up a couple of Devils, but as usual, he didn't budge.

We reached The Salt Grove in just over an hour and found Lonnie's home in one of those cookie-cutter neighborhoods where each house looked almost exactly like the next. We parked our bikes behind a black SUV in the drive, and I removed my helmet, slinging it over a side mirror. Beside me, Prospect climbed off his bike—far too limber for a guy who'd ridden more than a hundred miles, at twice the speed limit. Sure, he looked like a guy who'd sat in the same position without a break on crumbling and winding roads, but he wasn't falling on his face stiff or walking like a man with a double-edged sword between his legs.

Much to my disappointment, but there was always the return trip.

"Plan?" he asked.

At least he seemed resolved to keep our conversation to a minimum. "Nope."

His stern expression faltered, but he took a step back and motioned for me to take the lead.

Maybe we could get along.

I walked around the house to the saddest back patio I'd ever seen—a single square of concrete with one half-dead plant. Back doors weren't as well-guarded or fortified, but Lonnie must've heard us coming and would've been stupid to leave it unlocked.

He wasn't stupid.

When the knob refused to turn, I stepped to the side, looking to Prospect. He raised an eyebrow and smirked, then kicked the perfect sweet spot to bust the fragile door jamb half off the wall. Sure, these cookie-cutter houses were expensive, but that was mainly due to the location, not the craftsmanship. Certainly the housing community would appreciate our improvements.

"You've done this before," I said.

He shrugged. "We can work on the mutual commendations later."

I had to get paired with the smart ass. I rolled my eyes and stepped past him and over the debris left in the doorway. My hand rested on the gun handle hidden below my jacket. The house was deathly quiet, and I expected Lonnie to be hiding, or not even there. But Sawyer didn't leave things to chance. He knew schedules, habits, and usually the darkest secrets.

Trent and I walked into the living room to find Lonnie sitting on the sofa with a remote resting on one knee and his cell on the cushion next to him. He was too calm.

The skin on the back of my neck prickled with the intense electric energy in the room.

"Lonnie." I tried to get a read on his threat level.

"It was only a matter of time," he said in an even tone. "At least you waited until Madeline was gone."

"Sawyer wants his money. Cash."

Lonnie scoffed. "Sawyer always wants something."

"Then pay and be done with it." I, for one, wanted this over as quickly as possible.

"Done with it?" he said with an ironic laugh as he stood. "Have you ever known anyone to be done with your father, or for him to let it go after all debts are paid."

Only when they were dead. Even then, he had a hard time letting anything go. But I wished Lonnie would just pay up. I was good at violence for anger's sake, beating the crap out of a man apparently resigned to his fate was a different story. It threw the situation off kilter, and I suspected that was his intent.

"Pay or things get dirty." I had to find a way under Lonnie's skin, and when I spotted a picture of Madeline on the mantel, I had an idea. "Sawyer sent us here to hurt you and make sure you get the message, but I'm thinking the best way to do that won't be breaking your kneecaps."

His eyes flashed as the composure faded from his face, certainly regretting what he'd said earlier. He should have gone with fear. Resignation only revealed his hand.

I stepped forward until we were chest to chest. "See, I'm all about equal opportunity and it seems Madeline should stand as an equal partner in this little deal."

Lonnie's eyes narrowed, focusing on me. His jaw was so tight, I could practically hear him grinding his teeth. "Leave her out of it."

"What is it she does?" My voice almost purred and I wasn't sure whether to be proud or disgusted.

Lonnie's lips turned white.

"Doesn't she run that little private STEM school in town. What if something were to happen? An accident followed by a failed drug test? Maybe some rerouted money. I'm sure no one would stand for that. Especially when they realize the diverted money is going to pay your illicit debt. She'd be ruined. And, well, we all know how you make your money, so good luck dealing with an even more furious Sawyer after that."

"That's a lot of your father's blood and anger running through your veins." Of course, he knew my weak spot too.

"Pay and we'll be done here," I repeated.

A reflection bounced off the walls around us, and Prospect pulled back the curtain to look out front. "A Cadillac SUV just pulled in."

I stiffened. Lonnie's phone had been right next to him. What if he'd called someone? What if he had backup?

But then, I saw even more panic in his eyes.

Madeline is home, I thought.

Either Sawyer had his information wrong, or he intended for Madeline to walk in on us laying out her husband.

"Decisions, decisions," I said as Lonnie watched the front door. *Would he have been so calm if he'd known she was coming home?*

"I'll get him the money." His voice rattled. "I don't have it here."

"Then, let's go get it," I said, grabbing between his legs and squeezing as the lock on the front door clicked.

He looked from the door to me. "I need a few days," he grunted.

I squeezed harder. "Wrong answer. Get the wife, Prospect."

Quick footsteps crossed the room behind me, the door opened, then Prospect gasped.

Lonnie sighed and the blood rushed out of his face.

"Brooke," Prospect said cautiously. I snapped my head around to find out what his ineptitude was about, but what I saw was a very, very pregnant woman.

And not Madeline.

"You have a pregnant fucking mistress? Getting into bed with Sawyer didn't teach you enough?"

Lonnie didn't make a sound, but behind me his mistress squeaked, "Derek? Who's Sawyer? What—"

"Shut up," Lonnie hissed.

"Well...." I grinned releasing my death grip on his junk and taking a step back. "I'm guessing we figured out where the money is. Does Madeline know about this?"

"No," he said.

"What's going on, Derek?" the mistress stuttered.

And what is with this Derek bullshit? He brought this woman into his house, knocked her up while photos of his wife sat on the mantel, and she didn't even know his name. I nearly choked on my breath. She had to be a fucking dimwit. And it turned out Lonnie was scum on a whole new level—not a surprising one.

"I need a few days," Lonnie hissed.

Do we beat a man in front of a very pregnant and possibly ready to pop woman? I couldn't say it would be the worst thing for her. She needed a reality check as much as him. Sawyer wouldn't care about her, only results. We sure as hell wouldn't go back empty handed.

"Not good enough." I punched him straight in the nose. He jerked back, blood running down the front of his shirt as he covered his face.

Also not good enough.

"Derek." Prego-mistress waddled forward until Prospect grabbed her arm.

"Love," I said, turning to her. I found terms of endearment the most condescending things known to man, and in this case, highly effective. "You should really—" I took a step toward her. "Really." Another step. "Get as far from this as possible before your little one becomes a pawn."

"Little ones," she whimpered. Then she seemed to come to her senses. "I'll call the police." She fumbled around in her purse, her hands shaking so violently she almost dropped the bag and her phone.

I glared at Lonnie, hoping he'd tell her to wise-up.

"No, Kim. No police." He sounded like a dumb cartoon character trying to speak through the blood and broken nose.

"This is probably one occasion where you should listen to 'Derek.'" I used tacky air quotes, but she only blinked, looking more confused.

"Didn't choose this one based on brain cells, huh?" I glanced over my shoulder to Lonnie and nodded toward his mistress. For that, he rushed toward me. I widened my stance, preparing to fight, but in a blink, Prospect had him by the neck, slinging him around and down on the floor.

Jackass, stealing my thunder.

Mistress shrieked, so I grabbed her by the arm and slammed the front door. The asshole Prospect left me to deal with her before she drew unwanted attention from the whole neighborhood. I pulled her into the kitchen, yanked out a chair for her to sit in, and took her phone for good measure.

"Shut up. Chill out." I slammed her phone against the table. "Everything will be just fine if you do that. If not, daddy"—I pointed to her stomach—"will disappear."

I leaned in and whispered. "And it'll be the cops hauling him away. Not us. And that wouldn't be any good for anyone, would it?"

Wide-eyed, she shook her head.

"Best advice, love, run as far and fast as your pregnant little body can get you. And never look back or this—" A well-timed grunt carried through the doorway. "This will be the only future your children know."

She nodded—as much agreement as I figured I could get, but I put one hand on the back of her chair, the other on the table, and sealed the deal. "You're looking right at the product of a woman who refused to run when she had the chance. Don't fuck this up."

A bold-faced lie. Mom never had a chance to run.

Another grunt punctuated the silence. I offered her

phone back, and she quickly grabbed her purse and ran straight for the door without even a sideways glance.

Kids are always a weakness—especially before they're born. That's when their futures seem the brightest and most assuring. Then they're born and subjected to the same hell that breaks the rest of us.

I rejoined Prospect in the living room, pulled out my phone, snapped a picture of Lonnie's hunched form bleeding into the beige carpet, and sent it off to Sawyer. "If she has any brain cells, she won't be back, and if you have any, you'll let her go."

Lonnie didn't bother to look up at me, so I strutted over and nailed him in the balls. "One week, plus interest. Get it fucking together."

This time, he rolled his eyes up to look at me. *Good enough.*

"Let's go, Prospect."

Prospect followed me out the front door to our bikes, where he pulled out a rag and wiped off his knuckles. They looked battered, but none of the blood was his. He'd also lost that intense and bemused glare he'd had in his eye after kicking the door down.

"Thinking this job isn't for you, Prospect?"

He straightened, and that damn crass look appeared again. "My name is Trent."

"Around here, you go by whatever the hell we call you." I kicked up the stand on my bike, balancing the hundreds of pounds of steel between my legs.

Trent followed suit, then paused and glanced over at me. "So, how do I earn a better nickname than Prospect?"

I secured my helmet and squeezed the key but didn't turn over the engine. "Prove yourself."

Trent still held his helmet in front of him, rotating it

between his hands while giving me a smirk straight from the face of Lucifer himself. "Thought I just did."

I scoffed at his audacity. Any illusion of getting along with him faded. "You're an arrogant bastard if you think you just earned anything."

"Maybe a little gratitude."

I made the mistake of tracing his expression up to his eyes. That spark of green tainted with something I couldn't pinpoint. Cockiness? Flirtation?

The second would make my next assignment easier, but I wasn't ready for niceties, so I cocked my head. "Aww, little Prospect wants gratitude."

"What I want," he snapped. "Is for you to stop patronizing me."

"Get used to it because this"—I waved my hands— "doesn't change."

Way to make your next assignment worse, Brooke.

Trent raised his eyebrows briefly, as if he didn't believe me. Then again, maybe that'd make the next part of my orders more entertaining. After all, maintaining a semblance of sanity was all about finding enjoyment in the little things like irking the cocky bastards who thought they could one-up me so easily.

Chapter Four

DOIN' THE DIRTY GRITTY

Trent

I EXPECTED Brooke to lead me back to the clubhouse, but she pulled off the interstate just short of town and into the parking lot of a hotel. I stopped my bike next to hers and glanced around the parking lot. There were only a few cars on the other end, and no one else around.

"What are we doing?" Not that I expected an answer, but I hoped any response would help me get a read on her intent—and whether I should expect an ambush in the next few minutes.

Brooke hung her helmet over her mirror and swung her leg over the bike. "Remember what I said about questions? Just follow me."

My back and knees were stiff, but I forced myself not to show it as I followed her around to the side of the building. Brooke unlocked the first door and stepped inside. The dimly lit room was silent, but my body remained on high alert, watching the shadows and listening for any indication of movement.

"Shut the door," Brooke said, dropping her keys on the dresser.

At least that reduced the chance of an ambush, so I complied. I scanned the room again—it was a typical looking hotel room, simple and cleaner than the exterior, but that wasn't saying much.

Brooke pulled out her hair tie, shaking her head and letting her hair fall over her left shoulder.

"Shower?" she asked, tossing her jacket over the back of a chair.

When I didn't answer, she grimaced at me over her shoulder, lifting her shirt over her head. She tossed it aside to join her jacket. "Or do you prefer it dirty?"

"What?" I had a good idea what she had in mind, but it made no sense.

Her shoulders dropped, and her head tilted to the side. "Don't be so fucking thick."

"Thick? You could try making sense." My mouth started working faster than my brain. "Because if you're suggesting what I think, your foreplay sucks."

Maybe all that riding and violence did something crazy with her libido, but I wasn't feeling it. Maybe she had some hate-sex fetish, or this was another power play in her book. Either way, I had to find a way out of that room without making things worse.

"Didn't know dicks needed foreplay." She crossed her arms, and watched me for a long, uncomfortable moment. Her arms and chest were covered in ink. Black flowers bloomed on her right collarbone, the stems curling around her bicep through leaves, thorns, and drops of blood. At the base they wove through the Devils of Ashville insignia.

"Your turn." She pushed her hair back. Stepping forward and kneeling in front of me, she grabbed the closure of my jeans.

"Why are you doing this?" I asked, stopping her hand, but she jerked away.

"Questions," she snapped. "You want to prove something? Show me what kind of man you are."

Her voice was different. A hint of seduction, but hollow and unconvincing. This was an act she'd put on before. Several times if I had to guess.

"Not the kind to ride all afternoon with a cranky woman and then feel like dropping my pants."

"Welcome to the club," she smirked, tucking her hair behind her ear. Every movement seemed rehearsed and unnatural.

I reached behind me for the doorknob, but as soon as I did, she went for the button on my pants.

Buy time. "You welcome every guy this way? Does that mean you stop calling me Prospect?"

She lifted her head, and without a flicker of remorse, punched me between the legs.

"Fuck." I doubled over, reaching for the wall to balance myself before I hit the floor. Every muscle in my body tensed as the hot wave of nausea pulsed through me.

"Sorry." She shrugged innocently, but the look in her narrowed eyes was anything but as her gaze drifted down my body, stopping at my crotch. "Didn't think you had anything in there."

I gritted my teeth. "Honey—" I used the word on purpose.

"I told you not to call me that," she yelled, but it gave me just enough time and space to regroup.

"Honey—" I repeated louder, grabbing a fistful of hair

and pulling her to her feet—careful to avoid her swinging appendages. "I ain't provin' my manhood to you or anyone else with a random fuck. You're gorgeous, but your attitude fucking sucks."

When she slapped my arm again, I released her, and she shoved me backward. "You're not fucking my attitude."

"Not fucking you either." I reached for the doorknob again.

This time, she grabbed my collar ripping open the front of my shirt. "That's not how things fly here. You want a place in The Devils, you go through my family. Your first test is here."

"Fucking the President's daughter." I shook my head. "Let me guess, I'm supposed to jump at the chance, let my guard down and spill all my secrets? Or maybe you just want me to fuck you so you can run back and tell Sawyer so he'll kick me to the curb? Either way, I'm taking my chance and declining on... whatever this is."

I threw the door open and walked out, leaving her standing topless in the entryway. I figured exposure wouldn't be the part that would piss her off the most, but damned if I was jumping in bed with that crazy woman.

———

A MILE OUTSIDE OF ASHVILLE, Brooke didn't seem to be following me, so I pulled off the road long enough to make one call.

"Don't tell me Brooke's done with you already," Caine said immediately.

"Why didn't you fucking warn me?" My voice exploded into the phone—I could hear it through my own speaker.

Caine seemed to chuckle. He definitely knew her plan. "You said you were ready for anything. Didn't want to ruin the surprise."

Surprise? Like a fucking Venus flytrap. I wasn't sure anyone could be ready for Brooke. I never expected Caine to be a babysitter, but in this case, a heads up would have been nice.

And for what?

So I could have practiced my exit?

No, that wouldn't have helped. What I really needed was some indication on proceeding through the rest of the night without too much fallout.

"Did you finish the job?"

The one in the hotel room or Lonnie? "We delivered Sawyer's message."

And my knuckles were still sore from it. I knew that Lonnie wasn't an innocent bystander. I'd been quite familiar with his work in my previous life, but we could never find a way to nail him for it. I'd known coming into this that I'd have to get my hands dirty. But it was a strange feeling beating the crap out of someone. Added to that, the punches I took from the men earlier and Brooke's fist to the nuts. It'd already been a hell of a day.

"And Brooke?" Caine asked.

I didn't have much of an answer. "Last I saw her, she was shirtless in a hotel room."

Caine made a noise that didn't sound promising. "Get your ass back to the bar before Brooke does. Sawyer will be there, but he won't expect you to come back alone, so you better make it good."

That was far from helpful.

I pinched the bridge of my nose. *What did I expect?*

I needed to clear my head, but in the mile between me and the clubhouse, I wouldn't have a chance. *Regroup. Regroup. Think.*

I couldn't afford to lose it now, but Brooke had jacked with my head. And that was probably the point. What kind of initiation is being propositioned by the President's daughter?

One that seemed to end in ruin either way.

Pull it together. I strapped on my helmet again and took off.

By the time I got back to the point, the bar was over-flowing with bikers and women—most of whom I was hard pressed not to classify as hookers based on the way they rubbed their half-naked bodies against any man who passed. I dragged my hand through my hair. I wasn't particularly picky, but it desperately needed washed, and I wanted to go home and crawl into bed.

I wasn't in the mood for whatever this crowd might have to offer. I was sore. My shoulders were killing me. And after that little surprise from Brooke, my mind wasn't on the job at hand. I struggled to come up with an explanation that wouldn't land me in hot water or with an insane and ruth-less biker chick as my enemy.

But none of that mattered, I had to walk into that bar like I'd done it every night, and prove it was all I wanted to do every night for the rest of my life.

On paper, my goals looked much simpler. I needed one connection. One break. Before the club broke me. All the while surrounded by a group of men who all looked like they wanted to slowly eviscerate me.

The sign above the door to the bar read THE PIT: WELCOME TO HELL and it was beyond accurate. It aggravated the knot in the base of my spine that sent a tingling sensation down my legs. Every step closer to my goal was a step into a new ring of hell. Rock music thundered through the double doors of the front entrance as I approached. The original brick of the opera house remained throughout much of the structure, but the interior of The Pit had been remodeled with wood, which dulled some of the ambient noise once I entered. A long oak bar stretched the length of the room, with shelves of liquor from the back counters up to the base of the half-wall of Sawyer's overhead office. On the opposite side of the room, there was a section divided off by tall unfinished beams connected by thick planks at chest height, which were crowded with beer bottles and glasses while the men chatted around the pool tables.

Caine said to find Sawyer before Brooke, so I scanned the room until I spotted him in a booth at the back. His eyes widened as he saw me, then he nodded in my direction.

Before I could make it through the maze of tables and constantly shifting bodies to the table, a blonde girl stepped in front of me, pressing herself against me. "Ready to party, Prospect?"

As a Prospect, I had no sway, no power, and typically none of the perks, but apparently that didn't matter to some. I was a step up from hang-around and now ran with the elites of the Ashville underworld.

"Always," I said, hiding the wince as my sore knuckles brushed against her bare shoulder.

She lifted my hand and cupped it in hers, gently rubbing the bruised skin. "Hard night?"

I wouldn't say that I've ever been opposed to having a hot girl appear out of nowhere and offer a good time. I wouldn't even say that I'd refuse to entertain her to a certain extent. But tonight, it was all a lie.

She took me by the arm and led me to an open spot at the bar.

After Brooke's little stunt, and beating the shit out of that guy, I wasn't even in the mood to humor her, but I figured I may as well dull the pain in my body with a little alcohol.

As we took our seats, the bartender sat a dark brew in front of me. *Guess I don't get a choice in the matter.*

Sawyer and Fitch left their sanctuary in the corner and flanked me at the bar, stepping in between me and the blonde.

"Saw your work," Sawyer said. "Not bad."

I straightened my shoulders, leaning back on the stool so they were both in view. "I was hoping to do a little better than that."

Sawyer smirked and nodded to his friend. "You've met Fitch?"

I nodded at the man who'd stood by while the others attempted to make short work of my time here. Fitch offered his hand, and I reluctantly shook it. "What's next?"

"Next you wait. You'll do whatever we say. Whenever we say it," Fitch growled. He was going to be a treat. If I hadn't been told, I would have never guessed he was Caine's father. Then again, the overbearing harshness went a long way in explaining Caine's edgy insecurity.

I nodded, pushing back my own smirk and taking a swig of whatever I'd been served. It tasted like a bourbon beer and fucking strong at that.

"Enjoy it while it lasts," Sawyer said, slamming his hand down on the bar and sending a shock wave through my glass.

I raised my eyebrows in question.

"Our most popular brew." He nodded to the glass. "Every barrel takes several months to brew, so we can only get our hands on it a couple of times a year."

That was probably a good thing—too much of that circulating with this rowdy bunch would be trouble.

"Good stuff," I said. I guessed it was at least ten percent alcohol, and honestly, it tasted like I'd licked an old, burned bar stool.

As I waited for the real inquisition to begin, a ruckus broke out in the far corner near the pool tables, with a loud crack and a round of cheers. I suspected a bet gone violent, but when Sawyer shifted to look, I saw that it wasn't just any loudmouth ruckus. It was a fucking orgy.

With at least two women, including the blonde who'd approached me when I entered, piled on the pool table with a dozen guys around.

"Membership has its privileges," Fitch said, slapping his hand against the bar. He then headed over to join the fun while Sawyer returned to his corner table to watch. No one asked me about Brooke, so I sure as hell wasn't going to bring her up.

Instead, I sat at the bar, taking small sips of beer until it was too warm to stomach, making small talk with the bartender, Caine's Ol' Lady, Thea, and listening to the conversations around me. I needed time to sit back and observe, but the longer I did that, the more suspicious I'd become.

"You've been nursing that drink for an hour." Brooke's voice stood out from the crowd.

How'd she know?

Brooke took the stool next to me, shrugging off her leather and revealing the same black tank she'd stripped off in the hotel room. In this light, I saw even more of her tattoos, as well as black bruises peeking out along the straps of her top.

"Not loving the drink of the month?" she asked.

The turn of civility had me suspicious. "It's all right."

She leaned toward me and hummed in my ear. "I'll take that as a no."

Without warning, she swept my glass away and dumped it over the other side of the bar, then she lifted herself onto the counter, kicked her legs over, and jumped to the other side. "What would you like?"

Oh, there's definitely a trap brewing. I didn't trust less-bitchy Brooke. Not at all.

"Lager." At least I could stomach that without getting too buzzed.

She grabbed a frosted stein and filled it with a deep amber liquid. Then she took a second one and filled it with the same, placing both in front of me while she returned to her seat in the same manner—to the cheers of the men who remained close by. Those who hadn't paired off with women or joined the ongoing orgy around the pool table.

"Not like this back with Brothers of the Wheel?"

How do I answer that? "Just finding my place. Still a Prospect—as you've pointed out—waiting on my next order."

"One way of putting it." She took a long drink of her beer. "Prospects are usually a little more gung-ho than this."

I leaned off the bar stool toward her. "I rode more than three hours today, beat up some guy, and had a strange as hell stopover at a hotel. Now I'm drinking some beer and watching a gang bang over a pool table."

She pursed her lips. "So, you're saying it's been a long day?"

"Something like that."

She leaned her elbow on the bar and rested her chin on it, still facing me. Maybe it was the beer or the lighting, but she looked like a different girl.

"So, why aren't you in the middle of the party?" I asked.

She snorted. "You don't want to fuck me, but you want to see me get fucked, that's a bit ironic."

"Uh—" I glanced back. That did seem to be the only thing the women in the bar were here for, aside from a couple of waitresses and the bartender. "Hadn't really considered that."

Her eyes widened. "Sure about that?"

The look in her eyes dared me to answer—either way would get me in more trouble. So I took a drink of beer instead. A long drink.

"Another beer?" she asked. If she was so eager to fuck, I wasn't sure why she hadn't turned her sights on easier prey. Maybe even someone she could tolerate—which over the course of the day, I'd figured wasn't me.

No, fucking wasn't on her agenda, unless it was fucking with me.

"Come on, Mama." Out of nowhere, Gavin squeezed between us and grabbed Brooke's arm.

From the apparent familiarity, I assumed he was her boyfriend, but she shoved his hand away. "Why do I have to remind you not to call me that, or anything else?"

He whispered something in her ear, then jerked her clean off the bar stool.

I jumped to my feet, swinging in his direction before taking time to think. "She's not interested."

He cocked his head as an amused smile spread across his lips. "Prospect thinks he can make a claim?"

Gavin swung at me, but Brooke grabbed his arm,

yanking him sideways so he missed by inches. Within seconds, two others joined the brawl—all targeting me, but Brooke persisted in throwing some of her own punches.

I only got hit because I was trying to keep an eye on her. And the beer wasn't helping. The more sober side of my brain screamed about how bad this could turn out. But I had the choice of standing up for the Treasurer or standing down to the Sergeant-at-Arms, and neither seemed truly appealing.

Fist primed and ready to throw another punch, everyone around me froze.

"Sawyer," Brooke said flatly.

A heavy hand landed on my shoulder, and Sawyer made a tsking sound. "In-fighting already, are we, Prospect?"

Shit. "I'm not about to stand around and get my ass handed to me for no good reason."

"What's this about?" Sawyer's gaze flicked to Brooke.

She put her hands on her hips and scowled as if she couldn't even believe he was asking the question. "What the hell do you think?"

"Same old story," Sawyer mumbled. "Move along, everyone. Now."

The crowd dispersed and the two who had joined in on the brawl wandered away, but Gavin didn't move—neither did Brooke or I.

"Brooke," Sawyer said, his voice low with warning.

She shook her head and yanked her coat off the bar stool so violently the chair crashed to the floor and I had to hop out of its path. Gavin walked away too, but I watched to see if he headed toward the same door.

Sawyer held my shoulder. "Careful with that one."

Brooke or the asshole? I gathered this whole scene was common around here, but it was shocking that Sawyer hadn't made any effort to defend his own daughter or the Treasurer of the club. Sure, she'd proven herself as conniving and untrustworthy as any biker here, but in that instance, she had every right to stand up to Gavin.

When Sawyer turned his attention back to someone else, I slipped outside.

Gavin stood on a corner, smoking and laughing with some of his friends, so I went in the opposite direction, glancing up the alley beside The Pit. A swirl of smoke swept around the back corner of the building and toward me as it dissipated into the night air. I looked back, making sure no one was paying attention, before darting up the dim backstreet.

Behind the building, I found Brooke under a flickering light, leaning against the wall with a cigarette pressed to her lips. I still had to get to the root of this Brooke mystery.

"Sorry I jumped in," I said, certain I attracted the two additional attackers.

Brooke shrugged, staring forward as she blew out another cloud of smoke.

"I'm sure you could've handled yourself." When in doubt, why not try to stroke the ego?

She still didn't speak. Probably pissed that I hadn't fallen for her second ruse of the night since the classic bitchy Brooke had emerged again. As I turned to leave her stewing, she kicked off the wall. "You will regret turning your back on a Devil."

I spun back and closed in on her so I wouldn't have to raise my voice. "You didn't seem to rat me out to Sawyer. Does your dad know how you welcome Prospects?"

She jabbed her cigarette into the side of the building and dropped it to the ground. "Oh yes, dear old dad. How will I ever repay him for the train he got me for my sixteenth birthday? You think anything in this club happens without his input?"

She stomped away and threw open the steel door about halfway down the back of the building, leaving me alone in the alley with an echoing thud.

Chapter Five

SHE WHO SUPS WITH THE DEVIL

Brooke

I'D FOUGHT since I could remember to have some part of my life on my own terms, but it seemed like the only things I had any control over were the stock orders for The Pit. And even that was debatable. I submitted my final order of the day before noon, mainly because I wanted to enjoy the quiet of my office before the bar opened.

Lately, Sawyer had been spending most of his free time with his new side piece, Cissie. Young, blonde, naive. A simple but perfect recipe as far as Sawyer was concerned. She did whatever he ordered with a disgusting smile on her face. She wasn't going anywhere and thus far, he showed no signs of being bored. At least it kept him out of my face.

I sat up in my chair when I heard the sound of motorcycle boots clomping across the wood floors beyond my office door. I held my breath, hoping whoever it was would pass, but I knew better. The only one walking through the bar in heavy boots at this hour would be Sawyer, even though he had his own back entrance to get up to his loft office.

My heart pounded faster and harder until I couldn't hear the footsteps closing in on the office door. First the doorknob rattled, then the whole door shook. "Brooke, we need to talk."

My office had two doors, one that led out to the bar, and one toward the stock room. My nerves hummed under my skin, urging me toward the back door. But I'd learned many years ago that only made things worse. So, I pushed my seat back, letting it grind against the floor, flipped my hair over my shoulder, and stood tall like the officer I was.

Even though I felt nothing like an officer around him. I could fake the bravado when prepared, at times like this, I still felt like that young girl hoping he wouldn't barge into my room in the middle of the night.

As soon as I opened the door, his fist slammed into my diaphragm, knocking the wind out of me and sending me backward a couple of steps. Before I could right myself, he had me down on my knees with his arm wrapped around my throat, cutting off any opportunity of finding my breath again.

I clawed at his arm on instinct, trying to wriggle my way out of his grasp.

"That was a short night," he said. "Now, I know you ride at break-neck speeds, you learned that from your brother."

His words echoed in my head as the cold fog settled around my brain. Then, he released my throat for a second, allowing me one gasp of air so I wouldn't pass out before he was done.

"I gave you an order, and what type of club would this be if I didn't expect the officers to carry out simple tasks?"

Fuck a stranger. Simple tasks....

My chest ached. I stretched my arm back with what little strength I had left reaching for his head. Hair. An eye. Anything.

My movements slowed.

Just as the blackness threatened to take me, he released me, shoving me to the floor where I gasped, gagging on the air as it rushed into my lungs.

Self-preservation told me to keep my eyes down, but if I had listened to that instinct, I wouldn't have been in the situation to begin with. I would have run the first time Dixon told me to.

So, I lifted my gaze, planning to stare him down and prove I couldn't be beaten, but as I raised my head, my gaze stopped on his hand, rubbing his half-hard erection through his black jeans.

I swallowed the vomit rising in my throat and opted to keep my eyes on the floor.

"Your mother and brother thought they could defy me, too. Remember that and finish the job." He turned and left me on the floor, but I heard him mutter under his breath as he crossed the threshold back into the bar. "Cunt."

Chapter Six

DEVIL WITH THE BRIMSTONE TONGUE

Trent

THERE WASN'T much to be seen from under a Dodge Ram. Sometimes the only thing I could keep an eye on while working at Bone Grinders were people's feet, but when I saw a pair of calf-high leather boots step around the garage door while I worked to replace an old, busted clutch, I knew exactly who was about to walk in.

Caine stood in the corner of the garage organizing sockets and bolts.

"Is Gavin around?" Brooke asked in a hushed voice.

"Haven't seen him today," Caine said.

"Good." Brooke cut through the garage, heading straight for Cannon's office.

I half expected her to give at least one of my protruding legs a kick or stomp, but I took my time, lining up the new clutch and bolting everything back in place. I strained to pick up any of their conversation from the office, but I heard all of two words before the tapping and clinking from Caine's work drowned the rest out. By the time I had everything in place under the Dodge, Brooke scuttled out of the garage.

Once I finished cleaning up around the truck and moved it back out front, Cannon told me to help Cain strip down an old Hardtail he'd picked up for spare parts. Anything we might be able to use was kept in inventory, the rest was junked or sold for extra money.

"So, what's the deal with Brooke?" I began as Caine and I set to work, hoping to get some insight into her erratic tendencies and motives.

"No." He slammed his screwdriver against the concrete floor. "Best avoid Brooke and all things related."

I cleared my throat. "She's the Treasurer. I don't think 'avoiding' her is in the cards."

Caine rubbed the back of his arm over his forehead and tossed a handful of bolts into the bucket near his feet. "She's a disaster and getting swept up in her storm will only be bad for you. Shit changed after Dixon died. She's always been a bit...." He shook his head, staring off in the direction of The Pit. "Explosive. We all grew up together, probably saw each other more than our fathers. Dix was the oldest and he took care of us. Kept us out of trouble. But between him dying and her putting up with Sawyer and Vin's shit for years, Brooke doesn't care about anyone but herself. Kinda had to be that way to survive, but one day she's going to fully meltdown and I'd advise against being anywhere near it."

Right. But her comment the night before still niggled at me. "What's a train?"

"Train?" Caine snorted. "We need to work on your street jargon. You don't know about pullin' a train?"

It clicked. *Gang bang. Fuck. Did she really mean that?* No wonder she was wound so tight. "Never mind."

He gave me a flat look. "You walked out on her. I guarantee that moved you way to the top of her shit list. You get pulled down her rabbit hole and you'll find yourself beyond fucked around here. You think you've seen the worst of Gavin? Brooke brings out nothing but blind rage in him and half the men here."

———

MOSTLY CLEAN OF grease and grime, I sat back on the couch and kicked up my feet. Finally, a moment of quiet. No facade. No noise. Just peace.

Although no closer to figuring out the drug connections around here or lining up any suspects that might be feeding the group info from the police, I had plenty of suspicions about Gavin and his little subset of the gang. But my thoughts kept going back to Brooke. Did she really mean her father had given her a gangbang for her sixteenth birthday? *What the fuck is wrong with these people?* Beyond the obvious, of course. They were supposed to protect their own daughters. Not arrange gangbangs or send them off to fuck the new guys.

The last victim Detective Windsor had been working with mentioned a gangbang once, just before becoming too erratic and terrified to form a coherent sentence. Two days later, Windsor responded to a call and found her convulsing from a drug overdose. It appeared that while trying to assist, he got jabbed by the needle, which still contained enough fentanyl to give him a lethal dose as well. By the time EMTs arrived both Windsor and the girl were in respiratory failure.

I started to doze off on the couch when the door on my shabby apartment rattled with a knock. I didn't bother to grab my shirt off the back of the couch before opening the door, but I quickly regretted it when Brooke's dark eyes bored into me.

She lifted a six-pack of beer. "You owe me a drink for stepping in on my fight last night."

Before I could say a word, she stepped around me and into my living room. No invitation necessary.

Okay, so much for that peaceful night. I reached behind my neck, gripping my hands together. Even if, on the slightest chance, she'd come on a good-will mission, her sudden appearance wasn't promising. I pulled my exhausted mind back together and focused, knowing there would be no right answers or moves where she was concerned. Limiting the damage as much as possible was my only option.

Brooke dropped her keys on the coffee table and deposited the beer next to them, then continued around my living room as if it were some kind of museum exhibit. I didn't have much to look at, mainly garage sell rejects we'd collected so the place didn't look bare. After a few moments, she turned on her heel and plopped down on the couch. Then she pulled out the first bottle of beer, twisted the cap off and handed it to me. "Where were you born?"

Another inquisition.

"Ashville." I lied easily, but I'd spent most of my life there anyway. I had been four when Mom and I moved up here from Georgia to get away from my father's family. "Born and raised."

Her bottle opened with a hiss, as she got comfortable against the far arm of the couch. "You know Edie's Bakery?"

They really enjoyed asking questions about trivial shit in

hopes of throwing me off, but I knew that tactic pretty well myself. "Torn down five years ago. My family never went near the place though. Not into roach rolls."

Regardless of the reputation for bugs and even fingernails in the food, many considered it a local staple. I vividly remembered the uproar after the place was shut down due to numerous health code violations when the bribe money ran out.

Brooke dragged her tongue across her front teeth. "Who's your team?"

Team? I cocked my head. I thought I'd prepared for all scenarios, but I didn't have a ready answer for that one. I shrugged and shook my head.

"Bengals? Don't tell me you're a Browns fan. I'll have to deduct points." Her face hardened. "Steelers?"

"I didn't realize we were on a point system," *Really? Can we get off the football?* I rolled my head back and rubbed my temples. "I don't follow football."

"Then what the hell do you do? Baseball? Basketball?" She sat forward. Her eyes drilled into me as she dug, but for what? Sports? I'd never taken her for an avid sports freak. Her eyes rolled back, and she looked to the ceiling. "Hockey? Golf?"

"This is going to be a real bone of contention with you, isn't it?" I sat down my bottle to grab my shirt off the back of the couch as she plopped her feet—and dirty boots—on the table next to it. Then I joined her on the couch, slightly angled to keep an eye on her. "I guess if I have to choose, I'll go with hockey, but I still don't follow it much."

"You must have a lot of time on your hands," she mumbled, then took another long drink.

"Or not enough." I rolled my bottle between my fingers

then raised it to my lips, pretending to take a drink. "Why so adamant about the sports thing?"

She shrugged, then let her head to fall to one side. "You can tell a lot about a person by their sports interests. You play anything in high school?"

"Hooky."

Although she played the casual conversation act well, the features around her eyes remained tense and her gaze bore into me as if waiting for something. Given what I'd learned about her, I would have approached every man around here with suspicion as well, but whether punishment for walking away from her or just being the new guy, she had it out for me. Throw away answers weren't going to appease her, so I fabricated a nice little morsel for her. "Mom put me in martial arts when I was thirteen. She thought the discipline would be good for me."

James and I had actually come up with the idea of joining the Kendo Club after leaning how it was used to train police in Japan during a demonstration at our school. I don't know how we got it in our heads that we wanted to be cops, but the idea had been there almost as long as I could remember.

Brooke sighed, twisting into the corner of the couch and pulling her knees up under her. "That's not a word I hear around here very often."

"That's obvious."

Brooke laughed. It was quiet, and even a bit delicate like she wasn't used to the feeling, and for a brief second her features relaxed. "If you're so disciplined, why are you here?"

Does it ever end? I wondered if she chose tonight in particular because she knew I put in a long day and would be too exhausted to answer questions. I knew what she was alluding to but irking her was more fun. Poking at the wild lion. I should have had my head examined, but this lion had barged in and interrupted my quiet retreat into normalcy. It was well-deserved. And if I kept her on edge, that upped the chances of her being the first to drop a secret here or there. "Figured I was done playing gopher for the day, and I could relax."

She glared at me with her typical annoyed look. "I mean Devil's Point."

If my grandma had seen that face, she would have warned her it might freeze like that. I was brash and annoyed, but not that brave. "I've been drifting for a few years. My uncle was with the Brothers and wanted me to join, but I didn't get the chance. I found my way to Bone Grinders, and here I am."

If I didn't already have that story down pat, I'd repeated it enough in the last week to mumble it in my sleep.

Brooke's gaze continued around the room as if she'd stopped listening. She plucked another bottle out of the six-pack, replacing it with her empty. She drank as fast as she asked questions and although I had no intentions of keeping up, I took another sip to humor her and keep up appearances. "What about you? Not many women work their way up to officer, not even daughters of the President. They all give you hell, why are you here?"

Brooke slammed her bottle against the coffee table, spraying everything with droplets of beer. "I'm as good as anyone here, and I didn't get my position just because I share the last name of the President."

That time, I hadn't meant to set her off, but I'd discovered quite a sore spot. "I bet you spend more time trying to prove that than any Prospect ever will."

Her eyes narrowed as if she was trying to stare right through me. "There's always something to prove."

I lifted my bottle toward her and cocked my head. "That why you enjoy busting my chops?"

"That's the life of a Prospect. I didn't become Treasurer by being gentle or agreeable."

The room suddenly felt hot, and I leaned forward, pressing my forearms into my knees. My eyes were opened, but refused to focus, like I was underwater and moving in slow motion.

"Shit," I muttered. I shook my head to clear the fog, but that only made it worse as the darkness closed in around me like an inescapable tide.

Brooke stared back at me, utterly calm and unmoved.

The glass bottle slipped out of my hand and thudded against the stained carpet. With the slow nauseating heat building in my core, I realized she hadn't been interested in my answers to any of her questions. She'd been buying time.

"You drugged me?" My slurred words echoed in my head.

"You don't seem to hold your liquor very well," she said smoothly.

That wasn't it. I hadn't had more than a few small drinks. I tried to stand, but every movement was sluggish and clumsy. I couldn't coordinate my movements to shift my weight from the couch.

This isn't good.

As the room swam, I sat back, afraid of falling off the couch. *What is this?*

Brooke moved across the couch and straddled my lap, sliding her hands under the hem of my shirt and rubbing her fingertips over my stomach. "Told you it was a bad idea to turn your back on a Devil."

Chapter Seven

UNDER THE DEVIL'S BOOT

Brooke

ANGER DOES FUNNY THINGS. And not the laugh out loud kind, or even the chuckle to yourself kind. The kind that made the last fight I had with my brother even more pronounced. He'd shown up at my house in the middle of the night after a run I'd never learned all the details about, but I knew a lot of people died on both sides.

Dixon sat on my couch, head hung low. "Do me a favor and run. Run far away from all of this."

Run? I couldn't believe what I heard. I wouldn't give up everything I'd fought for. I'd just made Treasurer for fuck's sake. "You're supposed to have my back, Dix."

He whipped his head up, a crazy look twisted his face as he stood to look down at me. "I do. Never doubt that. That's why I'm telling you to get out."

"Seven years. I've worked my ass off for seven years to finally get a little respect around here and now you're trying to push me out?"

"Respect doesn't exist when you're a Devil."

"Well, it's better than my other choices."

He leaned in close. I could smell the mix of blood and gasoline on his soaked clothes. "You could get out. I have the money to get you far away from here and Sawyer."

I laughed in his face. "And if Sawyer finds out where you got that money or where I am? There is no escape plan. No. Not until I have my revenge."

"There. That." He shook his head, throwing his hands in the air as he paced away. "That's the problem. Is revenge really worth losing yourself to this place?"

"I lost myself after Mom blew her own face off, and I walked in to find her in a pool of blood." And after Sawyer started crawling into my bed every night.

"Brooke," Dixon grabbed me by the shoulders. "Listen to what I'm saying, please. One day the Devils will drive you past the point of no return. You'll wake up, look in the mirror and have no idea what you've done. That point will come from your own choices. That's the difference."

I stood there with my arms crossed believing I'd already crossed that threshold long ago.

"You keep thinking the blackness can't get any darker, but it does. If you stay here, it'll consume you, and one day, it'll be too late to come back."

I didn't listen. Taking advice was never a strong suit of mine.

Now, I sat in the window of Trent's bedroom in my bra and jeans, staring at the aftermath of my most recent sin. Chuck another one up to the Devil I'd been raised to be. But this was different, I'd finally hit that wall my brother had warned me about, and I wasn't the only person who would suffer because of it.

I lit a cigarette as the moon rose above the distant horizon.

Not far away, Trent dozed off the remaining Ash, our new local specialty. I'd laced the rim of his bottle with a strong enough dose to fuck with his head for a bit. With every puff of smoke, I wrestled with the thought that I'd finally gone off the deep end, just like Dix warned. Then, I heard an unfamiliar ringtone.

Snuffing out my cigarette against the metal frame of the storm window, I put my thoughts to rest. I still had work to do, and I needed to find Trent's phone before he woke up. I wasn't ready to stare eye-to-eye with my own aftermath. I searched the pockets of Trent's jeans which were halfway between his couch and bedroom door.

James, the screen read.

I tapped the screen and put on my sickeningly sweet voice. "Hello."

"Who is this?" he asked. "Where's Trent?

"Sleeping. Seems he had a rough day." I tried to sound playful, but it turned my stomach. I needed another drag from my cigarette to get through this. "Care to keep me entertained, James?"

"Seems you have me at a disadvantage already," he said dryly. "I'm afraid I'm not that entertaining though."

Oh, no. He wasn't getting off that easily. Not until I got something out of him. "So, what? Are you guys old football buddies?"

"Football?" The man laughed. "Where'd you get that idea? We've been friends since school. I was hoping he'd be up for a drink."

Oh, he's certainly not up for a drink. Prospect certainly had consistency going for him. I groaned and dropped onto the couch. I needed to dig up some info, but the facade I put on every word only exhausted my aching body and mind more. Lonny had been right. There was a lot of my father's blood in my veins, and maybe I'd never escape that fact as hard as I fought.

I drugged him.

I'm worse than all the pigs here.

Not that they hadn't ever been guilty of the same, or worse. But at that moment, I was so angry and hurt I didn't care. I refused to care. The only reason I kept going was to show these assholes they weren't better than me. And I did it by being just as evil. The pain, hatred, and spite made all that much easier. I fought pain with more pain.

"How about you tell Trent I called when he wakes up," James said.

"I'll try to remember to do that, but since you're not going to entertain me until then, I'm going back to my cigarette and finding something better to do this evening." I disconnected and slid the phone back into Trent's jeans.

I couldn't take being in Trent's space anymore. And I had work to do back at the bar. So, I left him to figure things out for himself. If he wasn't too hungover. I wasn't sure how long the cocktail would last.

But I needed one last thing... Well, two if I really wanted to sell this, and I had to if I didn't want Sawyer to bust my gut again. My shirt and Trent's leather. Sawyer was all for spectacle, and I'd give him one.

Chapter Eight

BALLS AND GUTS

Trent

I WOKE ON MY STOMACH, one arm hanging over the side of the bed. For a few long minutes, feeling like an elephant had taken up residence on my back, I didn't move. Instead, I listened to the traffic outside. The faint thud of distant music. It didn't sound like anyone else was left in the house.

What the hell did she slip me? And how? How did I get so stupid?

I'd underestimated her. Just like everyone else, I'd fucking underestimated her. I sat up, jerked into full consciousness by the memory of her hand down my jeans. Fingers around my cock. *Dammit.*

I'd turned my back, and in return, she'd turned the tides, leaving devastation in her wake, just like Caine had warned.

My brain was still caked with mud. All I could remember were tiny flashes, but nothing about coming to the bedroom, or what she'd done with most of my clothes. I went through every curse word I'd ever heard in my head, as I let my feet drop to the floor and forced my body upright. She'd left me in my boxers at least. *This is so fucking wrong.*

I pressed the heel of my palm to my forehead. As hard as I tried to remember what happened, I couldn't move past those brief fragments. Everything else slipped away like trying to grab a hold of the very darkness that dimmed the corners of the room. Staggering to the doorway, I felt the floor shift under my weight with every step. I'd suffered through some wicked hangovers before, but whatever she'd given me left a funk thicker than the sludge of an old motor. I bummed into the wall as I navigated the narrow hall to the kitchen. My pants laid in a heap on the floor nearby, and my shirt had been tossed over the lamp by the couch.

Fuck. I grabbed my pants, and the phone slid out, between the quiet sound and motion of bending over, I almost joined it on the floor. Once I managed to straighten again, I pressed the power button, but the screen remained black. The phone was dead, but at least she hadn't taken it with her. I put it on the charger in the kitchen and sat against the corner cabinet with a bottle of water, hoping to flush out whatever remained in my system.

I'm still alive. At least I could say that. I hadn't done or said something to get me killed on the spot, but that didn't mean I was safe. That didn't mean she wasn't taking the information back to Sawyer or someone who could hurt me worse. Or maybe she'd already gotten the very revenge she desired—but I figured that was wishful thinking.

After a quick shower, I pulled on a pair of track pants and a T-Shirt. I needed to get away, but I still didn't trust myself to climb on a bike, so I made my escape on foot.

Running shook the fog out of my head, but that, unfortunately, left plenty of room for reality to slip back in.

Fuck. What if I had already fucked it all up?

Not dead yet. That seemed to be the only assurance I could give myself.

After my legs carried me several blocks, and the world started to level out again, I dialed James.

"What the fuck, man?" he answered midway through the first ring.

I figured I should have been glad he hadn't called in the reinforcements or come over here and dragged me out himself. But if anyone understood my current position, it was him.

"You didn't check in, and someone else answered when I called last night," he continued.

"Dammit." I dragged my hands through my hair, shoving it out of my face. My skin was still clammy—not just from the run.

"She didn't tell you?" he asked.

"She was gone when I woke up." *Thank god.* I groaned. I had to get back home, get dressed, and find my leather. And my pride—that would be the hard part.

"Trent?" James sounded exasperated and I couldn't fault him. "Are you in trouble?"

Oh, I stared up at the cloudy sky, *in so many ways.* "I don't think so."

I tried to leave it at that, but I also knew he'd find out the details eventually. I already knew all of his demons, but this...

"You don't think so?" he snapped.

When you grow up with someone, practically spend your entire lives together, and then becomes partners on the force... Well, we knew each other and our tells, probably as well as we knew ourselves. He was overprotective, annoyed, and probably clawing at the walls, but that didn't mean I could walk away from this with nothing and ruin what might be our only shot. There was too much at stake to simply throw up my hands and walk away.

"She drugged me with... Something. I don't remember... much."

"Then get your ass to the hospital and—"

"James." Yeah, I knew the policy. Sit at the hospital for hours, blood work, questions, paperwork. That wasn't going to fly. It was the equivalent of giving up. I'd miss the meeting with Sawyer, and even if I finagled my way out of it, I'd likely get pulled from the field. "I told you that because you're my friend. I'm not backing out of this."

"You could be compromised. Get out," he yelled. "Or I'm going to come up there and haul your ass—"

"I can't. I just got in." I couldn't imagine Brooke leaving me for someone else to deal with. She'd enjoy it too much. No, if she had found out something, she'd play it smart and keep it to herself to use it as her own leverage, which gave me time to get to her first. "I think I'm good."

"Oh, really? And what percentage would you give that probability?"

"I'm a hundred percent not dead." I could hear him sputtering and growling something under his breath. If I got home alive, he'd kick my ass from here to Florida. "I can still pull this off."

James sighed. He also knew me too well to think that I'd give up. I could practically hear his foot tapping against the floor through the phone. "Anything else happen?"

I swallowed—more my pride than anything, but the words still wouldn't come out. "I only remember flashes."

My phone started buzzing and I pulled it back to check the number. *Fitch.*

"I gotta go, Fitch is calling."

"You better fucking fill me in."

I heard James cussing me out when I cut off the call, but I had to go with my gut. I still had time.

"Yeah," I said.

"Grab five specials from Donovan's and bring them up to my house." He hung up.

I rubbed the back of my neck, jogged back to the house and threw on the same clothes from the night before since they were handy, but when I went to grab my leather from the peg next to the TV, I realized it was gone.

Fuck.

My keys were still under the TV, so I grabbed them and headed out the back door to the junker pickup I used when a bike wasn't practical, hoping it'd start on the first try.

It wasn't exactly practical in itself, but I wasn't hauling six meals on the hog.

As soon as the engine sputtered to life, I called in the order to Donovan's and hauled ass across the Point to pick up the food and then get to Fitch's house on the opposite side.

It was a good forty minutes after the call that I pulled up to Fitch's house. There were a couple of cars, including Cannon's beat-up Camero, and three bikes parked out front. I grabbed the bags and headed for the door with no idea what I was about to walk into.

When I knocked, Cannon jerked open the door, and I saw a grey-haired man I didn't recognize pointing a rifle in my direction. I jerked backward, but Cannon pulled me inside. "It's not loaded," he mumbled.

Fitch stood and grabbed one of the bags from my hand

and I put the other on the only empty space of the coffee table, next to the line-up of guns and scopes. As I straightened a leather landed against my shoulder. Sawyer grinned —the kind of grin you see in horror movies, and it made the doubts in my head even louder. "Brooke said she grabbed it by mistake last night."

Accident my ass. I wondered if she'd laced the sleeves with acid or if she'd had fun searching the empty pockets.

"Thanks." I grabbed the coat before it slid off and put it on.

"Fun night?" Fitch asked.

There was no way I could describe the previous night, especially not to them, so I left them with a vague grunt and a slight shrug. I felt like I'd been dragged back to square one. Not just with the group, but in every respect. I felt like a rookie. "I probably had too much to drink."

Sawyer nodded toward the back hallway, beckoning me to follow as the knot in my chest grew.

"What is it with you and Brooke?"

How was it that one woman—half my size—unnerved me more than any criminal here? "Oh, she's something else."

He nodded slowly, narrowing his eyes. "Gavin's been trying to tame her for years—he's not the first, or only—but she's stubborn."

"I noticed." But as his comments really settled in my mind, I thought about what it must be like for a woman who'd not only rose to officer in this world, but had to deal with all the men trying to tame her along the way.

"She's got some great assets though, can't deny that." He lifted a whiskey glass, grinning at me over the rim. The glint in his eyes assured me he wasn't talking about her accounting or bar management abilities.

Did he just...?

He winked as the deep brown liquid sloshed to his lips.

Train for her birthday. Checking out her "assets." Some father.

"Don't know why I'd have to tell you though. Wouldn't it be ironic for a Prospect to be the one to put her in her place?"

I nodded, hoping the conversation would end. I wanted nothing more than to put her in her place after what she'd done, but I was certain that my definition of that differed from Sawyer's.

While Sawyer rejoined the group, I hung back, unsure of what they expected me to do, but if they weren't showing me the door, I'd take advantage of a few minutes to observe.

There were at least half a dozen guns on the couch between Fitch and Cannon, while the grey-haired man inspected each in turn. Now that he wasn't aiming a gun at my face, I noticed that he wore a cut from Defiance MC with the name Cutter on his patch. Another unfamiliar face, who'd been standing behind the door when I entered, wore the same cut with the name Cam.

"And you can get all we need?" Cutter asked.

Fitch snorted. "Depends on what you're offering."

Cutter eyed me for a long moment, scratching at the grey stubble along his jawline, then gestured to Cam with a flick of his wrist. Cam moved to the center of the room, pulling a plastic baggie from his coat pocket. Fitch snatched it away and as the two Defiance members lunged toward him, Cannon and Bull revealed the guns tucked under their coats.

Heat enveloped my chest. *I should have listened to James.*

The Defiance men stepped back, but neither lost their glower as Fitch opened the baggie, dipped his pinky into the white powder and sampled the residue. He then passed it to Sawyer who did the same. They both shrugged.

"We can get you two-thirds for what you're offering," Sawyer said.

"Are you nuts?" Cutter jumped from his seat. "That's pure—"

Sawyer turned on his heel, grabbing the man by the collar. "Our customers know their shit. Street value means two-thirds of the guns unless you want to double the shipment."

"Double? That's jacked. We can move this shit for twice the value of your guns."

"But, if you could get your hands on that quantity for base value, you wouldn't be coming to us." Sawyer threw up his hands. "On the other hand, we do have choices for B-grade flea powder."

"B-grade?" Cutter sputtered, his face turning bright red as his jaw ticked.

"Might want to have a talk with your chemists. They could do better."

Cam scowled. "Three weeks? You want us to double our offer in three weeks?"

"If you want all the guns, yes." Sawyer said.

Pissing people off who you're offering guns to. Smart.

"We can increase it by seventy-five, but you're asking us to take a big risk moving so much. We don't have a Barney watching our asses."

Barney? I'd heard that term used in reference to cops. *So they do have someone on the inside.*

"We'll give you the address for the drop the morning of delivery," Sawyer said.

"And how are we supposed to prepare to move that much dope to a location we don't know?"

"I suggest caution," Sawyer drawled. "Once you're in Devil territory, you'll be fine."

"Why not a neutral location?"

"Because I get what I want," Sawyer said, tucking the sample of drugs into an inside pocket of his cut. "For this kind of trade we need a secure location, and that's the only way I can guarantee that security."

"And what's to protect my club?"

"My word," Sawyer said. "This alliance is far too valuable to risk on not keeping you safe. Just focus on getting your shipment to the Point. We'll have everything ready for you. Three weeks."

Sawyer was getting the rich end of the bargain. Teaming up with Defiance could give him exactly what he wanted, ultimately, I had no doubt his goals would be to merge the clubs and rule over both. Defiance Club was far out of our jurisdiction, but their dirty antics and playing fast and loose were bad news. And here the Devils were inviting them over for a play date.

Chapter Nine

HELLBENT

Brooke

FOR THE NEXT WEEK, I left my apartment as little as possible, choosing to work from the couch in my living room. PMS was going to be the death of me, and if even one man gave me the side eye, I'd lose everything I'd worked for by taking a pencil to his eye. This was the only time I had penis envy, I mean it wasn't exactly like they spent an entire week of the month feeling like a gremlin was relentlessly kicking and clawing away at their manhood.

But this month seemed worse.

Karma, I figured.

Karma for truly proving I was exactly like every man in the club. But Trent still came back, the damn fool, also proving he was just as stupid and desperate as the rest of us.

"Brooke," Gavin yelled as he pounded on my door.

I had no intention of leaving my position, curled up on the couch, wishing for a cure for the monster ripping at my insides. Instead, I sank deeper into the cushions. It wasn't like Gavin could see me in any case. My apartment was on the third floor of the building in what used to be a large storage space for the opera house. Dixon had remodeled it to live in when he first joined the club, eager to get away from Sawyer, and I'd moved in with him when I was sixteen.

"Open the fucking door," Gavin yelled, slamming even harder against the steel door. Yes, there was an excellent reason I kept an industrial-strength steel door on my apartment. But not even that acted as a deterrent against Gavin. "I fucking know you're in there. You haven't left all day."

"Go away." *What excuse could be viable?* I couldn't have PMS. I couldn't be sick. All of those were non-options in my world. "I have work to do."

The next thud against the door rang out with the sharp tones of metal on metal, and I nearly fell off the couch with the jarring sound. I rubbed my hands over my face. The downside to my location was no back door.

Gavin never gave up. Never took no for an answer. But why would he? Sawyer set the stage when he served me up to Gavin and all of his friends for my sixteenth birthday. Since then, no matter what I'd done, he'd come back. I greeted him with a gun once, and guess who that landed in hot water.

"What the fuck?" I screamed.

"I'll break the fuckin' door down, Mama." It was no empty threat. If Gavin had to, he'd come through the brick wall next to the door.

I wanted to vomit in my mouth. I was no one's fuck toy or possession. And yet, as hard as I tried to fight it, the men around me had made damn sure I knew my place.

Gavin thought he was the chosen one—according to Sawyer, he would be. Gavin was the hot-headed son Sawyer always wanted, and his desire for power made him easily malleable. He'd be whatever Sawyer wanted, and what Sawyer wanted most was for him to put me in my place.

Gavin continued pounding on the door until the plaster around the frame shook, and dust flew out from under the trim. Unfortunately, I couldn't line my walls in steel, too.

I dragged myself to my feet and carefully approached the door. Keeping my distance, I looked through the peephole to see him swinging a crowbar. *Shit.* I jumped back before it impacted again. "Put down the crowbar," I yelled.

I peeked out again, and he held the crowbar overhead, ready to swing.

I unlocked the doorknob and slid free the deadbolt. It was either that or live without a door until I got a new wall and door installed.

On the other side of the door, the bar clanged to the floor. The only reprieve I would get.

I took a breath, twisted the last lock, and let my hands fall, stepping to the side and out of the range of the swinging door. Gavin took care of the rest—as I knew he would—bursting through the door, slamming it behind him, and resetting the first lock. "About time, Mama."

"I told you not to fucking—"

His hand smacked across my face before I could finish. "Don't be so mouthy."

The familiar taste of blood stung my tongue.

Grabbing my shoulder, he shoved me face-first into the wall. He held my throat, blocking off all but a little oxygen as he pinned me there and unbuttoned my pants from behind.

"Fucker—" I grunted with what air I could get and tried to push his hands away. His knees hit the back of mine and my kneecaps cracked against the wall.

"This was cute once," he growled, yanking my head back by my hair and slamming it into the wall again.

I saw lights. Tasted more blood.

But he didn't relent. Hell, I was certain it turned him on even more. He was a sick fuck like that. A sick-fuck I was sure no psychology book in the world could ever nail down.

He yanked down my pants and undid his.

Power-hungry sadist.

I squeezed my swollen eyes closed as he thrust into me.

Misogynistic bastard.

Chapter Ten

WHERE THE DEVIL DON'T GO

Trent

CANNON DRAGGED me into the shop Sunday morning. I wanted to get some sleep, but that described much of my existence here, especially since that whole mishap with Brooke. I worked through the day, although they still hadn't let me near the hot stuff, and most of the guys who brought in their bikes insisted on doing the work themselves. I, on the other hand, replaced brake lines in a minivan, several sets of brakes, and finished what seemed like hundreds of oil changes on all the Ol' Ladies' vehicles. I'd spent the week trying to stay under the radar, but I couldn't sleep well at night because I still hadn't figured out Brooke's fucking angle. If I got my mind off that, there were always incoming calls asking me to run here or there, pick up cigarettes, or deliver beer.

I learned as much as I could about their system over drinks with Caine or Cannon since they were at least tolerable, eavesdropping at work and volunteering for odd jobs whenever I wasn't inundated with orders to carry bags, pick up cigarette buts, or clean the disgusting bathrooms. It kept me busy, under the radar, and allowed me to work my way deeper into their system.

I finally understood why the members of the club were loaded. The money that came in, never left the Point. They had the means to handle practically anything internally. Club-owned mechanic. Club-owned bar. Club-controlled gas station. And those businesses didn't even scratch the surface, although I imagined they made some decent fronts for laundering money from the drug and gun networks. They'd put together an almost entirely closed system, and by the time they were ready to spend money outside of the Point, it had already been run through so many legit businesses, it'd be untraceable. Although, I still hadn't seen hide nor hair of any cops in the area.

The Devils weren't big enough to hit the national radar, even though many considered Sawyer to be one of the biggest rising MC Presidents in the area. They were a small-shot mosquito of the mid-west, but Ashville was feeling the brunt of those mosquito attacks, and without competition from the Gold family, they seemed to be inching their way into the inner-city.

Swat down one nuisance, and another takes its place. That was the bane of trying to be a good cop in a fucked-up world. There would always be another group waiting in the wings to take advantage of the vacuum and step in. But I figured it was good job insurance, as long as I survived. And with the frequency I tended to step into the shit-filled quicksand, well, I was probably my own worst enemy.

Sometimes I regretted the gung-ho persona I had to wear around here—like when Cannon requested that I deliver the accounting records after the shop closed

Saturday afternoon. Because that, of course, meant seeing Brooke, who I'd been vehemently hoping to avoid.

It was a weekend, and no one else seemed to be around. Something about a big event upstate—which is how I got dragged into the shop to finish up a few repairs in the first place. A lot of guys took their families for a weekend of fun. How they managed to keep families in lieu of the constant indiscretion and danger, would always remain a mystery to me. But I figured the drugs and power helped.

I knocked on her door several times, hoping she wouldn't answer, but the package was too thick to slide under the door, so I tried one more time. Just as the tension in my chest eased, and I turned to head back down the stairs, the door opened.

"What?" Brooke's voice cracked.

"Thrilled to see you, too." I held out the envelope.

Slowly, her gaze traveled down to my hand, then she blinked. She looked like she'd just climbed out of bed, and given her sweaty and matted hair, pallor skin and slow, jerky movements, I wondered if she was high. "Cannon said you needed this."

Her eyes widened like she'd forgotten I was standing there.

Definitely high. "Are you okay?"

I held up the envelope, and she reached for it, but her knees wobbled, and she fell forward. I dropped the envelope and caught her before she sent us both tumbling down the stairs. Her body was hot to the touch.

Dammit. So much for keeping it short. "Brooke?"

I carried her back inside and grabbed a wet towel to lay over her face. She moaned at the touch but didn't open her eyes. Her breathing was rapid and shallow, so I felt her wrist to check for her pulse—also rapid. I pulled out my phone and prepared to call an ambulance—how bad would the club freak over that?

But in her current condition, I didn't see another choice.

As I started to dial, she stirred, rolling to her side, and grabbing my wrist.

"I'm calling an ambulance."

"No." She swung her arm through the air, aiming for my phone and missing by inches. "No ambulance. I'm fine —I'm just..."

Her eyelids drooped as she tried to find her reasoning.

"Did you take something?"

"Tylenol," she mumbled, then glared up at me. Well, I wasn't sure it was a glare or the only expression she could manage. "You think I'm high?"

"You passed out, and you're running a fever."

She clutched her stomach and leaned forward. "Probably a bug. Now stop fussing and go away."

"You feel nauseous?"

"No," she snapped. "I'm cramping, if you must know."

Her hands quivered as she tried to hold herself together. Her eyes were glassy and distant.

"You need to see a doctor. You're white as a ghost."

"I am—" she grunted, curling up until she looked like she'd roll off the couch.

"Brooke," I tried again. She looked like death and, despite the contempt I held for her, I couldn't walk out.

"Fuck off." What was undoubtedly meant as an intimidating yell came out as a whisper.

"I'd love to," I mumbled. More than anything I wished I could bring myself to walk away and pretend I knew nothing. But even if my conscience would allow it, I wasn't taking the fall for it either.

Brooke slid to the floor, curled up again, and leaned against the couch. "No ambulance," she whispered.

"You can't ride, and my truck is on the other side of town."

"Sure I can. All I have to do is hold on if you drive."

I raised an eyebrow. "Is that the same confidence you had when you almost crashed into the floor a few minutes ago?"

With a scowl, Brooke climbed to her feet and stumbled down the hallway. A few minutes later, she reemerged in jeans and a T-shirt, steadying herself against the wall.

This is a horrible idea.

But then, trying to infiltrate a motorcycle club wasn't at the top of the good ideas list. Nor was refusing to get out after she drugged me. I was definitely riding a trend.

Brooke grabbed her jacket and headed for the door. If she was agreeing, she must have been in excruciating pain. But when I caught up with her at the top of the stairs, she refused to let me help, leaving me behind to watch her every shaky step with my stomach in my throat waiting for her to tumble down the long, straight concrete stairwell.

Out behind the bar, we both climbed on my bike, and she pressed her feverish body against my back. I could feel the heat through the leather.

I had to drive carefully, painfully slow on two wheels, but she managed to hold on until we reached the emergency room entrance, where I stopped for her to climb off. I had to hand it to her, she kept going.

I parked relatively close to the door, swung my leg over the bike and reluctantly went inside to find her. Not that it was difficult, she'd already found her first victim of the day —the registrar at the front desk. I walked in just in time to see her snap at him and then suddenly, she fell to the floor.

This time, I wasn't nearly close enough to catch her, but a nurse and security guard rushed over, pushing me out of the way. They took her straight back, leaving me to answer questions.

Birthday? No fucking idea.

Doctor? How the hell would I know?

Medical history? Still haven't caught on to the trend here?

Finally, they dumped me in a dim room with a giant empty space where a bed should be and ordered me to wait. They probably didn't want a guy in and MC leather scaring off the other patients in the waiting room.

But where the fuck was Brooke?

An hour later, the door opened, and two nurses wheeled in a sleeping Brooke. They didn't say a word as they hooked her up to half a dozen monitors and readjusted her IV line. All I got was a scowl as they left me with an unconscious Treasurer and the constant beep of monitors.

I crept toward the door, listening to the chatter outside the room. Although I only caught a few clear words, one phrase echoed in my head. S*exual assault.*

Damn. That meant they'd report it. Great under normal circumstances, not so much with Devils involved. That could put both of us in serious danger.

Standing between the curtain and the wall, I shot off a quick message to James.

Need to keep the heat off Mercy Hospital. Had to bring the P.'s daughter here. Can't elaborate.

As soon as the message came up as delivered, I deleted the entire conversation.

I knew James couldn't do much, but I was desperate not to have the police charging in right now for whatever reason. I considered contacting Captain Ainsley directly, but it was easier to hide conversations between myself and

James which couldn't directly be tied to the local police. He'd take the issue up with Libby, our own Captain, who could talk anyone into practically anything. I knew that from the experience of getting dragged out of bed in the middle of the night because her car broke down. Among other things.

My phone buzzed a few minutes later, but I ignored it since the doctor finally stepped in.

"You family?" His face was almost as stern as the scowl I'd gotten from the nurses. He didn't care if I was family or not. All they saw was the DOA emblem and wanted to wash their hands of us.

I nodded.

"We did an emergency D&C to clear out the products of conception." He babbled so quickly I could barely keep up, but the conception thing got me.

"Hold up? What?"

His eyes narrowed. "She had a miscarriage, but the tissue wasn't fully expelled. The infection started to spread, so she'll be in rocky condition until the antibiotics clear it up."

She was pregnant? I nodded again, trying to digest the news without asking too many questions. "How long until she can leave?"

What I really meant was, how long would I need to convince her to stay. As if convincing her of anything was feasible.

"Depends on her immune system." And with that less than helpful answer, he ducked out of the room.

How long until the club finds out? I couldn't begin to imagine their response to all of this. At least with most of the members out of town, we'd have a little leeway before anyone started asking questions, but Church was Monday morning, and it'd be pretty damn obvious if the Treasurer didn't show up.

I slumped in the chair, resting my head on my fist. *This is going to be a long weekend.*

Finally, I dozed off, albeit uncomfortably, at least I wasn't conscious to watch every single second tick by until a crash ended my reprieve. When I opened my eyes, Brooke stood, wobbling next to her bed.

"Brooke." I jumped to my feet, grabbing her before she made a nose-dive for the floor again. "You need to lie down."

"No," she muttered. "No, I need... I need." She rubbed her hand over her face and collapsed back onto the bed.

"I..." she started again, staring off and blinking. Her condition hadn't changed much since answering the door.

I pulled the blankets to the foot of the bed, leaving room to get her situated, but she grabbed my forearm with her hot, clammy hand. "Please, don't. Sawyer..." Her eyes fluttered closed. "What'd you give me?"

"Nothing. You're at the hospital. Now, lie back. You're sick and need rest." I pushed her into bed and pulled the blanket up over her legs.

"I need..." she continued mumbling. "I need to... What is it?"

"Sleep."

She shook her head and kicked off the blanket again. "That isn't it."

"Well, if you don't try to rest, I'm sure a nurse will be in soon to help it along."

"No drugs." She pulled at her IV. "What're they giving me. My head...."

Dear lord, I wasn't going to attempt to explain it in her

current condition. "You have an infection. They're only giving you antibiotics."

Her head dropped back like she didn't have the strength to hold it up any longer. "I can't stay."

"You don't have a choice right now." I pushed back the hair that had matted to her face with sweat. Her eyes finally closed, and her breathing fell into a slow rhythm that indicated she was asleep again.

As I stepped back to my chair, she moaned and curled up on her side. "Put out the fire before you burn the fucking house down."

She was in bad shape. I sat down, leaning forward onto my forearms. *What a mess. What a fucking mess. Trapped in a hospital room with the sadistic woman who drugged me.*

Chapter Eleven

BLOODY HELL

Brooke

I WOKE IN A DIM ROOM. At least, I thought I was awake. My head pounded so hard I couldn't see straight, let alone focus on details. *Karma is a sick, fucking bastard.*

Someone moved next to me. A tall figure with broad shoulders.

"Dixon?" I knew it couldn't be true, but at the same time, logic didn't seem to matter. That's just one of the things desperation can do.

"Sorry to disappoint you," he said, stepping closer, into the narrow beam of light that shone in around the curtain.

"Trent," I mumbled. Of course it was Trent. I tried to sit up, but my arms shook with every effort, and I finally gave up. "What's going on?"

Trent stood over the railing on my right side, rubbing his eyes and forehead like he hadn't slept in days.

When he didn't answer immediately, my heart jumped up into my throat. "Am I dying?"

The only disappointment in that would be that I hadn't finished what I'd set out to do. Those bastards would get away with everything.

"No." Trent stuffed his hands into his pockets. "You have an infection."

"Why? How?" Even the small words were a struggle, like my mouth had been shot up with Novocain.

"Uh..." His eyes wandered around the room.

What the hell had I picked up? What the hell had those bastards left me with this time? My heart thudded in my chest as the possibilities rushed through my head.

Trent still didn't answer.

"Prospect," I said as sternly as I could manage. "What the fuck is wrong with me?"

He stared up at the ceiling. "You had a miscarriage."

I shook my head. "No."

I took precautions. I didn't miss my pills. I sure as hell wasn't taking a chance that one of those ingrates would knock me up. *Fuck no.* A sudden wave roared through my stomach and rose up my throat. *Not again.*

"It caused an infection. They didn't give me any details, but after you passed out in the lobby, they did and emergency D&C, and have been pumping you with antibiotics since."

This had to be a joke. *Would he stoop this low for revenge?*

"Miscarriage. That's impossible."

Trent nodded and staggered backward, refusing to look at me. I knew then he wasn't lying. This wasn't a prank. *Oh, God.* "I was pregnant?"

Trent cocked his head to the side. "You didn't know?"

"Of course I didn't fucking know." I wished I had something to chuck at him.

How could... What if....

I had to get out of the hospital. I kicked off the blanket and pulled at the monitoring equipment stuck all over my body. *No. No.* I wasn't doing this.

Trent grabbed my arm before I could free myself from the IV. "You need to stay."

"I can't." It wasn't an option. If Sawyer found out.... If the police found out....

I was too vulnerable there. More vulnerable than I could handle. But as the monitors near me beeped in protest, I ripped all of the lines off, ignoring the stinging pain from adhesive, tape, and the IV tube violently exiting the back of my hand. The next thing I knew, the alarms around me blended into one long inharmonious sound. The room went fuzzy, and darkness crept in around the edges.

———

I GASPED FOR AIR, finally escaping the frigid darkness. Except the cold stayed with me. My muscles shook so hard, I heard the bed rattle under me, and as I reached out into the darkness, my hand hit something cold.

My brain stayed five steps behind my body. I couldn't remember where I was or how I'd gotten there.

Something moved beside me, and all I could think about were those chilly nights when Sawyer would open the door to my bedroom and pull back the covers. I clutched the thin blanket covering my body, waiting for the inevitable. A weight landed on my feet, then crept up my body as a dark, shadowy figure drew an extra blanket over me.

Hospital, I remembered.

"Trent?" My voice shook when I spoke, but at least I could blame it on the cold.

"Here I thought you couldn't remember my real name." His words were laced with dry sarcasm.

I was too tired to fight. "What time is it?"

"Ten am. Sunday morning."

We'd been there all night. Longer than all night. I couldn't remember what time he'd shown up, but I was certain it was closer to afternoon than evening. I couldn't believe he'd been sitting in the dark with me the entire time, but he probably just didn't want to lose his chance at earning a patch by leaving.

He'd probably filled in the entire club on my condition already. Sawyer might have offered him a lofty reward for keeping an eye on me and reporting all the details. It would have been fitting given what I'd done to him.

In my mind, I pulled myself out of bed, stormed out, and got back to my apartment to finish my bookkeeping. I had to finish before anyone found out what was going on, but I closed my eyes. "Did you update everyone in the club? I'm sure Sawyer was thrilled."

"Not my story," he said.

I silently laughed. A story. They'd all want a hell of a story if I didn't get my work done. Sawyer never stopped looking for an excuse to make me look incompetent and weak. Now this? Dear old Dad would never get over holding this over my head. It'd become a joke, a reminder of my "frailty", yet another failure brought on by challenging the boy's club.

He'd never own up to the fact that he'd set all this into motion himself. It started when I was fourteen with him coming into my room months after Mom died. The women in the bar—who he'd also enjoyed long before his wife died—weren't enough. When he'd forced me to have an abortion before my sixteenth birthday to cover up his illicit deeds, then handed me over to the club so they could have their own fun.

Find someone to take care of you. Claim you. Become an Ol' Lady. That's how you serve the club.

For a long time, I'd reluctantly conformed to the only life I'd ever known, the only existence possible for a teenage girl in my world. But I never stopped listening. I never stopped learning, and finally, I stepped up to prove I could be useful in other ways. I could do more than sex. I hated sex. But everyone does something they hate to get what they want. For Sawyer, that meant dealing with the fact that I'd earned my patch and I wouldn't let him forget it.

My brother helped, feeding me information the women usually weren't privy to and watching my back until finally, I got my chance to patch in and become Treasurer. But some things refused to change. I rode with them. Worked and fought alongside them. But I'd always be a second-class member.

Another chill ran through me, forcing out an involuntary whimper. "You open your mouth, and I'll slash up your testicles." I hoped it sounded more intimidating than I felt.

He snorted. "Got it."

I shook my head. He thought I was just as pathetic as everyone else did. "Right, until you're presented with an opportunity to benefit from my 'secret.'" I knew how things worked. "You and I both know that."

"Or maybe"—he held out the word—"I'll keep my mouth shut."

Yeah, that was a big fuckin' maybe. "Why? Because then you'll have blackmail on me?"

"You know, farfetched as it seems, have you ever considered the possibility that I'm not your enemy or your biggest threat?"

I clenched my jaw. "I gave you every reason to be."

"Then, there's probably nothing I can say to change your mind." He took a seat near the window, pushing the curtains back and flooding my room with light.

Why did that bastard always have a point? There was nothing either of us could say. Nothing we could do except protect each other's secrets, but suddenly I was at a disadvantage in that capacity.

———

A PHONE RANG, and Trent held mine up. "Looks like your dad."

"Don't call him that," I snapped, grabbing the phone. "It's *Sawyer*. Always Sawyer."

There wasn't anything remotely "dad" about him and never had been.

"Hello," I answered, concentrating on keeping my voice steady.

"I need you to run up to Hudson and pick up the package from Anarchy."

Icy daggers cut through my spine.

"Gavin will meet you at the bar and ride with you."

Gavin. Bar. You've got to be kidding me. I dropped my head back and stared up at the ceiling. Of course, I was already behind on the bookkeeping that he'd be expecting a full report on in church the following day. I needed a shower. I needed clothes. And I couldn't even imagine the state of my face and hair.

And to top it all off, *Gavin*. "Why not Trent?"

"You really have a thing for him." His voice went up a pitch. He was desperate for me to end up with someone— apparently even if it was a Prospect at this point.

"He's less insufferable." *And here.* And he already knew exactly why I looked like shit so there'd be far less explaining—and forcible flirting—involved.

"Gavin—" Sawyer began. He continued to look for every opportunity to stick me with that bastard, which in turn, only fueled Gavin's entitlement.

"Trent or find someone else to ride with Gavin. I'm not fucking dealing with him."

Sawyer made a low sound. "Mouthy, mouthy."

I shuddered as his words reminded me of my last visit from Gavin.

"Fine," he said. "Just get the damn package from Anarchy."

When the call disconnected, I let the phone fall onto the bed. "We have a run."

"You're in no condition—"

Poor fool was too concerned with my condition for his own good. "Doesn't matter."

I ripped the tape off my IV and gritted my teeth as I yanked out the tube again. It stung a bit more than I expected, but I managed not to wince too much.

"You need antibiotics." Trent blocked one side of the bed, so I wrestled with the opposite railing until it gave way and I flung my legs off.

"Last I checked antibiotics come in pill form."

"The only thing holding you up must be pure carbon-fiber obstinance."

And stupidity.

———

FORTUNATELY, my clothes were all in one piece and I managed to get dressed without passing out.

The hospital staff barely looked at us as we walked out —they'd dealt with our kind far too much, and usually valued their friends and families over getting in our way. From time to time, we ran into do-gooders, but that didn't seem to be the case this time.

Climbing on the bike behind Trent, I just wanted to fall asleep, and one look into his eyes said he wanted the same thing. As we hit the highway, I rested my chin on his shoulder, using the wind to keep my eyes open. For a moment, I zoned out, and my body swayed. I squeezed against Trent harder, trying not to fall off until I realized we were still going in a straight line.

"Trent. Stop." I dug my fingers into his leather, trying to stay on the bike until it came to a stop. In the midst of climbing off the bike, I found myself on my hands and knees, puking. The taste filling my mouth was so rancid I shuddered as I sat back on my knees. The worst thing was the tears. I couldn't stop the fucking tears that came with it.

I hated crying. It was worse than feeling weak and beaten up. It was everything I tried so hard not to be. Crying made those wounds visible, and it brought back every experience I'd fought to suppress.

I waited for Trent to tell me that I should've listened to the doctor, but he stood by me in silence, staring down. I hated the feeling of his eyes on me. Hated it more than anyone else's gaze because I knew exactly what they all wanted. Trent, however, I couldn't peg.

He probably hated me—as he should. That was my goal after all. But he might have saved me as well, and I couldn't handle being the focus of those dueling realities. As I climbed to my feet, he handed me a bandanna. I kept my head down as I took it and wiped my eyes, then my mouth.

"You okay?" he asked when I finally looked up.

"We need to take a detour to a pharmacy." I wanted him to think it was important—and picking up something to keep me from puking all over the Race Trap Bar wouldn't be a bad idea, but really, I needed makeup. I needed to cover the blotches and the purple bruise on my cheek and make my pink eyes less visible. The last thing I could ever do was let anyone see me this weak.

Chapter Twelve

CHEEK OF THE DEVIL

Trent

AT THE PHARMACY, Brooke headed straight for the makeup aisle.

"What on earth are you doing?" I asked.

"You don't get it." She threw one product after another in her basket.

Damn straight, I didn't. One night to hell and back and she was concerned with makeup. "Then explain."

"I can't look weak. Ever. You could get your ass kicked, and they might give you the benefit of the doubt, but me... I can't even flinch. I can't let them see the bruises or splotchy skin." She pushed past me to grab something from another shelf. "If they find out about this, the cause won't matter. It'll just be another excuse."

"Why do you put up with them?" She was smart, strong, and possibly the most cunning and determined of the bunch. I couldn't imagine that she couldn't devise a way out. That she couldn't find a better way to buck the system.

"Because if I back down, I admit they're right."

"You know that thing I said about you being stubborn? It's going to get you killed. You can't want to spend the rest of your life like this."

She straightened, wearing a death glare that cut right through the pale skin and bloodshot eyes. "That's a big challenge coming from a Prospect."

"I'm not the one dead on my feet. And like you said, their expectations of you are different." They were downright sadistic, to say the least.

"One day you might be, and you'll keep going. You're all alike, thinking I need to just lie down and take it."

That wasn't what I had said at all, so I threw my hands in the air. Surrender was less time-consuming. After she had a basket full of makeup—and at my insistence something for her nausea, she paid, then pulled me to the single bathroom at the back of the store.

Fifteen minutes later, she opened the door. "Do I look passable?"

"Aside from the bloodshot eyes?"

She slammed the door in my face. It wasn't as if bloodshot eyes were a rarity around here.

"Brooke." I knocked. "You look fine."

"Stop lying," she shouted.

What? I couldn't tell the truth. I couldn't fudge the truth. There was no winning with this woman. But little by little, I was beginning to understand her, and it made every nerve in my body tingle. Her frustration was probably a tiny part of what she dealt with on a daily basis when surrounded by chauvinistic bikers.

Her animosity with Sawyer was just the tip of the iceberg. I'd never know how many times this woman had been assaulted. How many times she'd been attacked by her own father, and probably every member of the club.

What did she have to feel facing those people every day? Every night when she walked into that bar?

Caine was right. Her storm was no safe place to be, but I'd already been sucked in.

An old lady in the corner glowered at me as she searched the incontinence section nearby, so I turned my back to her and leaned my shoulder against the wall. *Can this week get any crazier?*

As soon as I thought the words, I wanted to take them back. Putting that kind of challenge into the universe under these circumstances was just asking for trouble.

The door opened again, and this time the black makeup streamed down Brooke's cheeks and pooled under her eyes. "Why do you have to be like this?"

"Like what?" I dropped my head against the wall. I was exhausted. I wasn't even sure I had it in me to ride, let alone deal with her mood swings. "What the fuck did I do?"

She yanked me into the bathroom and closed the door. At least that got me away from the cranky old lady, but it also meant I was trapped in a tiny room with an extremely unpredictable woman.

"Why are you really here?" she asked, facing the mirror while she dabbed away the stray makeup.

"Because you dragged me along."

"I mean Devil's Point, smartass bastard."

This again? "Haven't we gone over this?"

Brooke snorted. "And you've given me all the answers you expect me to want. Give me the real one."

"Tell me something real," I challenged.

She cocked her head, grabbing a paper towel. "I just had a miscarriage. How fucking real do you want?" Her voice shook, and I thought about letting her get away with it.

But then, she'd want a convincing answer from me.

"You didn't tell me that, and I'm sure if you had any choice in the matter, I wouldn't know."

"Fine. How about this? I have no idea who the father was. I guess there's a good chance it was Gavin's since he's usually the one beating down my door."

I watched her hands shake as she dabbed more foundation under her eyes, and over the bruise on the side of her face.

Was that Gavin's work too? "He the one who gave you that shiner?"

She wobbled, looking away. "We had an argument."

"About what?"

She closed her eyes, and her jaw pulsed. She was silent for a long moment, then she took a breath and glared over her shoulder at me. "He wanted to fuck. I didn't, so he took it upon himself to put me in my place."

Her admission didn't come as a shock—I'd already figured out that much—but my throat burned as soon as she said it.

With her back to me, she dragged her fingers through her hair, tackling each section, knot by knot. "The club knows two types of women. I don't want to be either, but they don't care."

I huffed, dropping back against the wall. "So, you decided to turn the tables on the new guy?"

"Sawyer ordered me to fuck you and get you to talk," she snapped. "When you turned me down, I took a shortcut and..." Her voice went quiet, barely audible. "Goddamn it, if it were any other prospect...."

She faced me again, reclining back against the sink.

"There's something different about you and that's why I don't believe any of your textbook answers."

My turn. I had to make it good. Good enough to get her to stop asking questions, and vague enough to cover my trail. "I came up here looking for someone who used to know my uncle. He used to talk about a man named Marcus Hutchinson who used to ride with BOA, but last anyone heard from him, he was hanging around the Devils when the fallout happened."

I gave her just enough to satiate her skepticism and pique her curiosity. A small grain she—hopefully—couldn't trace back to my real objectives. Not immediately anyhow. I'd come to The Point with two names to get me in the door and give me a reason to ask questions; Vic "Hawg" Clevenger, the main I claimed as my uncle, and Marcus Hutchinson. A man with a reputation for getting rid of his problems by slipping hot-shots to his enemies. We'd turned up Hutchinson in several old Brotherhood records and some personal records from Clevenger's effects. While it wasn't likely he was responsible for the recent pattern of fentanyl deaths, we hoped it'd serve as a cover for asking about similar patterns.

"Never heard of him" She looked me up and down as if trying to gauge whether or not to trust me. "What's so important about him?"

"I thought maybe he or my uncle might have had friends up here, and I have some questions. I came by Bone Grinders a while back looking for answers, and"—I shrugged—"I needed work. I needed answers, not just about Hutchinson, about my uncle and why he went to the grave defending a *club.*"

Brooke narrowed her eyes and studied me for a

moment. Suddenly, she seemed perfectly calm—as if something about this line of discussion was relaxing. Although it probably was a good distraction from whatever was going on in her head.

This is her thing, I realized. Pulling at the loose ends of tiny secrets until she had enough information to leverage her position. The other men might've looked at her as the weak link, but there was a reason they hadn't just gotten rid of her. They just kept the lion caged, trapped, abused, and expected compliance.

What are they going to do when she pulls out that final screw that renders the cage useless?

"I guess that brings us to the end of story time." She tossed all of her makeup back into the shopping bag. "But if you're just being nice to me to get—"

"I'm being nice to you because I'd rather be on your good side."

She made a clucking sound with her tongue. "That's a political answer if I ever heard one."

I crossed my arms over my chest. She was one to talk. "What did you tell Sawyer about me?"

Her shoulders dropped. When she turned away, I watched her through the mirror, pursing her lips together as she took a ragged breath. "I told him we had a few beers and I spent the night at your dump. That I didn't expect you were anything more than what you seemed."

I licked my lips, gauging her shifting eyes. "But you didn't entirely believe that."

"Still don't. You're good. You're not some ratty uneducated guy off the streets. You have street smarts, but there's something else as well." She met my gaze in the mirror and held it for a moment.

I had dismissed most of the members of the club as oblivious enough not to notice the little things that might make me stand out, but I couldn't risk even blinking wrong in front of her. "You thought you might be able to use *me* if you kept the suspicions to yourself."

She cocked her head. "Guess we're even."

I wasn't admitting to that. "Not quite."

Brooke swallowed. "I don't ever say this, and if you ever tell anyone—"

"You'll slice up my testicles?" It wasn't hard to guess where she was going.

The corner of her mouth twisted up as she rolled her eyes. "Forget it."

"That's a lot of work for 'forget it.'"

She didn't respond, so I reached for the door, hoping we were finally done, but she blocked the door.

"Trent," she said softly. "Do not tell—"

I sagged against the door. "You don't have to keep saying that, Brooke. I'm not mentioning this to a soul because I'm sure as hell not facing that firing squad from you or any of the guys."

I almost believed I saw the start of a smile, and possibly a bit of relief on her face. If she'd have been anyone else, I might have even offered a hug, but it was Brooke and we had work to do.

WE RODE another thirty minutes to the Race Trap Bar in Hudson, known as a "neutral zone" for bikers of all colors. I shut down my bike in the gravel parking lot beside the old brick building.

"Sawyer does business with Anarchy, the owner of the bar," Brooke said quietly. It was hard to tell if she was trying to be quiet, or if that was as loud as she could speak. Probably both.

She stood at the back of my bike, pressing her thumb into the center of her forehead.

"What are we picking up?" I asked, hoping that if she had something to concentrate on, she might snap out of the distant funk she'd fallen into. Or she'd just start yelling at me again. Either was better.

"Mostly gambling money. Some info—blackmail materials, pictures, details on what the other clubs are running."

I looked away to hide my smirk. So much for the neutral zone. "So, the guy running the biker haven doubles as PI of the MC world?"

Brooke sighed. "You know Sawyer, he always has his hooks in somewhere."

She took the lead when I opened the door.

The inside reeked of stale alcohol, greasy food, and old cigarettes. The place was empty except for a couple of guys in hoodies hunched over a corner table who looked like they were left over from the night before.

Brooke took a seat at the edge of the bar, draping her coat over the counter between us. After about five minutes of sitting under the thumping beat of some screamo music that was impossible to understand, the bartender stomped out of the back, looking irritated that she had to work. When she saw us, her posture straightened and she smiled, revealing two rows of rotted and broken teeth.

"Nachos and two ginger ales," Brooke said.

"Not the usual drink?" The bartender raised her eyebrows.

"If you were paid to care what I order, you wouldn't be working here," Brooke snapped.

With a snarky grin, the bartender filled our glasses, winking at me as she slid them across the bar.

"Newbie?" She snapped her gum. Up close, I could make out the pitted skin on her forehead and cheeks, with paired with the teeth and her twitchy movement led me to suspect a meth addiction.

She leaned over the bar and whispered, "I have fifteen as soon as I run some appetizers."

She sauntered away, peeking back at me to see if I was watching as she grabbed two plates off the counter.

"Did she—" I started to ask but couldn't finish the thought. I almost asked Brooke for some of her nausea meds.

"She offered to suck you off in the back room," she said flatly.

I didn't even want to touch my glass. "And we're eating food from here?"

"Food's good. Syn doesn't make it. Gavin normally rides along, and as you can imagine...."

"Fucks anything that moves?"

Brooke flinched and scratched the back of her neck, staring down at the wooden bar in front of us. "I'm pretty sure that without him here, she's hoping you have her fix."

"I definitely don't." *Not in any way imaginable.*

Brooke shrugged.

Syn walked past us, giving me a wink as she slipped out a side door.

"Any chance of us getting out of here before she comes back?"

Brooke shrugged again. I preferred her smart-ass remarks to this.

A man brought out the nachos, slipping an envelope under Brooke's coat in the process.

Slick. Brooke picked up a nacho covered in chili-cheese, jalapenos, and sour cream. "This is life," she said, then mumbled, "And if I puke it up, I'm going to be pissed."

"Just give me a warning." I watched her out of the corner of my eye, but my real interest was the men in the back. There was something off about them. They weren't wearing the colors of any local clubs, but as they sat over their untouched plates, they kept an eye on us as well.

After one nibble on the chip, Brooke put it on the edge of the plate and took a swig of ginger ale. "That'll depend on my mood at the time."

I looked at her for a long moment. *Was she joking?* I kind of got the feeling she was, but her expression remained stoic. Even now, she was a beast. An unpredictable and extremely dangerous beast who had been beaten down so much she didn't care who took the brunt when she lashed out. It wasn't so long ago that I'd been bearing the brunt. And yet, here I saw a different side of her.

Probably because she was so doped up and sick that she was desperate, but maybe we could use each other. If we could figure out a way to accomplish that which wouldn't get either of us hurt, permanently maimed, or killed.

Sawyer's objective was to see her settle down, and he didn't seem to care who accomplished that as much as he desired someone to tame her. If I could convince Sawyer I was the man for that job and he would benefit from it, he might call in the dogs to play nice and give Brooke a break from their violence. If played right, it could give us the break we needed. But suggesting that to Brooke was another obstacle entirely, charms didn't exactly work on her.

How exactly does one go about setting up an alliance with a wild, possibly rabid animal?

The more I thought about it, the more it seemed like the most terrible idea I'd come with up yet. Riding out her storm and forging some unholy alliance also meant risking the animosity of every single member of the club.

Chapter Thirteen

DONE AND DUSTED

Brooke

I COULD BARELY STOMACH one bite of nachos, and that pissed me off. *Perfect, now I'm a She-Devil who can't even eat.* Weak didn't begin to describe how I felt

I stared at the Ginger Ale—I despised the flavor, but somehow it did the trick and took the edge off the queasiness. Sometimes, I felt like one of those bubbles, clinging to the inside of the glass. Real, but only for a moment, until the slightest vibration sent it floating to the surface and then, nothing.

Am I really more than the walls I cling so tightly to?

"Brooke." Trent grabbed my arm.

The two drunkards from the corner bumped into us as they passed, but it was more than that. It knocked me off balance—purposefully, and the room spiraled around me as I grabbed the bar to steady myself.

Trent grabbed the closest man by the collar and shoved him backward, knocking over a whole row of stools.

The second man charged headfirst at him, doubling Trent over, but Trent spun, using the momentum of the hit to swing his attacker crashing into a table in the middle of the room.

That left me with the first hooligan charging toward me again. I swallowed the nausea and braced to throw the first punch. My fist connected with his jaw—it was a weak punch at best. The hood fell off his head, but he laughed and came at me hard, knocking me back.

My head collided with a barstool, but that wasn't the worst of it. The worst was that damn nacho. It caught in my throat and the taste mixed with bile and ginger ale in my mouth.

I can't puke. Not now.

But before I pulled myself together, the guy standing over me grabbed the envelope from under my coat and made a dash for the door.

"Fuck." I scrambled to my feet, but the other guy blew past me as well.

And to top it all off, Anarchy burst out of the kitchen— shotgun in hand. "You know better than to bring a fight here."

"They started it," I shouted, pointing at the door.

I yanked my coat off the bar and threw it on as I ran toward the door to see what direction they'd run off in.

"Brooke," Trent called after me.

I ignored him, scanning the gravel lot and the sidewalk beyond. No sign of them. They'd already gotten away. I started toward the sidewalk, but Trent grabbed me by the shoulder.

"We have to find them." I shrugged him off.

But instead of helping he grabbed me by the arm and

spun me around, opening his coat so I could see the folded papers tucked into his pocket.

"But they..." I'd watched the other man grab the envelope.

"They'll probably have a great time looking over the cocktail menu. They were in such a hurry, they probably won't notice until they think they're safe. I suggest we get going."

I gasped. He'd seen it coming. While I was staring at the bubbles in my drink, he saw it coming and switched out the contents with a cocktail menu. "When did you...?"

Rather than answer, he glanced back at the door, where the shotgun-wielding Anarchy stood, staring us down.

"We should get out of here."

As I climbed on the back of his bike, part of me wanted to nail him in the balls while a much smaller part of me reminded I should probably thank him for saving my ass, again.

Did it bother me more that I'd lost my focus and been utterly unhelpful in the fight? Or that Trent had managed to swap out that envelope for a beer menu before I even noticed? Or that I, as Treasurer, was just one-upped by a Prospect?

He'd saved the information we'd come to collect, but we still had no idea who those tweakers were, or what they were looking for. They knew where to find the envelope, but did they know what was inside?

I had to sweep up this mess before I got the blame. It weighed on me the entire ride back to the bar. And it was probably the only thing that kept me upright and clinging to Trent's back.

Trent offered a hand to steady me as I climbed off his bike. With my feet firmly on the ground, I concentrated on walking to the door of my loft without crumbling. Never mind the stairs, I couldn't even think about those yet. All I had to do was get to the other side of that door.

"Forget something?" Trent asked.

When I turned back, he held out the folded papers.

I'm so fucking off my game.

"Not a word of this," I reminded him.

As soon as he released the papers, I felt something strange bubble up inside of me. This time it wasn't the food. I wanted to be alone, and yet, some part of me didn't. A part I told to shut the hell up. I hated myself for the very thought of wanting him to stay. The men around here were stubborn, but there was something else that unnerved me about Trent. He was low man on the totem. He had no power or influence, and yet, he continued to carry himself with an air of unalterable confidence. As if he couldn't be rattled.

If I could just figure out why he's really here. While I believed what he'd told me in the bathroom was closer to the truth, he crafted his stories well, knowing exactly what to reveal and what to keep hidden.

"You going to be okay alone?" he asked.

My head snapped up. *Am I getting that easy to read?*

"Always," I lied. But the lie wasn't my problem. The problem was how quickly he saw through that as well.

I had a shit-ton of paperwork to get through before morning and a few calls to make—regrettably the first would be my doctor. I figured my body needed more antibiotics than the round I'd gotten in the hospital, and I needed to kick this shit fast.

I didn't have the energy for any of it.

The information in my hand was just one of my worries, and it seemed to weigh a ton in itself. I had to take care of that, the payroll Trent had delivered, and Sawyer would be asking me for every detail of it the following morning. I had lost an entire weekend. Two days I was counting on since I'd spent most of the last two weeks curled up with what I assumed was my monthly cycle from hell.

Trent ruffled through the compartment under the back seat and tossed me the bag of makeup. "Want me to stay? Just in case."

"In case of what?" I asked defensively.

"Gavin getting the urge to beat your door down again. You passing out again. Should I continue?"

My stomach sank. Suddenly, I realized why it was so difficult to be caught under Trent's intense gaze. It wasn't just that I didn't understand his motivation. He saw me. He saw right through me. "You're better off not getting in the middle of that."

"Sawyer knows how bad he hurts you?"

Out of nowhere, I laughed so hard my sides hurt. "Why would he care? Did you forget that he ordered me to fuck you, your first day as Prospect?"

The somber look on his face told me that he had forgotten about that—just a little bit. I swallowed and fisted my hands. "He's not going to tell anyone to stop the very thing he started when I was fourteen."

I snapped at myself for saying that.

I heard Trent exhale, then he put down the stand on his bike and climbed off.

"I don't need you," I said, putting my hand up *Why did I even open my mouth about Sawyer?*

Trent cocked his head. "I never said you did, but I've barely slept in forty-eight hours. I'm too tired to drive home, and you owe me."

Manipulative jackass. And dammit, some part of me liked it—the part that desperately didn't want to do this alone anymore.

All the more reason not to trust the asshole fully.

But I nodded, yanking open the door to the stairwell. "Fine, but keep your mouth shut and let me get my work done."

When we got upstairs, he went straight to the couch, hanging his coat over the corner and stretching his arms up over his head. As his shirt rose, I got another glimpse at the tattoos hiding underneath.

Don't, I told myself, turning away. That was, in no way, the distraction I needed at the moment.

"I hope you don't expect to get much sleep out here." I held up the paperwork I'd piled on the bar just outside the living room. "You're in my office, and I have work to do before church."

Chapter Fourteen

HOT BLOODED

Trent

"THE DEVIL WON'T LET GO."

I could still hear Brooke mumbling that over and over as I put her to bed. Two hours later, she'd walked out of the bedroom with a distant look in her eyes. "There's blood everywhere."

Her voice had been broken and distant.

I jumped up from the couch, thinking it had something to do with the miscarriage, but she didn't seem to know I was there. "Brooke?"

She looked toward me, but not necessarily at me.

"Are you okay?" I asked.

Her forehead was beaded with sweat. "He's never going to let me go."

"Who?"

"The Devil." She collapsed sideways against the wall, her eyes falling closed. "He ripped out my heart, but he still wants more."

Is she awake?

Or just delusional?

I considered taking her back to the hospital. I slowly approached and brushed back her damp hair. "Brooke."

"The dreams," she said faintly. Her eyelids fluttered, and her head dropped forward.

"I—" She shivered, so I grabbed my jacket off the couch and wrapped it around her shoulders. She still felt hot, swaying on her feet as I took her by the arm and led her to the couch.

"I can't." Her voice shook. "I hurt. Please...."

"Just sleep." Lifting her feet to the couch, I slid in behind her.

How many times had she been raped? Used? Beaten?

From the moment I stepped into the club, she'd seen a threat and decided to get me before I got here. None of it excused what she'd done, and yet, here I was, helping with her work, trying to sleep on her couch, trying to make sure the woman who attacked me was okay.

It was fucked up.

As I drifted off, she elbowed me in the ribs. The next assault came with a pinched nut as she jerked. Then, a bruised shin. She was as dangerous in her sleep as she was awake. Maybe worse. Finally, she stilled again.

Two adults, one oversized couch, and one feverish sleeper made for a long night. I woke up before the sun but didn't wake her. I wasn't ready for that. The hot and cold. Anger and hurt.

The logical part of me still didn't trust her, but I'd thrown myself into a world where no one could be trusted. Brooke was a different kind of beast, though. The men of the club had no idea who they were backing deeper into a corner every day.

I carefully carried her back to bed and noticed a new alert on her phone.

Prescription ready for pick up.

If she slept as long as her body needed, she'd sleep through church. But I figured I'd have plenty of time to run to the pharmacy and sneak back in, so I took her keys to lock the door behind me and left a short note just in case.

Twenty minutes later, I returned, placing the prescriptions and a bottle of water on the nightstand next to her. Then, I picked up the living room, using my cell to snap a few photographs of anything that might come in handy, and left the keys where I'd found them, locking the door on my way out.

———

I THOUGHT BEING a detective left me with little downtime, but I found myself looking forward to that schedule again. I got home, ready to drop, but I only had time for a change of clothes and a quick phone charge before I headed out again. Church would be starting soon, and I had to be the first one there.

But before that, coffee.

I brewed a cup as strong as I could get it and sat down to check my phone while I drank. The scalding temperature did as much to wake me as the caffeine—except faster.

To my surprise, I didn't find a deluge waiting on my phone, but I still owed James an explanation and a proper check-in.

"Trent?" he answered after a couple of rings.

"Yeah. Sorry to leave you hanging." I pinched the bridge of my nose and sank into the chair. On the other hand, I could also say turnabout was fair play. It made up for all the nights I had to sit around waiting for him to get a chance to call. James knew exactly what it was like to be undercover. Every caveat of the job. And he'd wound up with a hole in his chest for it. Not exactly a comforting thought, given he'd gotten off easy for a guy who blew his cover at the last minute. Over a woman, no less. "It's been a long weekend, and I have to be at The Pit in twenty minutes."

"Before you do, I have news."

Great. I groaned and lifted my coffee to my lips, only to be disappointed by the few drops left.

"Someone in the hospital reported a sexual assault. Captain Ainsley is trying to keep a lid on it, but one of their new detectives took the call and she isn't taking no for an answer. There's only so much Ainsley can do while keeping your little tryst a secret, so expect a visit."

Tryst wasn't the word I wanted to hear.

"Noncomshits." It wasn't exactly like anyone at the hospital showed any concern for Brooke while she was there. They had to wait until we left. And if "Barney" got ahold of the information, he might take it straight to Sawyer. No doubt, Brooke would blame me if he found out.

"You know what happened?" James asked.

"Not in detail." I chose my words carefully. I hadn't found any bugs in the house since Brooke's visit, but I wasn't taking any chances either. "I really don't need this right now."

"I got the images you sent through. I'm passing them on to Ainsley and Libby—" James grunted, and I heard a loud thud over the phone. "Damn it, cat. The last thing you need is fucking coffee."

Ah, Trapper. His girlfriend's cat. I'd taken care of her for a while when James and Rose had to go into hiding. He was right, that cat was a high-strung wrecking ball on a lazy day. "Well, you have fun with the caffeinated cat."

"And you have fun with the drunken Devils."

I made a sound in my throat and dropped my head back. *Right*, even with destructo-cat, he was getting off easy.

"Rose says hi, by the way. And stay safe."

"Will do," I said. The call disconnected and I debated between one more cup of coffee versus getting to The Pit a little early—at least if I kept moving, I'd stay awake.

Chapter Fifteen

KISS A DEVIL GOOD MORNING

Brooke

BLOOD.

Everywhere.

My world was tainted red. Tainted by my family. Tainted by the club.

I sat up. The pain radiating outward from deep inside my gut. Worse than anything I'd ever physically felt. And that was a lot to be said.

Why didn't I pick up those prescriptions? I flicked on the light by my bed, ready to ransack the whole place to find anything to help, but two pill bottles sat next to the light with a bottle of water.

Trent? Had he done that?

Or had I finally lost my mind? Most of the night was a hazy memory. Hell, most of the last few days were a distorted mess. I popped one pill from each bottle and pulled the blanket up around me again.

Something about the dream stayed with me, keeping me

from getting comfortable. I remembered my mom. The blood all over her room. Burying her when I was twelve. The blood on my sheets the first time Sawyer raped me. My brother's blood splattered against a brick wall.

Blood was the theme of my life. The one constant. One day, I'd also have to face the blood on my own hands. As I sat there, trying to forget, my phone buzzed next to me. *Church.*

The paperwork. Sawyer would want a rundown, and I didn't remember putting myself to bed, let alone finishing the work.

Dammit. I rubbed my hands over my face and jerked them through my hair.

Dammit. I threw off my blankets and punched the mattress next to me. I didn't have the energy to rush around for clothes and paperwork, but that's exactly what I had to do.

After I threw on a fresh set of clothes, I dashed out to the living room, expecting papers everywhere and a Prospect on my couch. But Trent was gone, and all of my work was neatly stacked on the coffee table with my completed list of bullet points on top.

Paperwork in hand, I reached for the doorknob, but I couldn't bring myself to turn it. *My world had shifted. Miscarriage. Is this my path? Pregnant again. Not again.*

Every part of me wanted to go back to bed, curl up, and forget about the men waiting downstairs.

I'd been fighting so hard to have part of my life on my terns, but not even my body was under my control. No number of fists flying, pill popping, or book cooking seemed to change that. Apparently, I was on the wrong path and couldn't even fight my way off.

It just wasn't worth it.

Downstairs, the back room was ready for church. Most of the patches had already gathered, and all eyes were on me as I walked in. Gavin sat in my traditional seat—one I hated but still fought him for because I could—but I tossed my paperwork on the table in front of Sawyer, walked past Gavin and stood near the window instead. If I tilted my head just right, I could see Trent outside on the corner watching over the lot full of bikes.

"How's Trent?" Sawyer asked with a malicious grin, as if he'd known exactly what I'd been looking at.

I shrugged. "Not much to say."

"There's always something to say. Especially when you two are spending a lot of time together."

God. I sneered. I wasn't in the mood. Let alone for this to come in front of an audience. "We've gone on two fucking runs together. That's not 'spending a lot of time together.' He's tolerable. Which is more than I can say for anyone else around here."

That earned me a scowl from Gavin, but I didn't give him the honor of acknowledging it, crossing my arms and leaning against the window seal.

The heat in the room seemed to double or triple as Sawyer presided over general club business. I tuned most of it out, still caught up in my own crisis. But then, I heard my name.

Heat rushed to my face, and nausea followed.

Not now. Not now. I repeated. I pictured myself making a mad dash for the door just in time to puke in the doorway. But somehow, on autopilot, my mouth started to work.

"The payouts from the last shipment have all been integrated with the business accounts. With the offer Kerion put on the table, we're looking at a twenty-seven percent increase in...." The room dimmed. "...in drug distribution, but I'm working on funneling that money into the dark account until we can clean it up."

Blah. Blah. I felt like I was speaking into an empty tunnel. All I had to do was keep breathing long enough to finish my spiel. The details of which no one cared about anyway, I just liked to throw around the math and watch it go over everyone's head.

Then, Damian—AKA Spook, as if he needed a nickname—piped up, cutting me off. "You know, it's about damn time we make a bigger move in Ashville—especially since the Golds have been out for months. We need some entertainment around here, strippers, sex." He made a lewd gesture.

I could barely handle the fever and nausea from the meds, that made my stomach churn even harder.

"Oh, for fuck's sake." I charged toward the door.

"Exactly, supply and demand, baby." He winked but it looked more like a minor seizure.

"I'll let you discuss your little fantasies in private." I spun on my heels, facing his condescending, shit-eating grin. "But I guarantee, I'm not rounding up funding for anything that involves you sticking your disgusting, wart-infected dick near anything that moves."

"'Cause you know you want to be my one and only, Mama."

"Not in this reality or any other. Fund and build your fantasy on your own time when you're not putting the rest of the club at risk—that is if you can stop blowing all your money on meth. We have three big deals before year end, and not even a handhold on the Gold's former business or anyone who could take on the responsibility. Who the hell we gonna put in charge of it? You? Who would probably spend more time fucking around than doing business—

which you can do easily if you march down to Waller Street and pick up one of your regulars."

"Damn." Damian sat back, staring at me wide-eyed and shaking his head. "You know they make a pill for those mood-swings now."

Oh, yes, I'm the problem here.

Cannon, who sat next to him, pursed his lips, then smacked Damian in the back of the head. "Keep it up and you'll be scrubbing the shop floors with your tongue," he growled. "You can barely tell a wrench from a crowbar so shut your face and let the Treasurer do her job."

Gavin made a sound in his throat and rocked his chair back. "Equal opportunity at its best."

At least they had a knack for angering me enough to keep me going. "As if you can manage your own damn checkbook. Which of you can do this job better than me?"

Silence.

"Well?" I waited for anything, even a smart-ass remark. "Because I dare you to try so I can laugh my ass off when forty other men are jumping down your throat when the bar isn't stocked or you failed to manage the money properly and the heat comes down. Next time you want to fuck with me, I suggest you check your bank account first."

I was surprised Sawyer let us go on so long, and before I jumped down anyone else's throat, I slammed the door behind me and stormed over to the empty bar.

Cock-sucking mother fuckers. I let a lot of things pass. I weeded through the drugs and guns to stay on top of the game, but I'd be damned if we started selling women.

Not long after I sat down, the rest of the crowd emerged behind me in a roar of multiple conversations. But I still heard the insulting remarks.

"...definitely on the rag..."

"…maybe she needs a good bang…"

I tapped my fingers on the bar and waited in silence for them to pass. Last thing I wanted to do was give them more ammunition. When the room had cleared, I took in a gulp of air and headed for my office.

"Not done with you," Sawyer called from behind me.

I stopped in my tracks and spun around, not willing to get any closer, but he gestured toward the stairs leading to his loft.

Fuck. I stomped behind him like the petulant child he thought I was, but I was done. *Fuck this day. Fuck this club.*

Once in the office, he closed the door behind us. Then, he stared down at me like he was waiting for an answer to a question he'd never asked.

"I have work to do," I said. "The bourbon beer is running low, and if you and the boys want to keep getting smashed every night, I need to get my orders in."

"Orders," he repeated. "The girl who can't follow orders—"

"Hold the fuck up. If you're going to give me another lecture about following orders, save your breath because I'm doing everything I can to keep this club running without the federal fucking government coming down on our asses."

The punch to my jaw sent me spinning, and as soon as my back was to Sawyer, he grabbed me around the waist, jamming the other hand down the front of my pants. I reared back, nailing him square in the nose with the back of my head.

"You're club property, bitch," he growled, his hot breath lapping at my ear. "Not some princess."

"I'm Club Treasurer. And I dare you to find one of these god-forsaken ingrates who can do my job."

Sawyer smirked. "And that would be worse than a Treasurer who has no respect for the Club or her fellow members."

"I have no respect?" I elbowed him in the ribs, breaking free. "Why don't you take that issue up with your Sergeant-at-Arms? Oh, right, because he's your golden boy."

Sawyer charged at me again, but I mimicked the move I'd seen Trent take at The Race Trap, using his momentum to send him straight into his desk. It didn't stop him though, didn't even deter him. He spun again, nailing me right in the gut. I stumbled backward, into the wall.

His fingers wrapped around my neck, holding me there and cutting off my windpipe. This is how we went around, time and time again. The only way he knew how to assert his dominance was through violence.

I kicked my leg out, nailing him in the balls so he loosened his grip. But this time, I didn't stop there. I kicked again, a solid hit to his kneecap. Another to his stomach, knocking him back.

"You want to fight. I'll fucking fight," I yelled.

Fortunately, I had a good dose of pain meds already and couldn't say the same of him.

Sawyer chuckled as he straightened. The man had no soul. Hell, I wasn't even sure he was a man.

I waited for him to come at me again, but he crossed his arms and stared me down. "It's time you take on an assistant."

By assistant, he meant he wanted me to start training my replacement.

"I am not your problem. Your problem is walking around out there with a golden crown shoved up his ass. Half the trouble around here is caused by Gavin and his miscreants. And when it costs the club, I sure as hell am not lifting a single finger to clean it up. Dix kept them in their place."

Sawyer growled when I mentioned my brother's name.

"You can groan and growl all you fucking want, but the members of this club follow Gavin's lead and as long as you let him undermine me at every turn, this is what you're going to get."

I yanked the door open and descended the stairs, carefully listening for a charging war-horse at my back, but Sawyer didn't leave his office. When I got to the landing below, he yelled down, "You're just a defiant whore, like your mother."

I continued walking to my office, slamming and locking the door behind me.

How long do I keep banging my head into the same wall and expecting to finally break through?

But his last words wouldn't leave me alone. Mom had always kept me out of things, hidden from as much of the club as possible. There had been times I had wondered if he'd treated her in the same way, but now I couldn't stop thinking about it. I collapsed at my desk, running my hands over my face.

———

I SPENT the next few hours in my office under a pile of orders, bills, and the tap reports while Thea and Courtney stocked the bar and got it ready for opening. The night after Church was particularly chaotic, putting all the guys in rare form.

Thea knocked on the door and handed me a delivery slip. "You need some ice or something?" She gestured to her own face in the same location my newest bruise was beginning to form.

"I'm good," I grumbled. Then, I noticed the huge, red out of stock stamp on the slip and slid down in my chair. *Why'd it have to be the freakin' whiskey?*

"We probably have enough to make it through the night," she said.

"That'll go over well." With our tight supply of bourbon beer running low, Sawyer would down it all within an hour of opening, especially after our altercation earlier. I slammed my laptop closed and shoved the papers away. I needed some fresh air, so I told the girls to text me if they needed anything and stepped outside. The lot was full of Hogs, but the men had wandered off, probably getting a head start on getting smashed.

After lighting a cigarette, I headed over to the garage. A pair of legs stuck out from underneath a beaten-pickup truck. I shuffled past, hoping those legs didn't belong to Damian. I might have been tempted to do something stupid.

Something else stupid.

It seemed that was all I excelled at lately.

I found Cannon in his office with both feet propped up on his desk.

"Working hard, I see."

"I supervise a bunch of dimwits who all have better things to do after church—namely drugs and alcohol. This" —he gestured toward the mostly empty garage—"is me enjoying the calm before the storm."

I made a sound in my throat. "I arranged for a Wednesday delivery for that part you were looking for."

"It's not a part, actually—"

"I don't care, Cannon." I leaned my head back against

the door frame. I usually didn't bother with orders for the shop. Cannon was far more qualified, but whatever he needed was insanely expensive. "I have enough to keep up with."

"So you do," he said with a small nod. Then his eyes narrowed as he gestured to my cheek. "How'd things go with Sawyer?"

"Same as always." I scanned the garage, making sure Damian, Vin, or one of the others didn't get any ideas, but part of me was also disappointed. Pathetically disappointed, but I couldn't help it. There had been someone else I'd expected to see.

"Trent's out back," Cannon said.

I jumped at his comment and cleared my throat. "I didn't ask about Trent."

"No..." He held out the word longer than necessary. "But I didn't ask why he was in and out of your apartment at the crack of dawn."

I pursed my lips. *Great.*

"Don't worry," he said. "I know you have enough problems to deal with."

He put up his hands, but the smirk on his face continued to grow. Of anyone here, I wanted to believe that Cannon meant well, but I just saw another man who took too much interest in my personal life and gained far too much pleasure thinking I might finally settle down.

Although, I wasn't as worried about Cannon trying to push me down and out of the Club. Once, I'd thought of Cannon as a second father—or a first since Sawyer never fit that role to begin with. I'd sneak into his house in the middle of the night and sleep in Thea's bed when I couldn't handle things at home anymore.

But he was also Sawyer's friend. Well as much of a

friend as a man like Sawyer could ever find. It was complicated, but Cannon had always welcomed me when I'd stagger downstairs with my eyes swollen from crying all night. He always offered me breakfast before school. And most days, when Thea and I didn't feel like walking, he'd drop us off at school.

He didn't ask questions, so I wasn't sure how much he knew, but he never tried to stop Sawyer either. Never tried to save me from my hell.

I turned away from the door frame and made a show of heading straight for the front door.

Then, once no one could see me, I wrapped around the building and up the adjacent alley to the back. I couldn't help myself.

One more reminder that he needed to keep my secret—I convinced myself that was my one and only mission.

Chapter Sixteen

RAZING HELL

Brooke

AS I APPROACHED the back corner of Bone Grinders, I heard multiple voices—one in particular, made me want to turn around and pretend I was never there.

"Prospect. I need my boots shined...." I could hear the smirk in Gavin's voice. "See, I ran into a bit of a mess and it seems like your kind of expertise."

A quick breeze carried the smell of shit around the corner. Dog shit, I guessed—and hoped. Gavin was a fucking bastard.

When I heard footsteps in the opposite direction, I peeked around the corner and saw Gavin's back. He was followed by two of his favorite minions, Damian and Bull. Trent sat on a couple of cinder blocks hunched over some piece of machinery and scowling at the pair of boots next to him.

I groaned, and after a brief war with myself, stepped out

past the building to the chain-link fence that separated me from Trent.

"Now," Gavin yelled, not bothering to look back, but his word stopped me in my tracks.

So far, no one had noticed me. I still had time to escape, but my feet carried me onward. I reached my fingers through the fence, drawing them along the metal and making a rattling sound as I walked.

Trent's head popped up. "Feeling better?"

I narrowed my eyes. "Look, I'll tolerate your Prospect questions as long as you don't ask me *that* again. Ever."

I reached the end of the fence and circled the last pole. The whole back of the place used to be fenced in, but the back portion was now torn away to make more room for the trucks they used to haul bike parts.

"You know, I can give you a brilliant way of handling that." I pointed to the boots.

Trent raised an eyebrow.

I glanced in Gavin's direction, he was still caught up with his cigarette and conversation, so I grabbed a can off the rusty shelf behind him and watched Trent's eyes widen as I doused the boots with the gasoline-oil mixture.

"Uh...." His gaze flicked to Gavin, then back to me. "Brooke, are you—"

I dropped my half-smoked cigarette inside. The first boot went up in a woosh, spreading to the second. That caught Gavin's attention. "What the—" he yelled, running back to where I stood.

"Fuckin' whore," he growled at me. Then he scowled at Trent. "You stay out of it this time."

"They were a threat to humanity," I said with a smirk. I was on some roll.

"Since when do you care about humanity, bitch." He

shoved me back and I knocked over a rusty jack. His two friends flanked him, like the high school clique he wished he'd had.

"Trent." Cannon barged through the back door, but he froze when he saw us squaring off. "What the hell?"

"This cunt burned my boots."

Cannon frowned at the smoking pile of burned leather. "And I'm sure we'll all thank her for it later," he said calmly, but the wrinkles at the edges of his eyes told me he wasn't really amused. and worse, I'd been caught red-handed with Trent. "Damian, Bull, get out of here. You too, Gavin."

"I don't work for you."

Cannon closed in until he and Gavin were chest-to-chest, then he pointed to his cut. "What the fuck does that say?"

"VP," Gavin muttered.

"Ah, then you realize that two people here outrank you. And unless you want to make it three"—he nodded his head toward Trent—"I suggest you get the fuck out of here."

As Gavin and his lackeys wandered away, Cannon turned to Trent. "I need some help with something inside."

He waved Trent in but didn't follow, closing the door so we were alone. "And you're dangling hazardously close to getting someone hurt."

"Gavin—"

"Gavin deserved it yes, but you two... Why do you always push him when you know what his reaction is going to be?"

Maybe because I know I'm going to get the brunt of it no matter how I treat him. At least this way I can make him as miserable as he makes me. "He pushed me past the point of caring."

Not caring was a freeing thing.

"And how are you going to feel when Trent takes the brunt?"

I sure as hell wasn't going to admit to the tight ball that formed in my gut when I thought about it. In fact, I chalked that up to antibiotics just to make myself feel better. "One, he can take care of himself. Two, what the fuck makes him different from anyone else?"

"Why don't you tell me?" he asked, crossing his arms.

That stung a little more than it should have. "So, of all the double standards. You can boss Trent around and send him on little errands—like delivering your accounting—but I have him do a few things while I'm trying to wade through bookkeeping and there's a fucking conspiracy."

I threw my hands into the air and stomped back toward the bar. All the "fresh air" was giving me a headache.

But Cannon's words stuck with me like a deep itch that's as impossible to reach as it is to get rid of, it seemed that every move I made put Trent in Gavin's sights. It wasn't intentional. He just happened to be there. I hadn't asked him to step in on the fight in the bar.

Hell, I hadn't asked him for his help over the weekend either. And that was the problem. Despite all I'd done to keep Trent at arm's length, he kept getting closer. He somehow kept prying me wide open when no one else could. Appearing out of nowhere. Stepping in on my fights. Dragging my ass to the hospital. Saving my ass at The Race Trap.

All of that, I could attribute to the duties of a Prospect, but then there was the way he looked at me. The way he *saw* me. It was something different that both infuriated me and ignited my curiosity. *What the hell did he see?* Because he sure as hell didn't look at me like every other ragamuffin here did. He didn't see through me, only seeing a vagina in a dick world.

And the end all to beat all, he helped when I didn't ask or even expect it. He'd picked up my prescriptions. *Why?*

Why? I had to figure him out. I couldn't lure him with sex. Alcohol hadn't done it. Drugs hadn't done it.

I rubbed my temples trying to get the headache to abate, but a dozen more headaches waited for me as I turned the corner around the shop and saw a black sedan parked in front of The Pit. I thought about making a beeline for my apartment when my phone buzzed in my pocket.

Thea: Popo is asking about you.

The hospital. I knew it was a bad idea. I pressed my palm against my forehead. It wasn't even noon, and my body was spent. And yet, there was no escape, so I trudged across the street and up the lot in front of the bar. Inside, I found two officers, one male, about six-foot-five, the other female, barely coming up to his elbow.

"Can I help you?" I asked.

They hesitated, looking me up and down, before the female spoke. "Are you Brooke Covey?"

I returned the favor, giving her a long look over, then, I looked down at my vest. "Well, I assume that's what the B. Covey stands for on my cut."

They were both silent for a moment, then she asked, "Is there somewhere we can talk, in private?"

I rolled my shoulders back and waved to my office door, giving Thea the "all okay" signal as I followed them inside.

"You were checked into Mercy Hospital on Saturday?" she asked.

"Didn't know that was a crime." I crossed my arms and sat back on my desk. Both officers continued to stare at my cut, and I realized they hadn't anticipated they were looking for a full-fledged member of the boy's club. I almost laughed to myself. Whichever hospital employee who'd had the audacity to report my visit probably hadn't seen me wearing my cut—or they might have assumed I was wearing Trent's.

"You're the club Treasurer?" the male asked.

"Also not a crime." Likely they'd expected to find some young girl they could flip on the club, but I sure as hell hadn't fought this long to watch a few go down on measly sexual assault charges.

"Guess that would depend on what's in your books," he said.

"Well, if you want to see those, and I have no idea how the hospital visit has anything to do with them, you're going to need a warrant."

"Hiding something?" he asked.

I smiled. "Does anyone really fall for that? See, that's the thing with this whole checks and balances system. You want to see my records, first you have to prove you have a reasonable justification to do so beyond some fishing expedition. Now, can we get to the point so I can get back to work?"

"You were just released from the hospital yesterday afternoon," the female said. Now she seemed to be eyeing the newest bruise on my face. "You seem to be doing better."

"I'm fantastic. Since when does the hospital send the cops to check on patients?" I was trying their patience as much as they were trying mine.

"When they have concerns about a possible sexual assault." She cleared her throat, clearly unamused.

I'd have to try harder.

I laughed. And as irony would have it, I figured my new shiner looked great.

"They reported extensive bruising as well as—"

I cut her off there. "I manage a *bar*. Drunk men sometimes get rowdy and I catch an elbow or two breaking them up."

"An elbow between the legs?" she asked.

I cocked my head. "I'm sure it's happened once or twice, but if you really want to know what goes on between my legs, why don't you just ask? You sure won't be the first to get a vicarious thrill from my sex life."

"Ma'am," the male officer said.

"I ain't no ma'am in life or in bed, but since you obviously want to know all about it, I take it rough. You know, nails digging into the headboard, fist-fulls of hair as he slams deep into me and"—I moaned, picturing my fingers tangled in Trent's hair when I didn't have any other visuals to choose from. "Harder—"

"That's quite enough," the female said, putting her hand in the air to silence me.

"Oh, honey, it's never enough. Especially when his cock sinks in and hits *that* spot"—I gasped, delighting in the male officer's red cheeks. Oh, he was certainly a missionary man. "and sometimes—"

"I think we've heard enough," he said quickly.

"But I was just getting to the best part. God." I glanced at his ring finger and saw a gold band. "I guess your wife doesn't do a lot of throbbing. Pity for her."

He grunted, the redness in his cheeks marred with the wrinkles of a scowl. "That's none of your business."

I threw my hands in the air. "Oh, says the two who walked in here wanting to know about my sex life. Hypocritical much?"

"We weren't—" The female grunted, nudging her partner toward the door. "We'll let you get back to work."

I sighed and as they passed, I added, "Call me if you need any pointers."

Then, I smiled and waved. That smile quickly faded as they walked out of sight and I collapsed into my chair and buried my face in my hands.

I had found my wit's end, so I locked both doors and sat at my computer while the girls up front blared music, preparing for the men to come home to roost within the hours. I had inventory. I had bookkeeping. But most of all, I needed a distraction, and one little mystery was at the front of my mind. *Trent.* And that elusive single name he'd given me, Marcus Hutchinson.

I slid my chair back, staring off at the corner where the smallest of my filing cabinets stood. It had been a while since I'd found it necessary to move it out in the middle of the day, but the damn curiosity was getting the better of me. Maybe if I found Hutchinson, I'd find Trent's real motive, because I knew it wasn't as simple as he made it seem.

I checked the lock on each of the doors to ensure I wouldn't have any surprises, then I slid the small cabinet out and over. It weighed more than I remembered, but I'd added and shuffled a couple of years' worth of paperwork since Dixon died. Then, I pulled the back section of the paneling that lined the lower half of the walls until I saw the gleam of the lock on the safe. My brother had shown me his collection almost two months before he died and assured me that if anything happened, I'd find my way out inside. I didn't want to hear it. I refused to listen any time he brought it up. But when he died, I couldn't avoid it any longer.

Inside, I had found dozens and dozens of books, scraps

of paper, and a few envelopes filled with receipts, pictures, and more notes. Some of his notes weren't out of the ordinary; attendance records, transaction notes, logistics regarding the club and bar. But they were filled with little notes on random slips of paper and post-its. All written in the same code Dix and I had used as kids. I wondered if he wanted to make it look just like that—the inane scribblings of two siblings. We had symbols for words and letters, enough to mix it up and keep Sawyer from cracking our code. But as much as I racked my brain, there were additional symbols I didn't recognize.

If this was his idea of my way out, he must've anticipated me sitting here wasting away while trying to figure out the enigma he'd left me. Then again, if I had given him the chance to explain when he was still alive, I'd probably know what the fuck it all meant by now. The scraps of paper were similar, all scribbled in a hurry, some in code, some not. I didn't have the concentration to translate at the moment, so I shoved the contents around until I found a worn black book. Not a lot of codes there, just lists of known associates. Pages and pages of people the club had worked with—and against.

Chapter Seventeen

DEVIL MAY GLARE

Trent

I KNEW BETTER than to get any closer to Brooke. On one hand, her knowledge and records could be just the thing I needed, but after our altercation behind Bone Grinders, I also decided, once and for all it wasn't worth the risk. Not just yet. I wasn't sure it ever would be.

I wiped the sweat from my brow and tossed the wrench into a tool cabinet. The bike Bull had brought in now laid in an organized mess at my feet. Anything we might be able to use was stripped of VIN numbers and loaded in the "chase vehicle" that followed behind on runs in case anyone broke down on the way. I'd just gotten orders to make sure it was fully stocked because the club would be going on a long run in two weeks. That was it. All the info I'd been given. Nothing like cryptic orders to kick off the week.

"Trent." Cannon slapped me on the back of the shoulder. "Get cleaned up. Caine is running the show today. You and me are heading out in thirty. I'll pick you up at your place." He stepped away. "And bring your gun."

Gun? Not something they'd brought up, but of course it was expected. And I had one, usually close by, but thankfully they had yet to ask me, or force me, to use it.

I drove home, sending off the info I had to James, then wiping my phone.

Devils, an undercover cop, and guns. What could go wrong? I didn't even know where to start that list.

Cannon picked me up in front of my house in his beat-up Camaro.

"Got extra ammo?" he asked as I climbed in.

"Not really," I said. "Two clips."

He sat, half reclined, in his seat with one hand on the steering wheel, the other extended in my direction. "Let me see."

My heart pounded and I fought not to show it as I held the 35mm out for his inspection. Plucking it out of my hand, he shifted it around in his, feeling the weight. "Nice piece."

He handed it back, and as I slid it under my coat, he put the pedal to the floor. The sudden jolt threw me back, but after that, the car struggled up to speed, shaking violently until the transmission shifted.

"We'll have extra ammo," Cannon said.

"Are we going to a shootout?"

Cannon just laughed, neither affirming nor denying my dread.

Upon further consideration, Brooke wasn't the most intimidating biker around. At least I had begun to understand her motives. And despite her little trick with my beer, she seemed to be a straight shooter. The others were less predictable. Less readable.

Cannon made small talk as we followed a winding road out of town and through the adjoining forest.

No signal. No backup. But if they were planning an ambush, they wouldn't want me armed. Or would that make their game more fun?

We turned off the main road on to a dirt... well, path. It sure as hell wasn't a road. I swallowed, then reminded myself to breathe.

"This was an old CCC camp during the depression," Cannon explained. "They cleared it a few years ago when they started logging the area. Now, no one really comes out here."

Comforting. "Except us?"

Cannon chuckled, and as we navigated the final bend, bouncing over the rough rocky and pitted terrain, I spotted a group of cars in the clearing ahead, surrounded by bikers.

"Ready to get smashed?"

I hoped he didn't mean literally, but before I could answer, Cannon was climbing out of the car. He slammed his door so hard the car rattled—the only way it would latch. He was an adept mechanic, but never seemed to take the time to work on the thing. He grabbed his gun and a duffel out of the back and nodded for me to grab the large red cooler.

The clearing was well trampled and littered with old bottles and broken glasses, indicating this event occurred regularly. Dense forest surrounded the open field, and beyond the shooting range, the grass and weeds stood waist high, stretching to the tree line. The foliage was just beginning to bud and turn green again. Off to the right, the sunlight sparkled across the surface of a small pond.

We joined the others not twenty feet away where Fitch nodded me toward the back of his pickup, and I dropped the cooler off. The next thing I knew, four shots rang out, echoing along the valley. To the already volatile combination of Devils, a cop, and guns, I added alcohol, pot, and meth to the list. For god's sake, I hoped they kept the heavy artillery away from the meth heads.

Then my heart stuttered as Gavin stepped out of the trees. As soon as he saw me, his face hardened as well, and he charged in our direction. "What's he doing her?" *here*

"I brought him," Cannon said, stepping up next to me. "And I don't have the patience to explain why, but I will say, I'm not in the mood for comparing dick sizes, so don't fuck with me—*or him*."

Gavin scowled. "Where's Sawyer?"

"Probably banging Cissie," Cannon said. "He won't be here today, which means"—his eyes narrowed—"your shit ain't flying. Either put on your big-boy britches or go home."

Gavin grunted and walked away.

"You two need to make nice," Cannon said in my ear.

Of all the absurd, impossible suggestions I'd gotten, that was the kicker. Cannon handed me a bottle of beer and wandered off in Fitch's direction. *Make nice with Gavin?* Where would I begin? And how long would I be able to tolerate myself if I sunk low enough to manage it? Undercover in a MC was low, but that was crossing a line.

Another series of shots rang out, this time continuing for at least five minutes as the men took aim at a line of bottles and cans set up on a fallen tree in the distance. A few shattered or flew off, but the majority remained standing. The process continued for over an hour. Drinking, replacing the busted bottles, shooting, more drinking, until half the men could barely stand, let alone hold their gun steady. Fortunately, they had also started running out of ammo.

No one paid much attention to me, so I found a good seat off to the side, settled in, and watched. I wondered if it was because they were too entwined with booze and bullets to remember they had a Prospect to order around or if they left me alone because there was some significance in Cannon bringing me here. But then, my luck ran dry.

"Your turn," Damian said, gesturing toward the log. "Get off your ass and restock the targets."

His voice wasn't slurred, so I took it he was one of the more sober ones, but that didn't make walking out into the middle of their shooting range any easier. I glanced in Cannon's direction to make sure he was paying attention. He seemed to have a knack for being on top of things, and by my count, he'd only had two beers—although he'd gone through at least a dozen rounds of ammunition—and was the best shot of the group by far.

I gathered the empty bottles nearby, and when my arm was full, I trudged across the field to the log. Keeping a careful ear on the movement behind me, I lined up the bottles, holding my breath until I turned around to face the group. A shot went off sending a spray of grass and dirt up less than a foot away from me.

"Goddammit," Cannon yelled.

"Sorry," Gavin said.

Of course it was that rat bastard.

"I had a twitch"—he waved in my direction—"and no harm done."

No harm? For fuck's sake, my chest was about to explode, but I kept my composure as I walked back to the group. Cannon grabbed Gavin's gun, removed the clip, and tossed it in the small lake nearby. Then, piece by piece, he disassembled the piece, throwing each into the water until all that remained was a shell of a gun, which he handed back to Gavin with a smirk.

Oh yeah, this is going to help my case.

Gavin scowled at me, and for that, Cannon punched him in the face. "You know, Vin." Cannon jerked him forward by his collar that for an instant, I thought I saw both of his feet leave the ground. "You'd have far fewer problems if you realized that the source of your trouble is *you*. Not Brooke. Not the Prospect."

Gavin started to walk off, but Cannon grabbed him by the throat and pointed to me. "Gun."

I straightened, pulling my handgun out from under my coat where I'd kept it tucked away all afternoon. Then, Cannon pointed toward the targets.

Cold sweat ran down the back of my neck, past my collar, and down my spine. *What is he trying to prove? And what does he expect me to do right now?*

I stepped up to the area they'd all been shooting from, swallowed, and raised my gun. Shot number one hit the left bottle dead center. Shot two took out the next. Followed by the third, and fourth. I took a breath and fired the fifth bullet, purposefully aiming a bit off center so it just missed the next bottle. I couldn't be *too* good. By the time I fired off seven rounds, six of the bottles were demolished.

Gavin's eyes were wide, but Cannon wore a satisfied smirk. "Now," Cannon said to Gavin, "as Sergeant-at-Arms, is that the Prospect you want to run off?"

Gavin's jaw pulsed, but he shook his head.

"Go," Cannon said, shoving him backward. "Damian, drive your friend home. And the next time I hear either of you causing trouble, I'm going to make sure you're the ones standing at the end of the firing range until someone with an itchy finger makes you piss yourselves."

I put my gun away and rubbed the back of my neck. As Damian's tires spun on the dirt logging road, Cannon fished out two more bottles of beer, handing one to me.

"I'm not sure whether to thank you or go into hiding," I said.

Cannon grunted, then took a long swig of beer, staring off into the distance as everyone around us murmured about what had just happened. "We need brothers who care for our own. That's a lesson Gavin has yet to learn."

And probably never will.

"Can I ask what his issue is?" I asked. Brooke's repeated warning that Prospects don't ask questions echoed in my head, but Cannon was usually more lenient on the issue. And, as a Prospect, it was my duty to learn as much about my future brothers as possible.

"Undiagnosed," he replied.

I figured that was the end of it, and we sat in silence for a few minutes before Cannon spoke again.

"His father was the former VP. When he was killed, Gavin expected to rise in the ranks, but I was elected VP and Brooke's brother, Dixon, took my place as Sergeant-at-Arms. Gavin took it all personally. Gavin takes everything personally. To him, everything is an attack against him and his father's legacy. But truth-be-told, his father wasn't all that either. His ego cost the club as well, but those are the footsteps Gavin wants to walk in."

"If he's a threat, why is he Sergeant-at-Arms?"

"When you have a loaded pistol, you make use of it in the best way possible. He appeals to the deviants, so of course, he had their support. The rest of us figured it'd be good to have him in a place he'd be held accountable." He scowled. "If only Sawyer would follow through with that, but he wants to use Gavin as a tool for his own agenda."

Brooke.

I also wanted to ask exactly what he'd been trying to prove when he'd put my shooting on spotlight. Or how he seemed to know I'd be a good shot and fall in line with his plan. What if I'd shot with the same accuracy as the others, or worse? Most of those questions weren't even possible to ask, but I already knew I'd been pulled in as a cog for some plan. Even if I asked, I didn't figure he'd give me the whole story.

Even if I knew, would it make a difference? I'd joined a gang of outlaws; it was all part of my role. Bide my time. Watch my back. Those were the only options I had.

Chapter Eighteen

THE DEVIL'S IN THE COCKTAILS

Brooke

THE FIRST COUPLE of days on the antibiotics, I could handle, but by mid-week, I was a walking puddle of nausea. To make matters worse, Thea had a problem at home—no babysitter for their three-year-old daughter, Cori. Thea's grandparents usually took care of her, preferring to keep her as far away from club business and our life as possible, but they were both out of town at doctor's appointments, and Caine wasn't answering his phone.

Something that happened with increasing frequency over the last year.

Fortunately, Ashville Point was uncharacteristically quiet, so I intended to enjoy my limited opportunity at peace. After I made a list of everything I needed pulled from storage, I grabbed a bag of pretzels and shoved a couple into my mouth. But as I bit down, expecting crisp, salty goodness, all I got was stale, tasteless yuck. I chewed as quickly as possible and swallowed anyway. *What the hell else do we have?*

Then, I remembered Danielle's daiquiri craving and headed for the fridge at the end of the bar. I shoved the bottles aside and found the half-empty carton of strawberries. Breakfast of champions, and if I threw them in the blender, no one would be the wiser.

With the blender filled with strawberries and ice, I pushed the half-broken button, and it blazed into deafening action. The strawberries bled red and shot to the top. Then, the blender clunked, shifted, and the top flew off like a volcano, coating me with icy berry guts.

Fucking perfect. I growled, wiping the juice and pulp from my face. Then, I heard a snicker from behind me, and my insides went as cold as the slurry melting off my skin.

"We're closed," I snapped, turning on my heel to see Trent leaning over the bar.

"Is this a new spa treatment?" he asked. If he was trying to hide the goading smirk on his face, he'd failed miserably.

"What the fuck are you doing here? We're closed and you're supposed to be fixing shit." I waved him off.

"Then, you probably shouldn't leave the front door open." He shrugged. "Cannon sent me to check on the equipment you ordered."

"Haven't seen it. It's supposed to come to the garage this afternoon."

Trent left his coat hanging over the bar, stepped closer, and pulled a chunk of strawberry out of my hair.

"You've been working all week without it." I grabbed a bar rag and wiped my face and shoulders. "Don't tell me you've run out of things to do."

"Well," he paused. "The shop is shut down for, uh"—he looked around—"damage assessment."

"Damage?" I stood a little straighter, searching his face. "What the hell happened?"

Trent drew his bottom lip between his teeth, something that held my attention far too long. "A certain someone decided he didn't want to wait on the delivery and insisted he could fix the equipment himself, just like he insists on always fixing his bike by himself and wondering why it never works."

"Gavin," I said dryly.

"Cannon thought he tripped the breakers, but it seems...." Trent trailed off, waving his fingers in the air.

Ironically, I grinned, hoping that Gavin would be getting his ass handed to him not only by Cannon but Sawyer, for once. "So, you're saying Gavin fried the whole garage?"

"It appears that way, and it smells worse than burned popcorn in there."

I wanted to laugh. I wanted to see Gavin finally get what he deserved, but the wave of heat hit me again, and I had to brace myself against the bar. On second thought, what I really wanted to do was curl up on top of the bar until this damn feeling went away.

Antibiotics suck.

"How are you?" Trent asked.

I flinched but didn't answer.

"You have schmutz everywhere." He pulled another clump of strawberry from just above my ear.

"Fancy word for a guy who can't read." I pushed past him to grab my list, but my knees wobbled as my face grew hot again. *Mother fucker. Don't vomit.* "Go away and get out of my hair."

He smirked, obviously about the strawberry pulp in my hair. I needed a shower.

"You're fucking lame," I snapped when he wouldn't lose the damn grin.

Trent reclined against the counter, eyebrows drawn together, as his focus remained trained on me. "And you never answered my question."

"I said it'd be here this afternoon." I slammed my hand down on the stock list. "That's all I got."

"That's not the question I meant, and you know it."

My jaw ticked. "You were supposed to forget that ever happened and I told you to never ask me that question."

"You could have died," he said under his breath. "That's a little difficult to forget."

Was that concern? Why the fuck did he have to be so confusing? And why the fuck had he been the one I'd imagined while fucking with the cops? "Well, I'm fine now. Congratulations, you can leave."

Instead, he straightened and picked another piece of something out of my hair. "Sure. Looks like you have everything under control here."

I swallowed and took a couple of deep breaths—which was harder than it should have been with him invading my space. "Fine, Prospect. If I have to put up with you, be useful." I slapped the list against his chest. "How about you bring all this shit up from the back."

He plucked the list from my hand and studied it for a minute. "Am I supposed to know where you keep all this?"

I pointed to the back door that led into the storage room. Thea organized it on a regular basis, so it was really just a matter of looking around. "You can read, right?"

He narrowed his eyes. "Not according to you."

"Closed." I waved my hands toward the door, unable to keep my cool around him any longer. "The fucking sign says closed."

Trent snorted again and nodded toward the front doors. "Maybe from this angle."

I whipped my head around so fast I almost doubled my nausea. *Smart ass.* Sure enough, the sign hadn't been flipped. "Go"—I gestured to the stock room—"and bonus points if you find non-stale pretzels."

"Aren't stale pretzels the standard around here?"

"Don't get smart." Again, I poked him in the chest, hoping he'd take the hint and get out of my space.

He smirked and left me alone behind the bar. I poured what was left of my strawberry puree into a daiquiri glass and took a seat at the end of the bar, propping my feet up on the stool next to me.

"Where you want these?" Trent called out, hauling the first keg through the door.

I could have told him there was a dolly in my office, but that'd ruin the fun. Instead I pointed over the bar to the cooler under the taps. "Kegs there. You can stack anything else on the side of the bar."

He dropped off the keg, then headed back around again.

"Was Caine at the shop?" I yelled after him.

"No." Trent paused at the corner. "Haven't seen him since Cannon left him in charge yesterday for the..." His face scrunched. "Shooting party?"

My jaw dropped. "Cannon took you?"

And he remained in one piece. My eyes raked over him one more time just to make sure.

"Yeah." He made a clicking sound with his mouth and rolled his head back. "Whoever came up with the idea of mixing Devils, booze, and guns was a real thrill-seeker."

"Sawyer," I mumbled. "He says it's a great for blowing off steam."

"You've been?"

Once when I was sixteen, but that'd only been to prove a point. "No vaginas allowed." And that was one battle I wasn't fighting. I had no desire to see any of that again.

Trent snorted and leaned against the edge of the bar. "Then why was Gavin there?"

My strawberry puree almost shot through my nose and I covered my mouth to compose myself. "At least you didn't take a ricochet to the leg like the previous Prospect."

"No," he lowered his voice. "Gavin just tried to take off my foot with his twitchy finger."

I sat a little straighter. Cannon was right, but it wasn't just that my actions had the potential to put him in danger, what startled me was that I cared. "Gavin always has a problem with shooting off prematurely."

"Yeah." Trent smirked, obviously catching my reference, but his eyes remained narrowed, lined with deep wrinkles. "I didn't bring it up to Cannon, but I wonder if Gavin's little stunt over at the garage might have been revenge for what happened after."

"Which was?"

"Cannon broke up his gun and tossed it in the pond. Then elected me to prove a point and take a turn shooting at the targets I'd just set up."

"You showed them up?" After seeing him fight, that wouldn't surprise me.

"A little bit."

I realized I was smiling again. At Gavin getting a well-deserved lesson, of course.

"Cannon gave him hell, but he would've been better off talking to the gun for all the good it did."

And Cannon had been the one lecturing me about putting Trent downrange of Gavin's anger. Maybe he knew what he was doing, but it was more dangerous than roasting Gavin's old boots. Trent disappeared through the employee door again and resumed stacking supplies on the far end of the bar, while I stared off, wishing the strawberries and ice had lasted long enough to do something for the nausea. Then, I heard a swoosh next to me and a bag of pretzels slid down the bar, stopping just before they reached my arm.

Trent gave me a wink, then went back to work.

What is with him? Maybe he is trying to get the same thing as everyone else around here. But Dixon was the last person who'd ever asked me if I was okay. The only one concerned with my well-being outside of empty conversation filler. If he were here, he would have been the one dragging my stubborn ass to the hospital. He would have been the one stepping in to defend me from Gavin.

Countless times I'd told him I needed to stand on my own to make my name. I figured they'd never respect me with someone else joining in on my battles, but even going at it alone got me nowhere. In fact, I felt myself sliding backward. The boys club stuck together, and with no one at my back, that pitted me against the entire club.

As I munched on the pretzels, I looked up again to find Trent standing across the bar staring at me, so I flipped my hair back, left the empty glass and open bag on the bar, and started putting away the stock. As I emptied boxes to fill the liquor cabinets and coolers, Trent moved them behind the bar, giving me anything but space. And I returned the favor, stepping in his way, bumping into him, refusing to give him room to pass by.

"You're impossible," I yelled when I took a step back and ran into him.

He laughed. *Laughed.* The sound deep and rumbling.

I grabbed a damp towel from the counter and swatted him with it. The towel snapped in the air and cracked against his hip. He lowered his chin, putting his shoulders back and glaring at me with that damn smile still on his face. Any other man would have erupted long ago. Hell, any other man wouldn't have helped in the first place.

Fuck me.

No. No.

Don't.

What the fuck am I thinking?

I huffed. "You realize this is why Gavin took a shot at you, right?"

"This?" he asked, moving a step closer.

I felt like squirming, but with my eyes locked on his, I found it impossible to move.

His head tilted to the side. "He doesn't like bar-stocking Prospects?"

"That's not what I mean." I could've easily moved left or right and yet, I couldn't budge.

"No?" He closed in again. One more step and he would have been standing in my boots, leaving me pressed against the counter with no room to move.

Would that be so bad?

Shut the fuck up. I told my brain as it raged out of control.

"You know what I mean." I couldn't breathe. I put my palm on his chest and pushed him a step back. "What are you doing?"

He shook his head. "Exactly the opposite of what I keep telling myself to do."

That response threw me—as if I wasn't struggling to make sense of him anyway. "Which is?"

"Stay away from you before Gavin takes another shot and doesn't miss."

"Fortunately, his aim isn't that good." So, he did know exactly what I was talking about. "Maybe you should listen to yourself."

"Maybe," he mumbled, but his eyes didn't leave mine.

Fuck. I could smell him. I could feel the heat radiating from him.

Fuck. My chest tightened like a corset, trying to keep everything in. Trying to keep each broken piece from that one final blow that would mean obliteration.

"Sorry," Thea's voice filled the room. And I turned to see her come to a dead halt as soon as she saw us. "Um, guess that's why you didn't see my texts."

She spoke in that high, playful voice I remembered from our childhood.

I pushed Trent back again and increased the distance myself by moving in the opposite direction. "Where's Cori?"

"Caine's with her." She tossed her bag into a cabinet under the bar and flipped her apron in the air a couple of times before tying it around her waist. "He mumbled something about the shop blowing up, but if you would've told me you had help, I would've gladly taken my time."

Trent's Adam's apple bobbed as he swallowed. Why the hell was I still staring at him.

"Right. Like I'm leaving him behind the bar." I tried to keep it nonchalant, but I'm sure my voice sounded higher than normal. I certainly felt wound tighter than normal.

Trent made a sound in his throat and crossed his arms, leaning back against the bar. "Why, you think I can't pull a stein of beer?"

"The guys wouldn't find you"—I looked him up and down—"bartender material." Most of my employees were wives of the club members for good reason. Eye-candy but off limits, and they made a killing in tips.

"You know how to make a long island iced tea?" Thea asked.

Trent frowned. "Who the fuck around here drinks that?"

It was my turn to clear my throat.

Trent shook his head, wearing that damn smirk again. "I took you for a Virgin Mary girl."

Thea squeaked, quickly turning away so I couldn't see her face.

"But." He held his index finger up in front of my face. "I do know how to use a blender without wearing the contents."

I narrowed my eyes on him, dragging my tongue over my teeth. I let my response seethe for a minute. "The lid shattered, dumbass."

Okay, that wasn't the best retort.

"Yeah, no operator-error to blame there at all."

I had to remind myself Thea stood two feet away just to take my eyes off his lips.

"This is about to be a shut out," Thea said, looking at me. "And not in your favor."

I glared at her, gave her a quick, sarcastic grin, and chucked the bar rag into the sink. "Someone wants to be unemployed today."

"Just calling them as I see them." Thea shrugged, pulling her long blonde hair into a ponytail, and adjusting the Property of Caine shirt she'd had made up. She thought it'd be a brilliant idea if all the girls had property of... shirts. "So, what happened at Bone Grinders, anyway."

"Electrical issue, I guess." I glanced at Trent but didn't let my eyes linger on him for more than a second, fearing I'd get trapped by whatever that was between us. For once, Trent said nothing.

I, however, wondered what Caine had said about the garage. Had he told her he'd been working when he hadn't been at the shop? Or was I reading too much into it? He could've been working on something outside of the shop; pickups or deliveries. Just because a Prospect didn't know, didn't mean much, but it still nagged at me.

Caine had been off since Dix died. At some points, way off. Drinking more. Staying out nights. Showing up drunk at my apartment in the middle of the night. That was the kicker. And the kick-start to our awkward air these days.

But something else was going on. Distance from his wife, certainly. More and more, I didn't even see him in the bar.

"Everything's stocked," I said.

"Cool, Danielle should be here soon, so I can handle this until then. Especially if you want to leave me your helper." She winked, eyeing Trent.

I laughed, but it sounded as strained as I felt. Every nerve in my body was on fire. Thanks to Trent. Thanks to her.

She's married. I told myself. *With a kid. And why, for fuck's sake would I be jealous anyway?*

"Stay out of trouble," I said to no one in particular as I headed straight for the back room. "Text me if you need anything."

I charged through the storage room, out the back door, and into the door leading up to my loft. My legs carried me faster and faster away from Trent.

But even in my apartment, locked away, all alone. I could feel him. I'd hoped the distance would give me clarity, but goddamn it, he did something to me. Something unsettling, and even in my own space, surrounded by familiar and not at all Trent-related smells, I could still feel the heat on my skin.

I could taste his smell.

I raised my fingers to my lips. *What is happening to me?* He'd fuck up my plans. All the things that had kept me going. He was...

He was infuriating.

And unsettling.

And hot.

No. He was just trying to get to me. By hauling my ass to the hospital, picking up my meds, and helping stock the bar without so much as a groan.

Groan. Oh, fuck, why did I have to think that?

He's mind-fucking me. Bastard.

Or am I doing it to myself?

I ran a warm bath and sank into the water.

I don't do this. I don't get wrapped up in desire, but dammit, my body didn't want to hear that logic. My core throbbed. I'd have to watch what I said to cops from then on because that damn act was biting me in the ass. I slid my hand between my thighs, finding that well-neglected sweet spot. Whatever this was, I intended to purge it from my system.

I closed my eyes and pictured Trent's tattooed chest as I massaged myself. Lending me his image was the least he could do, all things considered. He was the reason I was in this mess.

My hips shook. My heart raced. But nothing. *Come on,* I begged my body. *Just once. Just one time.*

And yet, nothing but frustration guilt within my veins. I growled and smacked the surface of the water, sending a shower of droplets to the floor.

Nothing.

The only thing I'd managed was a sopping wet floor and cooled bath water.

Maybe I was incapable. Broken beyond the ability to experience pleasure. I lifted the plug with my toe, letting the water drain. It left me clean, but far from satisfied.

Damn Trent. Damn his green eyes. And damn whatever ulterior motives he had. He just didn't make sense. If he wanted an easy way in, why me? Why wasn't he spending his time sucking up to Fitch, or even Gavin? That'd make his life easier, unlike helping me. That only put him in the spotlight, in a terrible way.

Like Dixon.

Like the old Caine.

Why can't I figure him out?

I checked the time, fifteen after four, the bar was open for business, and I had a long evening to kill and a lot of frustration to work off. If I couldn't get one thing out of my system, ink therapy was the next best thing.

——————

AFTER THE HOUR spent with my tattoo artist, filling in the demon wing that stretched around my ribs, I returned to The Pit with the dull, euphoric buzz of adrenaline and endorphins. I stopped up front to check on everything then locked myself in my office and pulled out Dix's old files again. This time I picked a new notebook, and as I scanned through the entries, I noticed little missing details. Details that he'd recorded on other occasions that seemed like they should be present. Dates that seemed like they should be present.

A knock on the door sent a shock wave through me. I

scrambled to stuff all the papers and journals into the safe and slid the panel back to hide it.

The knock sounded again.

"Yeah," I called, wiping the sweat from my palms down the front of my jeans. Then, I closed my eyes, hoping I wouldn't regret it, and opened the door.

Cannon stood over me. "Thea said you were in here, but I was beginning to wonder if you'd slipped out the back."

"Not yet. How's the shop?"

Cannon grimaced. "Wiring's shot. We're gonna need an electrician."

"Great," I said sarcastically, painting a fake grin on my face to match. A group of contractors running around the chop shop would be fantastic. "All over a damn thing scheduled to be delivered today."

"I think Fitch knows a guy, but we'll be down for a while." Cannon scoffed. "Gavin is footing the bill, and if I have anything to say, it won't be the only thing he's footing for a while."

I nodded, but I wasn't convinced it would happen. It was wishful thinking. As much as Cannon wanted Gavin to squirm, Sawyer would find a way to make any consequences meaningless.

Cannon stepped inside, shutting the door behind him. "That's not what I came over here to discuss though."

I managed not to squirm in my seat as a tingle crept over my shoulder blades. "Oh?"

Cannon's tongue pressed against the inside of his pursed lips. That was never a good sign. "The cops? Thea told me a couple of cops stopped by."

"It was just a mix-up," I said, pretending to need something on the shelf behind me to put some distance between us. "Mistaken identity. It's all taken care of."

"Mistaken identity?" He paced toward the back of my office and my heart sped as he approached the corner where Dix's documents were hidden. "They came into Devil territory, right up to the hangout, for a case of mistaken identity?"

"Yes, and I took care of it." *I hope.* At the very least I'd mortified the hell out of them, and there wasn't a crime without a victim. They were sniffing around the wrong woman for that. "Who else knows?"

"Thea said she mentioned it to Caine. So as far as I know just the handful of us, but if it's no big deal why does that matter?" Cupping his fingers around his chin, two of his fingers traced his lips. "I need you to be straight with me. Why didn't *you* tell anyone?"

"Cannon, it's no one else's business." I spoke through my teeth.

"Cops in the hangout is club business. Unless you can give me a good goddamn reason to forget I heard anything."

My heart pounded as I considered my options. If I refused to tell him, or failed to make it believable, he'd take it to Sawyer without a doubt, but the truth didn't guarantee he'd change his mind. That'd leave him with the leverage. I decided to gamble on Cannon's sympathetic side. "The day you pointed out you'd seen Trent leaving my apartment. He had to take me to the hospital because I had a raging infection. Since I spend most of my life covered in bruises, the doctors noticed and called the cops, but the dunderheads had no idea who they were dealing with and I got rid of them. If Sawyer finds out it's going to turn into a big unnecessary thing."

"If Sawyer finds out?" He spun away, throwing his hand into the air, then pressing it to his knitted forehead. "You're gambling Barney isn't going to bring it to his attention."

Barney, Sawyer's inside man, as if man described him. I'd never met a cop who wasn't a bastard, but one who played both sides didn't deserve the label of human. "He hasn't yet, and I highly doubt he reviews every single case that comes through the department. He wouldn't have time to blink. It doesn't fall under drugs or guns so it's fine."

Chapter Nineteen

I'M NO GOOD

Trent

THE SHUTDOWN of the garage gave me time to regroup but wasn't helping me gather any info, so I volunteered to help Cannon clear the building when Caine didn't show. When the usual storage shed was full, we started moving things over to the bar, stacking boxes and crates along the back wall of the meeting room. I saw Brooke in passing several times, but we didn't speak. She mostly kept herself locked away in her office until the bar opened. She seemed to be back to her usual distant self. And after the dangerous game we'd played in the bar Wednesday morning, that was perfectly fine with me. I couldn't afford that distraction.

The other men who worked in the garage—all friends with Gavin—hadn't set foot in the bar or garage since Cannon lost his temper with Gavin. To be honest, that made the work much more relaxed, even if it meant more to do. The other members were all preoccupied with the big annual ride coming up to a resort up in the hills to get away from "the man." By Friday afternoon, we had everything moved out, and Fitch's friend came in to strip the wiring and replace the system while we were away for the weekend.

I updated James, so he could have a contingency plan in place, but with a week left until this big deal was set to go down between Defiance and the Devils, I still had no additional details to work from. I hoped that while drinking and cutting lose for the weekend someone might slip up and reveal some details.

By evening, the streets around the bar were packed with members and new hang-arounds who apparently sensed the excitement. I kept to the perimeter, watching the new hang-arounds take my lace as club lackeys. We'd roll out the following morning, leaving the bar and most other club-run businesses closed for the weekend.

In twenty-four hours, the Point would be a ghost town.

I left the bar just before closing—even with the hang-arounds gleefully taking the brunt because they wanted attention. I learned it was always best to beat the crowd. I paused at the corner of the building when I heard the metal door on the back side slam, followed by another thud and a series of expletives.

Brooke. I closed my eyes. I had to admit, I hadn't just been okay with her keeping to herself, I was glad. And it wasn't just the trouble that seemed to follow her, or the prospect of getting my ass kicked because of being near her when that trouble struck, it was the possibility of losing my mind and blowing my cover because I couldn't keep my sensibilities around her.

There was something about her that drew me in, intrigued me. And I didn't have time for intrigue. And yet, I followed her voice and found her out back, under the dim light mounted between the doors. She shuffled around a pile of papers and books that had apparently burst through the bottom of a cardboard box that laid mangled nearby.

"What are you doing?" I asked.

She jumped, clutching her chest as she leaned sideways against the wall. Then, she let her breath go and slumped. "Of course it's you."

I got the feeling she'd intentionally been avoiding me as well.

"I'm..." Her voice drifted off. Her eyelids drooped, and she giggled, throwing her head back.

That was certainly a Brooke I hadn't seen before—and never expected. "Are you high?"

"Way to deduce, Mr. Sherlock."

Voices from around the building sent her scampering to collect everything she'd dropped, so I mended the box well enough to hold some of notes and journals and crouched to help.

Her eyes widened as our hands collided over a leather-bound book, and she froze.

"I have a feeling you're more worried about them, than me." I nodded toward the sound of a crowd gathering around the corner.

She nodded but gave me another long look as I collected the last of the items.

"Why do you always do this?"

I held out my hand to pull her up. "What?"

Without an answer, she jerked the door open and staggered toward the stairs, pulling herself up hand over hand by the railing. *God, she was toasted.*

She didn't look drunk, just deflated, and slow, and judging by the smell of roast skunk as we approached the top of the stairs, I figured she'd been smoking pot. The high-dollar kind.

Outside of her door, she pressed her back against the wall, staring down as she fiddled one-handed with her keys, which of course clattered to the floor.

She stomped in my direction like it was my fault. "You..."

Oh, good grief, it's the bathroom all over again. "What?"

"You rattle me," she said quietly, her brow furrowed. It wasn't her talking, it was the pot. "You..." her voice drifted away again.

I joined her on the stoop, brushing her long hair away from her face. She leaned into my touch before she could catch herself. Once she did, I took a step back.

"I should go," I said. Oh, it was tempting to see what I could get out of her, but that felt like taking advantage. My chest constricted. *I'm undercover and running out of time. This is exactly what I need to do.*

And I couldn't. Not where Brooke was concerned. This also explained my compulsion to creatively leave her out of my reports to James. She couldn't just blow my cover, she could wreck me. Whatever drew me toward her, whether intrigue or something else, could get me killed.

It defied reason and logic.

It defied my orders.

It defied my better sensibilities.

But being a good detective meant listening to your gut. *Do I really want to stake myself on some feeling in my stomach this time?*

"You came all the way up," she said. "You may as well come inside."

Groaning, she squatted to pick up the keys, then she

randomly snorted and started laughing again. "You're not going to tell me I'm a mess?"

"I'm refraining for now." Mainly because I didn't know what to say.

She stood, tucking her hair behind her ear. "I needed room to breathe, and of course, you showed up."

Her head tilted to the side, causing the hair she'd just tucked back to fall in her face again as she attempted to find the key. She leaned over to line it up with the lock, twisted, and pushed the door open. "Why do you have to be you?"

I chuckled at the ridiculous question. "Well, it's really the only option I have."

This time she laughed hysterically. "And therein lies our problem... somewhere..."

She dropped her keys onto the kitchen counter and headed to the living room. I followed with the box and saw numerous other notes and journals littering the floor and coffee table. "Did you blow up a library? What on earth are you working on?"

She scowled and plopped down on the floor next to the coffee table. "Wouldn't you like to know."

Yanking the box out of my hands, she dumped it in the middle of the couch. Whatever her mission, she hadn't wanted anyone else to find her. I should've been more focused on the opportunity to get some information, but I was concerned with her. And that was the very reason I'd been glad we hadn't collided again. She was the enigma that vexed me, one that I didn't have time for, and yet... inside me a war raged. The information I could get from her versus the trouble that came from being near her. And that wasn't the worst of it. I felt this clash inside me anytime she was near. The very thing that draws two storm fronts together and creates disaster. And I couldn't explain that. Not to James. Not even to myself.

"I couldn't concentrate with all the noise downstairs," she said, staring down at the journal in her hands.

I'm going to screw this whole thing up if I don't stay away from her.

No matter how many times I thought that, I couldn't bring myself to walk away. I couldn't bring myself to listen to reason. I'd made the excuse that I found her intriguing, and I did, but that wasn't all there was to it.

She flipped a book open, and I noticed the quick messy notes in someone else's handwriting. Brooke took a deep breath, held it for a few seconds, then blew it out. "What a mess," she mumbled. "What a fucking mess."

"Want some help?" I asked.

Her head jerked up and she looked at me, wide-eyed, like she'd forgotten I was standing there. Then she closed her eyes and dropped her head backward against the couch. "Do you know anything else about this Hutchinson guy?"

Is all of this to find him? My attention strayed as my gaze traveled over her bowed form until she snapped her fingers. "I'm the one with a short attention span right now."

I hadn't prepared for this and my mind went blank. "He, um, was known for slipping his enemies hot shots. They referred to it as the Hutch."

"That's all you got? It's not exactly original." Her head bobbed to the side as she turned the page in the journal. "And how did your uncle die?"

My tongue clicked against the roof of my mouth. "Hot shot."

Brooke slammed the journal closed and threw it on the table. "You joined the Devils looking for the murderer, didn't you?"

"He's gotta be dead by now. I'm just looking for answers."

Brooke's shoulders dropped and she blew a puff of air through her pursed lips, plucking another book from the box on the couch. "Looking for answers is a stupid idea around here. That's how Dix—"

"Dixon?" I knew who he was. I'd seen the files on Dixon Sawyer, all of the police reports on the accident that took his life, but Trent Clevenger wasn't supposed to know him. "That's what you called me at the hospital."

She pulled her knees up and leaned against them. "He was my brother. These were his." She waved her hand over the pile.

I hadn't noticed it before, but several of the records in the box and scattered across the table seemed to be in code. No wonder she hadn't wanted anyone to catch her. "What happened to him?"

"Sawyer," she began, then went silent again. "I..." She looked up at me, blinking slowly. Guaranteed she wouldn't be telling me any of this if she wasn't high.

Dammit. This is what you're here to do.

"I think Dixon was getting close to something," she said. "I think he figured out something Sawyer didn't want him to know. He kept giving me cryptic messages, and then Sawyer stripped him of his cut, kicked him out of the club. Dix went dark for a few days, then turned up dead. Ran his bike in to a brick wall. They say he skidded. Lost control. He was going too fast. But I know there's more to it. Just this feeling, you know?"

"Yeah," I took a seat next to her on the floor since her couch was covered in papers.

"Why is it you always show up like this? When I'm in the middle of something or..." She stuck out her chest and made a sound in her throat, leaving the rest of the sentence up in the air. "You should be avoiding me at all cost, not stocking the bar or"—she grunted, then whispered—"saving my friggin life."

I shook my head and stared off toward the table. She was right. Brooke was someone to be reckoned with, but despite that, I couldn't bring myself to look at her as the enemy. However naive that sounded coming from an under-cover cop talking about a patched officer of an outlaw MC. We had similar goals. And there was something about her that made her impossible to shake. "I don't really have an answer for that."

"Nothing happened."

I heard her swallow and glanced over. She stared down at her hands, twisting together in her lap. "The night I drugged you. I mean aside from jamming my hand down your pants because I figured that'd be the last thing you remembered. I stripped off your clothes, scratched up your back, and dragged your stoned ass to your bedroom, because Sawyer had to believe me, and I couldn't have you going around discrediting me."

She kept her face angled away from me so I couldn't see, but her voice began to shake. "I was so fucking pissed. Sawyer had already strangled me and threatened me for not getting the job done the first time. I intended to go through with it... but apparently it all backfired completely, because I can't fucking get rid of you and even when you're not here—"

She stopped herself, slamming her palms against the floor as the faintest hint of blush crept up her neck.

How could a new blood excuse siding with the enemy within? She was the black sheep of the group. Everyone thought of her as an obstacle. That made our relationship even more dangerous, putting me in even more of a precarious position. And no matter what I did or told myself, I couldn't fucking help myself around her.

Brooke frantically shuffled the papers around until she found another joint. She lit the end and drew the smoke deep into her lungs, tilting her head back and blowing the smoke up to the ceiling. Then she offered it to me.

I shook my head.

"I'm not going to drug you with the joint I'm smoking."

"I uh..." I rubbed the end of my nose, trying to hide my laugh. "You realize how ironic that statement is, right?"

She looked at the joint and it seemed to take her a few seconds to get what I was saying. "You're really dull for a biker."

"I think it's best one of us keep their faculties."

"Mmh hmm," she moaned.

I tried to shift my focus away from her back to something, anything, that might help my case. I stared at the notes closest to me, scribbled details about church. Who attended. Who was absent, the topics of discussion, meetings and deals. It was all vague enough not to help my case on its own, but it could provide connecting evidence if I got it somewhere I could use it and linked any of the information to something illegal or helpful.

Why is she letting me anywhere near this?

Because she's high.

As soon as I shifted a pile of papers on the table, I saw a stack of printouts with Ashville Woman's Center on the header and Brooke's name. I debated whether or not to cover them up or mention them since Brooke probably didn't realize they were laying out, but her hand slammed down on hop of them, wadded them up, and chucked them across the room.

"I didn't—" I began.

Brooke shook her head. "Nothing to see. Miscarriage. Infection is clearing. No other infections or diseases detected...." Her voice trailed off, but I sensed there was something more to it.

"Okay..." I held out the word, wondering if she was just rattling on because of the pot.

Brooke slammed her hand on the table. "What's okay? You thought it was bad when Gavin took a shot at you with a gun. I dodge a fucking bullet every time one of them—" Her eyes went glassy and she looked away.

"Brooke, I—" I reached for her shoulder, but she knocked my hand away.

"Don't touch me."

"Fine." I sighed, sinking back to my own side of the table.

"And stop looking at me."

I rubbed my hand over my face. *Should've gone home.* Instead I was sitting in Brooke's apartment at almost two in the morning, forbidden to look at her, and completely uncertain what the hell I should do. Comfort her, push her, back off, with Brooke they all seemed to have the same outcome, rage.

I glanced up, hoping she wasn't looking in my direction, but she was staring down with her arms folded around her middle.

"Who are you?" she asked quietly, and I got a sinking feeling there was no way I could satisfactorily answer that question. "You don't leave me anywhere to hide. If you were any other man in the club, you'd be forcing your way in, but you don't and it's almost worse."

As soon as I moved my arm, she flinched, so instead of

touching her, I held out my hand and waited. "I don't want to hurt you."

"Therein lies our problem." She stared at my hand skeptically. "I feel like you're fucking with me."

"I'm not."

Brooke snorted. "The hell you're not. How else would you explain me nearly flooding my bathroom?"

I drew back slightly wondering of the pot was laced with something. "Huh?"

"I'm not supposed to have this problem," she yelled, pounding her fists against the couch. "You're infuriating and distracting and—"

Next thing I knew, she closed the distance, pressing her lips against mine. I expected her to pull away just as quickly, but she threw herself into the kiss, needy and wanting more. Our tongues collided as she shoved me sideways, knocking me to the floor and pinning me under her.

Pot—the remnants on her breath brought me back to reality. Usually, my gut and dick didn't work in tandem against common sense, but they were both going to get me in trouble. I pushed her back, just enough to breathe. "You're high."

Brooke put her finger over my lips. "And I assure you, I'm in full possession of my faculties. I'm not helpless—"

"Believe me, I know."

Brooke pushed herself upright, sitting on my hips. "Do you?"

I got the feeling that this—like every battle with her—would end with an unwinnable situation. Maybe I didn't want to win. God, she got to me. The way she stood her ground. The way she'd flirted the day I helped her stock the bar. Not traditional flirting, but every time she'd stand in my way, every time our bodies bumped together, it got harder to control myself.

"We shouldn't," I said, reluctantly.

"Of course not." She jerked back, taking a ragged breath and that sight felt like an icepick through my chest. "The only guy I want to fuck has scruples."

She leaned to climb off me, but I held her hips, keeping her there.

James always kidded me about my penchant for women. And what could I say? I enjoyed a good fuck, but I usually kept things in perspective. An undercover cop fucking the Treasurer of an outlaw motorcycle club was not smart. Hell, an undercover cop flirting with said Treasurer was not smart, but I couldn't help myself.

You're going to lose your job.

"What?" she asked. "Were you flirting with me"—her face twisted—"or fucking with me?"

Flirting. I was definitely flirting, but before I could say anything, her rant continued.

"Don't answer that." Her gaze dropped to where her hands rested on my chest. "I'm just the club whore."

I couldn't listen anymore. I flipped us over, rolling her to the floor and covering her mouth with mine before another word escapes.

"I was flirting." I kissed her again, long and hard. "You're not a whore."

"Why do you have to be so confusing?" she whispered.

"This coming from a girl who yelled at me for looking at her and then jumped me?"

"I'm tired of holding it all together. I don't fuckin' want to." She pressed her hand to my chest, not pushing me back, just holding it there. "You're always watching me, but it's not like the others."

She squeezed her eyes closed. "You look at me and I feel everything falling apart. You flirt, disappear, kiss me, push me away. What the fuck are you doing to me?"

"I should ask you the same thing." I cupped the back of her neck and pulled her to me for another kiss. She closed her eyes, arching so her body rubbed against mine.

This is a bad idea. All of it. Coming to The Point. Coming to her apartment. Touching her. Holding her. Kissing her.

My cock throbbed against my jeans, but one thing I was sure of. "We wouldn't be doing this if you weren't high."

She slammed her foot against the floor next to me. "That's the fucking point. When I'm high, I'm free. I don't have to be uptight, on-guard Brooke. I don't know if I can fuck someone for the sole purpose of wanting to fuck someone, but if you're going to keep arguing, can you please leave so I can unsuccessfully try to get myself off again?"

I buried my face in her neck trying—probably unsuccessfully—to cover my laugh. Frustrated Brooke was too fucking sexy for my own good.

She hooked her leg around me, shoving me sideways until we landed in our original position. Brooke stripped off her shirt and sat back. For a moment, she looked like she was going to ask something, but I had a feeling my dick was once again doing the talking as she pressed against the bulge in my pants.

She grabbed the hem of my shirt, then stood, using my shirt to pull me with her toward the bedroom. At the doorway, I put my hands on the door frame.

She turned back, grabbing the back of my neck, locking me in a kiss until I dropped my arms and pushed her toward the bed. But just as we were within inches of the mattress, she widened her stance stopping me.

She wanted to be in control.

Needed to be in control.

And I found something insanely sexy about that.

Her fingers slipped under my shirt, exploring my skin as she inched the material higher. I ran my fingers through her hair, following it down to her shoulder. Then, I traced her bra strap down, slipping just the tip of my finger into the edge of the cup. As soon as she pulled the shirt over my head, her lips were on mine. Her fingers dropped to my waistband, and a sudden jolt went through me.

I wanted her. But was that want worth sabotaging everything?

Chapter Twenty

LET SLEEPY DEVILS LIE

Brooke

FOR A MOMENT, Trent stilled against me, his muscles tense, his spine stiff.

Maybe he didn't want me. *Why would he?*

But when I inched back, he grabbed my hips, pulling me against his bound erection. He pressed his lips to my neck, and his hot breath caressed me as I rose on my toes, wanting closer to his touch. I pushed him backward onto the bed and watched his eyes follow my movements as I stripped off my jeans, leaving them in a pile on the floor.

His cock pressed tight against his jeans, but despite that, he let me lead. He could take control in a split second, and I waited for him to turn. For the beast he kept hidden to break me. And he could, so easily.

I straddled his hips as he sat up, bracing himself on one arm and pressing the other hand to the small of my bare back, drawing the top of my breast in his mouth. A moan escaped his throat as I rubbed against him.

Still no glimpse of the monster.

I moved back, undoing the button on his jeans, and slowly pulling down the zipper. Trent lifted his hips so I could remove the thick material, setting free his erection. Ink covered every inch of his thighs, stomach, chest, and arms. I traced the lines along his lower abdomen, then pressed my lips to those same lines, tasting the salty sweetness of his skin as I nipped at a small piece of skin. I felt him flinch, but he didn't move to take control. His head lifted enough to watch me, his eyes narrowing with need.

I swallowed; the back of my throat was dry with the need for another hit. But for the first time in my life, the hit I wanted was a man. This man.

I crawled up him, kissing his collarbone and neck and taking one more bite. He growled, pulling me down so his cock pressed against me, and I momentarily froze, my chest constricting as I fisted my hand against the bed.

Trent's fingers caressed my cheek, then lifted my chin.

"You know." His voice was deep and gravely. "I'm really resisting the urge to flip you over and take you now, but I'm not going to... this time." He added with a smirk.

God, that look.

But as much as I wanted to act like I knew what I was doing, I had no idea. This was not the kind of sex I'd become accustomed to.

His fingers trailed down my sides, leaving a line of tingling skin and goosebumps. Then, his hand pressed between my legs, finding my clit.

Fuck. My core burned and insides ached as if I'd been turned on since that day in the bar. My back arched, and I moaned, a long rumbling sound that'd been waiting years to escape.

His lips pressed to my neck again, and I grabbed a fistful of his hair, pulling him closer.

His other hand moved up my back, undoing my bra with a simple flick. As the material fell, his lips moved to my left nipple. The sensations lipped down my spine to my throbbing center, and I threw my head back. Leaving that nipple fully erect, he moved to the other. Lips, tongue, teeth. I didn't know what to expect next, but it was all exquisite.

God, my imagination didn't do him justice. I raised my hips, moving back until the tip of his cock pressed at my entrance.

"Fuck." My mantra became audible. I groaned as I slid down his shaft, his hardness stretching and filling me. I braced my hands against his chest as my hips moved. I squeezed my eyes closed, fighting to hold myself together as I slammed against him, taking his full length inside me again and again.

Trent took my hips and matched the pace of my thrusts until my toes curled into the blanket.

"God," I squeezed my eyes closed at the feeling of him swelling inside me while his body tensed under me. He moaned, his hips shaking.

Please let me come, I begged my body as I ground against his.

Then, his hand left my hip, leaving a cold spot in its wake, and found my clit again.

I cried out as my entire body untethered. My thrusts became harder and more erratic as my body desperately searched for a release. One I was still convinced I could never find. My fingers dug into Trent's chest, leaving long, red welts, while his fingers clenched my hip.

"I'm going to come," he gritted through clenched teeth.

I slowed my movements, taking in every detail of his

strained body. The tendon that stood out on his neck. His half-open mouth as he licked his lower lip. The sound of every ragged breath. And that look deep within his eyes. Hunger. Need. Desire.

All in my control.

I bent forward, kissing the edge of one of the scratch marks and dragging my lower lip across his skin as I moved to kiss higher.

Trent's body shook beneath me. "You really are trying to kill me, aren't you?"

I smiled, thrusting my hips slowly as I took him in.

He stiffened under me, letting out a growl that raised the hairs on the back of my neck. Then, his thumb pressed harder against my clit. He circled it, then massaged it until my hips shook with one final thrust that turned my world black for an instant. Drained of everything, my last few puffs of marijuana hit me full-force and I collapsed on top of him.

He didn't shove me off, push me to the side and leave. Instead, he let me lay there, brushing my hair back, and kissing my jaw just under my ear. He wrapped his arms around me, holding me to his hot chest as I drifted off.

———

WHEN I WOKE to my alarm, the faint smell of Trent still clung to the air and my sheets. I rolled over, but the other half of my bed was empty and cold. If not for the smell, I would've convinced myself it was a crazy pot-induced fantasy.

And then, I remembered Dixon's records in the next room.

What if it'd all been a ploy to get to them?

I wrapped myself in my sheet and rushed to the living room. It was a mess but looked exactly as I remembered. He hadn't taken off with my records, but he had taken off without a single word. Probably for the best. And then, I remembered what he said. *I'm not going to.... this time.*

As if there would be another, I thought cynically. *I just needed to get it out of my system. And who would want to take another crazy ride like that?*

Me. Sadly, me.

But men were full of empty promises.

The roar of motorcycles shook the walls and reminded me I had somewhere else to be. I got dressed, threw my overnight bag over my shoulder, and ran down the stairs to join them.

We'd have an hour drive up into the hills to a resort that turned a blind eye to our exploits as long as we greased the right palms.

A crowd waited outside The Pit, ready to roll, and no-doubt we'd pick up stragglers along the way. This was our most popular ride, attracting both hang-arounds and members who hadn't been active in years.

The ride excited me. I loved the freedom of the open road and the rumble of my bike between my legs, but when I started my bike, the rumble only reminded me of the sore-ness down there. Of Trent between my legs.

Damn.

So much for hitting the road and forgetting him—espe-cially when I glanced around and saw him just behind Cannon, Caine, and Thea.

Nope. High fucking definitely didn't get him out of my system. But when I remembered that he'd left without saying a word, seeing him across the crowd like nothing happened brought that Devil who lived in the back of my brain to life.

I revved my engine and joined the crowd, roaring off in front of them.

What else had I expected?

I'd given him whatever he wanted. I'd let the pot slow my racing brain, numb my worries, silence my devil, and I'd served myself up to him on a silver platter. It was my fault.

———

AFTER THE OFFICERS, originals, and patches checked into our rooms, we gathered at the bar for lunch and drinks. Mainly drinks, but the lodge put out a nice spread of finger foods and the fixing for burgers.

The hang-arounds and prospects were sent to guard duty around the building. We were in the middle of nowhere with nothing to defend ourselves against, so it was more of a test than a precaution. Plus, it kept them out of the way. When we were done they'd get the leftovers.

The same went for rooms, and with the lodge full, even some of the members were camping outside, leaving the grunts to figure their own shit out.

And despite the hour-long ride, open road, and fresh, cool air. I still hadn't sorted myself out, so I threw myself into the party. I didn't have to worry about stocking or managing employees, so I leaned against the corner of the bar and waited for my beer, mingling with a few other members I hadn't seen in a while. The absence of Gavin and his crew made the afternoon more relaxed until an arm draped over my shoulder.

I froze, catching a whiff of Sawyer's cologne—a smell that would be embedded in my mind until the day I died. "Where have you been hiding out?"

"Nowhere in particular." As if he had room to ask questions. He'd been incommunicado far more than I in the last week. I stepped sideways and his arm dropped off of me, but he didn't stop staring.

"And the Prospect?"

I grabbed my beer from the bartender before it could touch the counter, then pivoted so I was facing Sawyer. "What about him?"

Sawyer shrugged, disturbingly casual about the whole thing. That never signaled a good outcome. "Just keeping tabs on my Prospect."

My Prospect? The way he said it irked me. "Then Cannon would know far more than me."

His lips scrunched to one side. "I hear it was your bar he was stocking this week."

I made a clicking sound with my tongue and tapped my nails against the beer bottle. "After your golden-boy fucked up the garage. What was the final bill on that, by the way? I'm going to need those figures."

Sawyer's forehead head twitched. "Cannon would know far more than me."

Something on the back side of the room seemed to catch his attention, but I wasn't turning my back on him to see what. His neck stretched as he looked over the crowd, then he waved and leaned closer to me. "I'll have some friends to introduce you to later."

I turned as he walked by me, keeping an eye on him as he headed straight for the door. Whoever he was going to meet must've already stepped out because no one was waiting there.

My desire to socialize disappeared with him, so I took a long chug of my beer and waved for the bartender to bring me another. For an instant, I wished we were back at The Pit and I could just walk through and grab my own. I drummed my fingers against the counter as someone squeezed in next to me.

"Dish," Thea said.

With no clue what she was on about and hoping it didn't have something to do with Sawyer, I shook my head. "Platter?"

Thea grimaced and shoved me in the shoulder. "Spill it."

"What the fuck are you talking about?" I tossed a couple of ones in the tip jar as the bar tender handed over my next beer. This was a double-fisting day if I'd ever had one.

Thea immediately grabbed me by the arm and tugged. I managed to hold her off long enough to finish the first bottle and slam it down on the counter. Then, she yanked again, and preferring not to lose my second drink in the battle, I followed her to an empty space along the wall.

Thea leaned into the wall, crossing her arms over her chest. "When you're on the back of a bike rather than driving, it leaves a lot of time to take in the sights."

"And?" I waved my beer through the air.

"And Trent can't keep his eyes off you."

I shrugged, trying to be as dismissive of her observation as possible. Fucker had left without so much as a see ya. And the fact that it bothered me was a bigger problem than his early escape.

"You two in the bar. The way you ran off after. God, Brooke, if any other guy talked to you like he did, he'd have been wearing a keg."

I wondered if she knew to what extent she was right about that, but I wasn't going to admit it. No one else came remotely close to talking to me like Trent did. I leaned into the wall and sipped my drink.

"You like him." She practically squealed with excitement. "He likes you."

I wished I could be that excited over the whole thing, but I didn't see the allure in all this... allure shit. But Thea had been waiting since high school to dote over me and anyone. We always gossiped about her crushes. I was always there when she prepared for first dates. I celebrated with her when she and Caine got engaged. When they had their tiny wedding to the chagrin of her grandparents while she was three months pregnant. I was fine with being a wingwoman. "I think you're reading too much into this."

Thea's shoulders sagged and her face fell into a matching pout. "Brooke, my dearest, bestest friend"—her words, while I knew she meant them were laced with a sarcastic tone—"you don't have to be a total hard-ass bitch every second of the day."

I gave her a flat look.

"I love you," she said sweetly.

I sighed, but the moment I relaxed a smidge, she hit me with the next assault. "Is he totally covered in tattoos?"

I looked up at the ceiling and shook my head. "How the hell would I know?"

My voice was tight. My stomach swam. I did know.

"I'm going to interpret that as a yes," Thea said.

"I need a goddamn cigarette." I reached in my pocket, but it was empty, so I patted each in succession. I'd left them in my room. I hoped I'd left them in my room. I was not going an entire weekend without a smoke, and I didn't want the shit most of these guys puffed on.

"Definitely a yes."

"Thea, I don't need this. Not this weekend." Or any weekend ever. "If anything, he's a distraction."

"If he's as well hung as he is hot and snarky, you definitely need it. More than you need a fucking cigarette."

"Oh, my god." My brain stopped working and my mouth hung open for a second while I tried to shake away the shock. I started to walk away, but she grabbed my elbow.

"Seriously, Brooke. I saw that spark—one I haven't seen in you in a long time—and if he could do that with clothes on..."

"Thea." I couldn't explain why I suddenly wanted to cry, but I had to get out of that room and get my head on straight.

"Fine." She shoved me back. "Go smoke, but if you happen to run into something very tattooed that you'd rather suck on, maybe give that a try because it might be a healthier distraction."

"You are a fucking—" When I couldn't come up with a word, I just grunted and walked away. Thea's grin didn't fade though, even when I peeked back from across the room.

Just as I faced the door again, a cluster of men entered, stopping my escape—Gavin and his crew had arrived. And from the look on Gavin's face, he'd seen me too.

They should've been banned—or hung.

I took a step sideways and took an errant elbow to my beer bottle, which emptied the remainder of its contents down my front and shattered against the floor. That was reason enough to leave.

The man who'd bumped me called over one of the hang-arounds who'd gotten table-bussing duty, to clean up the mess. "Sorry, Mama," he said with a tip of the head.

Done. I stormed past Gavin and his crew before he had

an opportunity to say anything. *Done with this party, this day, this entire shitshow. And every goddamn question about Trent.*

But that thought smacked me in the face when I rounded the corner heading toward the main lobby and saw a little girl chucking her show at the very man who'd somehow made my life even more complicated. A feat which should have earned us both a spot on a world record list somewhere.

Ruby was the four-year-old daughter of Sawyer's current... I had no idea what to call her. Sex toy? Fling? Whatever title I could think up for Cissie at the moment wasn't harsh enough for someone who'd brought her little girl to a Devil party. At least Thea had the sense to send her daughter to her grandparents' house for the weekend. Not that the kid didn't practically live there.

Ruby, understandably unamused at being left with some strange man, screamed at the top of her lungs, and ran toward the hallway, crying for her mom. Trent scooped her up, but she screamed even louder, attracting the panicked attention of the few employees who remained.

"What's going on?" I yelled over her screams. Trent looked slightly relieved when he turned and saw me, but Ruby kicked out of his arms and ran toward me with snot and tears running down her face.

"Sawyer dragged me in here and told me to watch her," Trent said.

Poor kid didn't even know the guy. At least Sawyer hadn't left her with Gavin. Occasionally, Cissie left her in the bar while she and Sawyer "talked" in his office. Thea usually took care of her, seeing as she had kid experience. Now, the tiny human stood at my feet, staring up at me with her hands outstretched.

My jaw clenched so hard I could already feel an oncoming headache. "I need a change of clothes."

My front was soaked with beer, wet, sticky, and uncomfortable, but suddenly, that was the best part of the situation. I sighed, knowing Trent didn't have a room and I couldn't leave them both out in the lobby while she threw a fit, so I pointed to the stairs off to the right. "My room's up there." ·

Ruby grabbed my hand, squeezing her tiny fingers around mine. This kid... I wondered if she'd end up even more fucked in the head than me. With Sawyer banging her mom, the obvious answer was yes.

I also wondered what the chances were that the dampness I felt from her tiny palm wasn't snot.

Trent followed behind us with a pink backpack slung over his shoulder. I didn't find it as amusing as I normally would have.

Inside my moderately-sized suite, I directed Ruby toward the couch in front of the TV. "Wait here while I change."

"I want my mom," the four-year-old whined, stomping her foot.

"Yeah, me too, kid." I tried to shake my hand away, but she refused to release me.

God, I don't know how to deal with kids. Most of the time, I felt like I'd never been one.

No hand holding. Few hugs. Tough "love."

"Come on, Ruby," I growled, shaking my hand loose. "I reek. I'm sticky and I'm just going to the bathroom."

Ruby refused to budge.

Trent knelt next to us. "Ruby, is it?"

She nodded, still giving him a scowl she'd apparently refined since birth.

Go kid. Never trust a guy.

Trent held up her backpack. "Did your mom pack anything fun in here?"

Ruby shook her head. "I packed myself."

"Okay," he said, sitting the bag on the couch next to her and unzipping it. "What can we play with while Brooke washes up?"

She stared at him skeptically for a few seconds, then released my hand and dug into the bag until she came up with a doll whose hair stood straight up.

"What's that?" Trent asked.

As Ruby explained, he nodded for me to escape, so I grabbed a change of clothes and took my chance. What a party this was shaping up to be. Once I had cleaned up and pulled on fresh clothes, I pressed my ear to the door gauging the chaos level.

"... and her dog jumped up and..." She made a growling noise.

"Wow," Trent said, as if enthralled by everything she said.

I huffed. *Fucking pretender.*

It was a good thing I already had a little alcohol in my system, but it didn't help the churning in my stomach as I joined them in the living room. Ruby stood on her knees in front of the couch, laying out her toys next to Trent. She continued chatting as if I wasn't there, telling Trent each of their highly elaborate stories.

I crossed my arms and leaned against the far wall. I wondered if he had a secret love child hidden away. Yeah, I was looking for marks against him. "Experience with kids, huh?"

"I've met a few," he said, wearing that sexy expression of his.

I was in deep shit. "Well it seems you have everything under control, so—"

Ruby, who I'd thought hadn't been paying a bit of attention to me, stood up, dropping the toy in her hand. "Don't go."

Her eyes were wide, head cocked slightly to the side, and her bottom lip jutted out. I figured that was the expression kids used to get whatever the hell they wanted, and yet, I didn't feel a damn thing. Probably one of things that required a heart or empathy—two things beat out of me a long time ago.

Or so I thought, until I looked back to Trent.

I grabbed the back of my hair and gave it a tug. I didn't want to be here. I didn't want to be trapped in this tiny room with him and Ruby. I really didn't want to be at the party either, especially since Gavin had crashed it. "Look, I at least need a smoke before I lose my damn mind."

"Can I come?" Ruby's voice almost squeaked.

"Why?" I dropped my head against the wall.

Ruby shrugged, then said quietly, "I'll be good."

Good, yeah. Good wasn't what I worried about.

"Come on, Ruby," Trent said. "You didn't finish your story."

He gave me a flat look as she climbed onto the couch next to him. He picked up a stuffed horse and handed it to her, but she didn't say anything.

"Fine." I sighed, giving up on my escape and collapsing into the armchair in the corner. If I couldn't leave, I was giving myself a large buffer zone. "What's the horse's name?"

I had to remind myself not to call it a *damn horse.*

Chapter Twenty-One

WHERE THE DEVIL FEARS TO BED

Brooke

WHEN RUBY LOST interest in her toys, I turned on the television and she fell asleep less than fifteen minutes into the stupidest show I'd ever seen.

Were cartoons that stupid when I was a kid? I wouldn't know because I was hardly ever allowed in front of the TV and if I did get screen time, it was interrupted by a fight within seconds, forcing me into my room to hide. Yeah, some good old days. But as I breathed my sigh of relief and thought I'd get a chance to slip out—and away from Trent—my phone rang. And of course, I had the volume turned up.

"Shit." I dashed across the room to where I'd tossed my jacket and fished my phone out of the pocket. *Thea. Thank fuck.*

Next to Trent, Ruby sat up, her wide eyes searching the room while her hands reached for her toys. "Where's Mommy?"

Oh, kid, you don't want me to answer that.

"Where is everyone?" Thea asked as soon as I answered.

"Uh—" Between the skull-drilling voices on the television and Ruby's shrill cries, I couldn't focus on answering.

Trent tried to calm Ruby, but she fussed more with every second.

"What the hell?" Thea asked. I knew she could hear the screaming.

I slapped my forehead. Hell was an appropriate description. "Sawyer invited Cissie, who brought Ruby, who is now in my room."

Thea gasped, knowing very well how I handled children —or failed to handle them. "I'll pop up and get her."

"Great." That sounded like a win all around. Ruby was used to her and Thea could calm the kid's tantrums in seconds. "311, please hurry."

I heard her laughing as she hung up, but what I hadn't considered was Trent. Thea's inquisition was bad enough already, and I considered telling him to hide in the bathroom until she had come and gone, but I couldn't trust Ruby to keep her mouth shut either. Dropping my hand with the disconnected phone, I tried to sound excited. "Ruby, Thea's on her way up."

Ruby slid off the couch, grabbing her half-open backpack and an armful of stuffed animals. Then, she charged past the narrow hallway to the bathroom that divided the living area from the bedroom.

"What the—" I threw my arms in the air.

Trent put a hand up, cutting me off before I cursed again. "She's just a kid."

"She's heard far worse than anything I'm going to say."

"It's not *what* you're saying that's the problem," Trent hissed. "Her own mom just brought her up here and abandoned her to get passed around like a communion tray. It's not her fault she's inconveniencing you."

Stunned into silence, I looked past Trent's shoulder and saw Ruby standing near the window. "That's not it."

"She makes you uncomfortable. How do you think she feels?"

I realized that I came across as not giving a damn about the kid, but I knew exactly how she felt. I didn't have to think about it. I felt it in the pit of my stomach, and I didn't know what to do about it for myself, let alone her.

"I'll take care of her." His stance relaxed slightly, and he gestured toward the door. "Do you want to get some air?"

I had my arms wrapped around my center. I wasn't sure when I'd done it, but I felt like I had to untangle myself just to reach for the door and step outside. The air wasn't any cooler or fresher in the hallway. It felt just as thick as the room I'd left. I dropped backward against the wall, letting my feet slide forward.

"Is it really that bad?" Thea's voice broke me out of my trance, but I didn't have an answer.

"Is she alone?" she asked. "Why didn't you call earlier?"

"She's not alone," I snapped. "I'm not incompetent. I just need a minute."

A minute away from the Prospect who'd just lectured me inside. It was his fault I had a kid running around my room in the first place.

"Okay," Thea said slowly.

I still hadn't lifted my gaze from the floor, but I felt her examining me. Then, the door to my room opened and Trent stepped out with Ruby on his hip. Her head rested on his shoulder, the stuffed horse tucked between them, and her backpack slung over his other arm.

Thea nudged my arm and made a humming sound in

her throat as I rose. "No wonder you wanted off kid duty."
She held out her arms toward Ruby. "Wanna come hang
out with me?"

Ruby shook her head. "I want my mommy," her whine
turned into a scream by the end. Then, she lifted a stuffed
horse over her head and chucked it at Thea.

Good grief. Of course this couldn't be an easy handoff.
After some cajoling, Trent handed off Ruby and retrieved
the weaponized horse as Thea flashed me a crazy smile and
a wink. "Enjoy your kid-free evening."

"Uh huh, thanks, Thea," I said dryly.

As she disappeared down the hall, I turned back to
Trent—bad idea. He stood against the doorway with his
arms crossed over his chest.

"You need to leave," I said.

"Anyone ever tell you your hospitality needs work?"

"Hospitality is not my industry."

"You run a bar," he said dryly. "By definition it is,
actually."

Couldn't just let that one slide, could he? There'd be no
saving either of us if we were caught standing in front of
my hotel room arguing. Too many people were already
asking questions. "Last night is not going to happen again,
so go find someone else to bother."

Trent sighed and pushed off the wall, but he just
grabbed my wrist and yanked me back into the room,
closing the door behind us.

I froze, stiff as a pry bar, but he immediately backed off,
putting his hands in the air. "I'm not here to hurt you, but
maybe we should talk."

Talking with him turned to flirting and always landed us
both in trouble. I scoffed in his face. "No."

Moving away from him, I turned off the TV, both

because I couldn't stand the high-pitched voices for another second and I needed a front to put some distance between us. "I'm not—"

I wanted to give him a hell of an argument—a verbal slap in the face, but my words disappeared. *I'm not what? The girl who's fucks practically anyone her father orders her to? Easy? Broken? A fucked-up mess that even time couldn't straighten out?*

My nerves screamed just under my skin. *Not now. Not now.* I fisted my hands so tight that my nails cut into my palms. I wanted the pain. I needed the pain to erase the constant scratching of all my broken pieces against my skin.

I wanted to escape it, needed to escape it, but how do you escape your own body?

My consciousness knew how, that's for sure. Suddenly, I felt like a spectator, unable to control my own body as my arm flew through the air and collided with the hard plaster wall. The pain shot through the tiny bones of my hand, circled around wrist, and spread up my arm.

"Brooke," Trent shouted, charging toward me.

I dodged his grasp, staring at the crater I'd left in the wall. "I'm fine."

"You don't look fine," he said.

"I will be fine when you *leave*," I growled, shoving him backward.

"So, you're going to physically shove me out? After almost putting your fist through a wall. Why? Because you'd rather be downstairs with—"

"Don't," I said through clenched teeth. "You have no idea what I've done to get this far. You have no idea that I—that I..." *intend to bring down this damn club.* I intended to watch it, and everyone involved burn. Everyone who I made nice with during the day, even though they turned their back on me long ago. Everyone whose worst offence was far from turning their back.

"I do know," Trent stood inches behind me, speaking in that low, grumbly voice that sent prickles down my spine. "I know that if you want revenge—and trust me, I figured that out a long time ago—you can't keep fighting on all fronts with no one to have your back. Either fight yourself, fight me, or fight the club. Choosing all of the above will get you killed."

For a brief moment, I felt nothing except the faint rush of air escaping my lungs. "If you know that, why in the hell are you still here?"

"Trust me, Brooke, I keep asking myself that. I'd love to know the answer, because my life here would be a hell of a lot easier if I were downstairs brown-nosing the shit out of this party."

That was a bit literal. I chomped down on the inside of my cheek.

Trent reached for my shoulder and pulled it gently back, so I would turn around, but I didn't look up at him. That would be my end. Those damn eyes. That damn mouth.

"I *punched* Gavin my first day as a Prospect—"

"Because of me?" I asked sarcastically. I knew it wasn't, and I was beating him to the lie.

"Because he was being a jackass." He laughed. "But everything I do, I wind up back here. In your company."

I flattened my lips. "Don't tell me you're going to give me a fate speech."

"No. I've been around long enough not to believe in that." His fingers grazed my jaw sending a cold shiver through me. Goosebumps erupted over every inch of my skin. I stood no chance of hiding my reaction to him. "But I do believe in my gut. And my gut tells me that whatever happens, I'm where I'm supposed to be."

Regaining my senses I pulled his hand away from my cheek. "So, your gut's telling you to *save the damsel in distress.*"

"Oh, honey, you're no damsel, and I've seen you handle your own distress."

"Honey?" My voice was high and shrill, but he didn't budge. In fact, a devilish smirk crossed his face. He'd done that on purpose. I would've nailed any other man for It. But I never wanted to nail anyone the way I wanted to nail Trent.

"Can I see your hand?" he asked with the same collected evenness that always seemed to throw me.

I held it up. "Why are you a doctor, now? That could've saved a lot of time a few weeks ago."

He took my swollen fingers, cradling them in his palm. It would have been so easy to give in and let his touch consume me again, but why? So he could sneak off afterward?

"If you're so concerned, why the fuck and run last night?"

He raised his gaze back to my face. "Fuck and run? First, remember you instigated all of that. Second, I fell asleep next to you but around five a.m. you kneed me in the nuts so hard I almost vomited on you."

Squeezing my eyes closed, I tried not to laugh. I couldn't deny that I was a violent sleeper.

"Third," he continued. "I remembered that within a couple of hours all of the Devils would be gathering right outside The Pit and I figured it was probably best *for both of us* if I left before that happened and gave Gavin yet another reason to take a shot at me."

Fucker. Why'd he have to be so… logical?

"I wasn't running from you, Brooke, and if you would've given me the chance, I would've explained all that earlier, but you took off out of town like a bat out of hell. I figured it was because you came to your senses and got all pissed off because I listened to your pot-induced reasoning and actually fucked you while you were high." His voice lowered, taking on a rough, gravely texture. "Sorry I upset you by leaving."

"I wasn't upset," I snapped.

"Uh huh."

I didn't have to look at him to know the face he was making right then. And it was a good thing I didn't because it might've been the last straw. "I was glad to not have to deal with you."

He lifted my chin slightly. "That's not what your face said this morning."

"This can't happen." I closed my eyes, the only way I could *not* look at him, but even that could only last a second. "What're you doing to me, Prospect?"

He lowered his head, tilting it slightly to the side. "Anything you want."

I grabbed him by the collar with my good hand, yanking him forward a bit. "And what do you want?"

That question was all the permission he needed. Instantly, his hands were on my ass lifting me up his body. I wrapped my legs around his waist, as my back hit the wall behind me. Our mouths collided, tongues tangling as my hands found his neck and my fingers twisted in his hair. He took a step away from the wall, then carried me to the back of the hotel room where he tossed me onto the mattress. I scrambled up the bed while he stood over me, peeling off his shirt. Then, he crawled over top of me, his hands sliding up my sides, taking my shirt with them as his lips found mine again. He leaned up on one elbow as one hand cradled my breast.

"I hate sex," the words slipped from my lips as I watched him explore my skin.

"Then, we should fix that." He kissed between my eyebrows. "You know I'm not going to do anything you don't want me to."

"But you are." Wrapping my legs around his hips, I pulled him against me. "You're destroying me."

"Do you still want me to leave?"

What if I said yes? Would he? Would I be able to take it?

"No." I let my head roll to the side, staring at the black TV screen and wishing there was something there to distract me. But all I saw was our reflection. The tattooed, muscular man crouched over me. "That's the problem. I'm a fucked-up mess."

"Yeah," he said on an exhale. My eyes snapped to him. "But I'm sure I could point out several dozen people in this building far more fucked up."

"And one little girl on the road to being more fucked up. Do you really want to be a part of this?"

"The club this? Or us this?"

He made me smile at the stupidest things. But I wasn't answering that. And I certainly wasn't admitting there was an us—because there wasn't. "Stop talking and kiss me, Prospect."

His head dipped, lips pressing against my neck as he mumbled into my skin. "If you insist."

Kisses trailed down my neck, and he pulled down the collar of my shirt to kiss my collarbone. He shifted his weight over me, inching my shirt up as my back arched into his touch. Slipping his hand under me, he pulled me upright, then yanked off my shirt. I kissed his chest, tracing my lips down his sternum, then across to his nipple, rolling it between my teeth.

He grunted and stiffened. "Is that how you want to play?"

He unlatched my bra, then pushed me back down into the mattress, palming one breast while his mouth explored the other. Tender touches, tender kisses. I pushed my head into the mattress, pushing my chest up, wanting more. And not getting it.

"Trent," I growled, grabbing a handful of his hair, and pulling. I felt his smile widen against my sensitive breast as his green eyes peered up at me. His tongue swiped over my nipple, then his teeth pinched the tender flesh.

"Yes," I moaned my body twisting and jerking of its own will as the sensation rippled through me. His painfully slow assault continued, kissing, licking, sucking, and then finally, another bite came, bringing the grounding jolt my body needed until I squirmed under him, completely at his mercy.

He sat back, over my thighs. I reached to pull him back, but he was out of reach faster than I could move. His fingers worked at the button to my jeans, slowly peeling down the zipper. His hand slipped under the fabric, moving against my folds while he kept his eyes up, on me, watching me, taking in the detail of every reaction.

"Fuck." I pulled at him with my legs, but he wouldn't budge.

Instead, he took a step back.

"Fuck me, damn it."

"Don't worry." His finger slipped inside me and I gasped, my hips rocking forward so he impaled me even deeper. His finger moved in and out as his thumb massaged my clit in time with each thrust. Then, he slipped another finger in and twisted his hand, hitting a spot that me whimper as my eyes rolled back and my fingers dug into the bedspread.

He had me panting, squirming, and bucking from just a finger fuck.

Then, he pulled his hand free and slid my jeans off my hips, stepping off the bed as he slid them down my legs past my feet, and tossed them onto the floor.

I expected him to remove his own as well, I could see his bulge waiting for release—in so many ways.

Fuck, he's hot.

Fuck, that's the first time I've ever thought anything like that.

But he returned, crouching between my legs, still half clothed. I reached for him, but he caught my hands, pushing them down to the bed next to me as he resumed torturing my taut nipples.

What would happen when he saw the rest of my broken pieces?

Would he be so forgiving, then?

How long until he loses interest?

As if he'd noticed as soon as my mind strayed, he bit the underside of my breast and I bucked.

"Fuck, Trent." I gasped.

Every word I tried to say just came out as a pant or expletive. His lips moved down my stomach, around my belly button, lower…

"Oh, my god," I screamed as his tongue found my clit. His fingers slid inside of me again, hitting that sweet, sweet spot. My thighs tightened against the sides of his head. His stubble stung my tender flesh, while his mouth moved against me as if he knew every square inch of my being.

He wasn't ruining me—he'd already done that. Like the bubbles fleeing a shaken bottle of Ginger Ale, all of my thoughts floated to the surface and exploded into nothingness.

My hips shook, my body writhed, and my toes dug into the mattress. And suddenly the sensation was gone.

"Don't you dare stop." I was so breathless my words were almost without sound.

"Patience, baby," he said, kissing the inside of my thigh.

I squirmed and poked him in the ribs with my toes. "I don't do patience, *Prospect*."

He pressed my knees down and nipped at the skin on the back of my leg.

Fuck, I couldn't believe I was about to say this... "*Please.*"

His eyebrows lifted, but he didn't make a move.

I growled. "Trent, don't make me say it again."

"Oh, you're going to say it again. Again, and again, and again," he mumbled the final words as he buried his face between my legs, taking my clit in his mouth and sucking.

I screamed, feeling the onset of my orgasm shaking through my body again.

But again, all sensation disappeared.

"You're. A. Fucking. Sadist," I growled, slamming my hands into the bed in frustration.

His tongue slid inside me, licking me from core to clit. "And you're fucking enjoying it."

Am I?

Not this part.

Maybe this part.

"Please," I breathed. "Trent." My hips thrust forward, desperate for more. "Please."

He grabbed my hips and took me in his mouth one final time. Every lick and suck pushing me closer until my nervous system exploded sending an overload of messages to every part of my body. Trent's mouth never stopped until my body quivered with the final fading sensations of my orgasm.

When my muscles stilled, Trent crawled up me, planting one final, long kiss on my lips, and rolled to lie next to me. "Now, would I be wrong in my observation that you didn't hate that?"

I tapped him in the chest with the back of my hand and shook my head. Once again, I felt as if my body wasn't truly mine, but this time, it was relaxing.

My fingers trailed down his chest and abdomen, hooking into the front of his jeans. "What about you?"

"I didn't do this for me." He grabbed my hand, holding it where it was.

"But—"

"No." He lifted my hand to his lips and kissed the back of my fingers. "No 'but.'"

I rolled to my side to face him. "You certainly are something else."

"Nah, you've just been surrounded by selfish, ignoramus, pricks your entire life."

What is this? My brain struggled to understand. My eyes closed, and I felt the bed shift as Trent pulled the comforter up and wrapped it around us.

Chapter Twenty-Two

CHALK OUTLINE

Trent

I COULDN'T TAKE my eyes off the somber look on Brooke's face as she lay silently next to me. It made me question my sanity. My inability to pull away from her. Not only hadn't I pulled away, I'd done the complete opposite. I'd landed in bed with her again.

My phone buzzed, and I rolled to my back, slipping it out of my pocket.

Cannon: Lookout duty. Get down to the hill overlooking the lot entrance.

"I have to go. Prospect duties," I mumbled.

"Yeah." Brooke propped herself up on her elbow, letting the blanket fall to her waist. "I should get down to the party." She stared up at the ceiling. "I'd just have to kick myself if I missed the fun."

I chuckled, but my attention was on the rise and fall of her breasts, which were accentuated by the tattoos rapping around her skin. A patch of rough skin stretching down her right side indicated the work there was recent.

I don't know how long I lay there silently staring, but it was long enough for Brooke to notice. When she giggled, sending a subtle vibration over her chest, my cock twitched in my jeans. A not so gentle reminder that it felt neglected. *So which is it? Am I really listening to my cock or my gut?*

"You keep staring and walking out of here is going to be very awkward," Brooke said.

I took a breath and shook my head. This Brooke was a completely different woman to the one I'd met weeks ago, but I could still see the question in her eyes. The uncertainty. There were more walls to get through, but something inside told me I wouldn't be able to stop until I'd crashed them all.

But if I walked away from this Brooke, I wondered if I'd see her again. Tonight, she'd rebuild all of those walls—possibly stronger than before. And I couldn't blame her.

Get your head together. You're a cop. She's an outlaw.

And yet, she was an outlaw with the same goals as me. She wanted revenge on all the bastards who'd given her the foundation for those tough girl walls. And in part, I thought she wanted redemption as well.

I sat up, adjusting my jeans over my uncomfortable dick, but before I could stand, Brooke's hand slithered over my shoulders and she pressed her breasts to my bare back.

A growl rumbled low in my throat. "You're enjoying this, aren't you?"

Her lips caressed the back of my ear. "What's not to enjoy?"

"You're going to be the death of me, baby."

She caught my earlobe in her teeth and skipped right over gentle nibbling to a bite that straightened my back and stretched my jeans even further. Before I could collect myself, one of her hands rubbed over the top of my leg, stopping inches from my erection. "I thought I told you not to call me any of that shit."

I picked her wrist up and dropped it on the bed next to me. "I like annoying you."

Her touches moved up my back as she shifted behind me draping her arms over me and leaning fully against my back. "That's a dangerous game."

"Oh, I know it." I twisted to look back at her—even though that wasn't good for the growing mass of desire. "Now, will you please let me get dressed before Cannon hunts me down?"

She made a humph sound in her throat. "If he were looking for you, I'm sure he'd know where to check first."

I squinted, questioning what she meant.

"He saw you in and out of my place the morning you picked up my prescriptions. The day I torched Gavin's boots, he'd told me where you were, suggesting I was interested in paying a visit. I told him I wasn't, but obviously he caught me back there anyway." She sighed, sitting back on her heels.

"Is that why he took me to a shooting party with a guy he knows wants to blow my dick off?"

"Cannon likes you, but I'm sure he enjoyed the opportunity to put Gavin in his place." She patted me on the shoulder and flopped on the bed, staring up toward the ceiling. Her eyebrows pinched together. "You should watch your back though, he's not the only one who suspects something. Apparently I don't give you enough hell."

I grunted. "Based on whose definition of hell?"

"The one in which I don't tell you"—she rolled toward me—"there's a green envelope on the microwave with my other key card. If you're brave enough to sleep in the same room as me, it might be less conspicuous if you can slip in here without waiting on me, and I'm sure it'll be better than roughing it outside."

"How could I resist an invitation like that?"

"If you were sane, you'd find a way." She grinned up at me and I realized my pull to her had nothing to do with my head, dick, or gut. I was screwed. That tattooed, confusing, devil was tugging at something dozens of hookups never touched.

She nudged me in the hip. "Have fun pointlessly standing guard."

Once I stood, I still couldn't move. Unable to take my eyes off her, I feared that when I saw her next, she'd have buried this Brooke under all that crass and attitude again, deep inside that deadly shell of hers.

"This isn't you getting dressed." She waved her hand at me.

Brooke teasing. I never thought that'd be something I'd experience.

I had to remind myself why I was really there as I grabbed my shirt and dragged it on. "I hope you're still in this mood later."

"Oh." Her eyes darkened immediately. "I can guarantee I won't be."

———

MY KNEES ACHED as the first hour passed and the sun began creeping behind the trees. I shifted my weight again. Standing out here with nothing to see, also left me with too much time to get lost in my thoughts. For the first time in a very long time, my mind went back to Stephanie.

Even with so many other pressing issues, I couldn't shift my focus.

Stephanie. James's little sister. The little girl who always wanted to tag along with us, even on the days she could barely climb out of bed or walk through the house without hacking her head off.

The first girl I ever loved—even though we were both kids and everyone insisted we didn't understand. It's been a lifetime since she died, and in that lifetime, I've realized we did understand. Stephanie knew far more than people gave her credit for—one of the effects of growing up with a chronic illness. From the time she'd been born, her life had been breathing treatments, frequent doctor's visits, chest PT to clear her airways, feeding tubes, a port in her chest, syringes and needles, cups filled with medication multiple times a day.

Some would think that's no way to live, but to her, it was the only way to live, and I think she showed us all up in her short life.

Despite every precaution and intervention, her cystic fibrosis worsened. Even living one virus away from dying, she didn't let anything stop her. She stole my heart and took it to the grave with her when she was fourteen. I was a couple of years older than her. I missed a week of school with James to stay in her hospital room with her that last week.

Maybe next year I'll get over it. That's what I always thought. *Someday I'll meet someone.*

Well, I'd met numerous someone's, and no one has ever held a light to the spark I saw in Stephanie.

And now, I'd lost my goddamned mind. I just left the devil's bed for the second time in less than twenty-four hours. A devil I should have been investigating, not going down on, but damn it, I'd do it again. And again. Because something in that woman stirred something in me that I thought had died a long time ago.

And it wasn't just my overactive libido. I could admit when that was the case. Honestly, that would actually make all this less difficult. Less conflicting.

No, it wouldn't. Even if it were fucking just for the sake of fucking, it could still ruin any chance I had of making any evidence I found stick. And then, I'd also have to face the reality of Brooke splitting as soon as she found out who I really was.

My thoughts were interrupted by the sound of a rough engine coming around the bend. Seconds later, a busted up black sedan appeared, chugging its way up the hill and pulling over near the turn off leading to the resort. James stepped out and yelled up the hill where I stood about ten feet above him. "You wouldn't know how to change a flat, would you?"

I glanced around, then climbed down the steep incline. None of his tires were flat and if anyone saw us, they wouldn't buy that cover long. "I hate to tell you this, but—"

Just as I started to speak, James took the cap off the front driver's side tire and let the air out.

"Right." Then, I noticed more movement in the car as the passenger door opened and a brunette stepped out.

"Pretty please," Rose said, leaning over the roof of the car.

In an instant, my breath was trapped in my lungs. I was glad to see a familiar face, but I tensed. "What the hell is she doing here?"

"Don't worry," Rose said. "I agreed to stay put if anything happened—and it's not like I haven't been in

worse situations than aimlessly driving through the hills."
She waved her arms at the woods around us.

That girl. Too stubborn for her own good, and a perfect
match for James. I remembered James's first call when she'd
been abducted and ended up in the same sex retreat where
he was undercover. After getting her out, I'd been on her
protective detail for a while, and that experience alone was
proof enough she wouldn't back down from going toe-to-toe
with anyone to get what she wanted—even James.

They weren't supposed to work out either, but he
couldn't let her go. Maybe I wasn't the only hopeless one,
but she hadn't been the outlaw either.

"Good to see you," I said tightly.

"Good to see you in one remotely put together piece—
for the walking disaster you are." With a smirk she retreated
back into the car, giving us room to talk.

"I assume you have a jack and a spare," I said.

James followed me to the back of the car and popped
the trunk, revealing a jack, tire iron, and a brand-new full-
sized tire. He'd really thought this out. He grabbed the jack
and iron, while I dropped the tire to the ground and rolled
it to the front of the car.

"How's the party?" James asked as we positioned the
jack under the frame just in front of the driver's door and
lifted the car slightly.

I groaned. Between babysitting, Brooke, and standing
on a hill watching the occasional car pass by, I hadn't even
set foot in the main event. "I'm going to need a knee
replacement from all the standing and doing nothing."

"So, you don't even get to eavesdrop?"

"Not yet. I assume Cannon will send someone out here
to relieve me eventually. And then I'll get to fetch cigarettes,
and maybe even shine a few boots."

"Exciting stuff." James caught his laugh in his throat. "Are you any closer to figuring out who their insider is? Or anything we can make stick? Libby's getting antsy."

"Nothing solid, but I do know where there's a cache of journals and notes kept hidden by Dixon Sawyer while he was Sargent-at-Arms. I got a glimpse last night, but there are piles of info." I latched the tire iron onto the first of the lug nuts before too much pressure was taken off the tire. "I have a problem."

James stopped fiddling with the jack and glared at me. "What kind of problem?"

"I um..." I leaned against the quarter panel of the car, bringing my foot down on the iron to break loose the first rusty nut, then I continued, loosening each in turn. "You know, that Treasurer problem."

James still looked confused, probably because I'd been leaving out as many details about Brooke as possible.

"Daughter of the President. You spoke to her." With each nut loose, I continued around the tire, removing them, then I waited for James to finish jacking up the car. He didn't move though. His gaze was locked on me, the wrinkles across his forehead particularly deep.

"The one who drugged you?" he asked under his breath. "Does she know—?"

"Not what you think," I mumbled, motioning for him to get jacking. I couldn't stand out here all day. "She isn't suspicious, she doesn't know about *this*."

Although I'm sure she was quite suspicious over why a Prospect would have no trouble helping her rid the world of the Devils.

"Trent," James growled, but fortunately he started jacking up the car—albeit slowly.

"Don't give me that tone, especially given how you met the girl sitting in this crap car right now."

"She wasn't a criminal," he hissed, reminding me of what I already knew. "You need to get your head on straight or get out."

He shook his head backing away from the car.

"My head is on perfectly straight." *Sort of. Not really.* Was it? I knew how close I was to fucking everything up and losing Brooke one way or another. The shitty part was, that concerned me slightly more than fucking up the case. "Look, she's the Treasurer, she has info on everyone, and her living room was littered with those journals and notes from her brother."

He looked me dead in the eye. "And if you screw her enough, she's going to hand it over?"

I didn't answer, focusing instead on shaking the tire free and rolling it off to the side. James' face softened and he returned to our facade of working on the car. "Okay, under-cover cop got himself involved with the Treasurer of the club. Please explain how that isn't thinking with your dick."

"She's been abused by the club her entire life. Particularly that shit-head President father of hers. She became Treasurer to get revenge on the whole lot." The words weren't sounding any more convincing coming out of my mouth than they had rolling around in my head.

He gave me a skeptical glare. "So, you've partnered with the club rogue. Sounds safe."

"Not at all, but we also partnered with the Gold family rogue, and that worked out fine. Besides—"

"You can't help yourself." After a few seconds, his scowl turned into a smirk. "You should really get that libido of yours checked out."

"Mmh hmm." I straightened, then leaned back until my spine popped. "I wish that were my problem."

James's expression went flat, and he shook his head. "You always have to chase the impossible ones, don't you?"

He rolled the spare into place, and we lifted it, lining it up with the hub. While he held it there, I threaded the lug nuts back in place, hand tightening each as much as I could. This was a lot of fucking work to have a simple chat. "I don't chase. It seems like every time I try to avoid her, I end up getting pulled in deeper. Besides, we can't keep up this shanty little gig much longer. Right now, her information is the closest thing we have to a break."

"I'll talk to Libby, see if she can work some magic with the DA if she agrees to cooperate. But you better damn-well not get yourself killed." James released the jack, and when the tire was firmly on the ground, I tightened each nut with the tire iron.

"What the hell you doin'?" Someone shouted from the top of the hill.

"Flat tire," I yelled back, waving him off. Then, I smacked James in the shoulder. "I think you can handle the rest."

I got a running start at the hill, using small trees and brush to pull myself up over the crest. "Ever heard of PR?" I asked the hang-around who'd probably been sent to take my place.

He scoffed and crossed his arms. "Tag, you're it. Cannon wants you back at the party."

———

BY THE TIME I headed back to the party, the unlit grounds were almost pitch black, so I followed the edge of the winding road to the side of the building. There was an external door on the edge of the large building that led almost directly to the ballroom where the lodge had set up the food for the party. Just outside that door, I saw a group of smokers—including Gavin and Damian, so I paused behind a cluster of tall bushes waiting for them to disband.

"It's almost time," Gavin said. "You sure your crew can pull this off?"

Gavin spoke to two men with their backs to me. The first a scrawny, blond-haired man in a Defiance MC cut. Next to him, the man had a black hood pulled over his head.

"There' in with no questions asked," the blond barked, seemingly annoyed at the line of questioning or the entire situation in general. "I got everything set up, now do your part."

The cluster of men tightened, and the blond handed something to Gavin. I had to struggle to catch any of the following words. "Be sure Sawyer gets the message. I'll be expecting the call this week."

"Just make sure you handle this shit better than what you pulled at The Race Trap," Gavin said.

My gut sank. They were up to something, and my hands were tied unless I could figure out what.

"*You* were supposed to be at The Race Trap," the blond said. "Who can't handle their shit?"

Damn it. I needed him to shift so I could get a better look, but I suspected he'd been one of those who'd attacked Brooke and me at The Race Trap.

Then, the hooded man turned, looking over his shoulder and scanning the surrounding area.

I sank deeper into the bushes. I recognized him as well, and he had a damn good reason for wearing a hood.

Chapter Twenty-Three

NAILED TO THE WALL

Brooke

THE PARTY ECHOED through the halls long before I reached the doors to the ballroom. I was late—not even fashionably late—just plain late, because I couldn't get Trent out of my head. *Why'd he affect me like that?*

Why did I let him?

Part of the answer to that was easy, I enjoyed it. As disconcerting as it was to have a man see through my walls, and as infuriating as he could be with all those stupid terms of endearment, he set me free. He pulled me out of the darkness where I hid, deep in the back of my mind, shook off the broken pieces, and dragged me out. It was terrifying that a man could have so much power over me and read me so easily.

He could send me to a worse hell at the drop of a hat, and despite that awareness gnawing at me, it wasn't the source of my queasy stomach or clammy hands.

I never lived in a world without ulterior motives. I lived in a world of orders, violence, and hidden selfish desires. A world where I couldn't trust Trent further than I could kick him. And yet, part of me wanted more than a couple of good fucks. Something I didn't stand a chance of getting.

There would be no settling down for me. I was Treasurer of an outlaw motorcycle group—one I had secretly plotted against since my sixteenth birthday. And it didn't matter how good Trent was with that damn tongue of his, I had one goal that I'd worked too hard to give up on. Sooner or later, this club would fall, and as Treasurer, I'd go with it. I'd resigned myself to that as well.

So that meant whatever enjoyment I got out of this whole Trent thing, there was already a doomsday clock hanging over every encounter.

I leaned into the door to the banquet room and shoved it open. The party was already in full swing and had easily doubled in size—especially in terms of barely-dressed women. For those who didn't have Ol' Ladies, or bring them along, there were plenty of choices—all eager to entertain a biker, or several, for the night.

From the looks of the one flustered bartender and the crowd stumbling around him, they were all well inebriated. Most of the crowd was gathered in the center of the room, carrying on in a slurry of conversation. Some sat at tables, beers in hand. Then there were the corner huggers at each end of the room. To my right, the tweakers, high strung and erratic, shouting and shoving each other around. To the opposite side, the speedballers, who preferred their high with a constant cycle of cocaine and heroin. Some of them swayed to the music, and stared off, and others leaned casually against the wall, chatting about whatever someone who had fried their brains found interesting. Probably murdering unicorns.

I was so busy observing the outside of the room, I never noticed Gavin emerge from the crowd.

"Where have you been, Treasurer?" Given he never called me that, I prepared for the impending assault. He cocked his head and grinned. "Room 311, right? I'm in the room right under you."

I sneered, but deep inside, my heart sank. All he needed was more ammunition. From the way everyone had already been talking, it was only a matter of time before all the details made it to him, but I had hoped for a little more time. "Hope you enjoyed the radio show, then."

I sidestepped him, heading for the bar, but Gavin grabbed me by the shoulder, jerking me back just as I caught the bartender's attention. "You're fuckin' the Prospect."

'Let's get this clear." I spun, knocking him back. "Who I fuck is not your business. Haven't you gotten into enough trouble lately?"

"Look here, Mama—"

Over Gavin's shoulder, I saw Caine break away from a small group and head my way. "Hey, Brooke, I need to talk to you about Ruby."

He gestured for me to follow him out to the patio. I threw my hands in the air and followed, I'd already been there far too long to still be without alcohol. Caine headed to the corner of the patio, where the sound of the party was muted, leaned against the railing and crossed his arms, but he didn't say anything.

"What's up with Ruby?" I asked. *Please don't tell me this is going to be a second lecture about handing her off.*

"Nothing, she's at the pool with Thea since her mom is

toasted out of her mind." His forehead pinched as he glanced back toward the party. "Just getting you away from Gavin. He's already been on a wild tear this evening about something."

I pressed my lips together. *Talk about a strange day.* "Been a long time since you've had my back."

"Has it?" Caine rocked on his feet, stepping away from the railing. "Look, I know things have gotten fucked up between us, but"—he glanced around, then shook his head—"we both have to choose our battles carefully."

I spotted Cissie propped up against Sawyer in the far corner and looked away from the scene as quickly as possible, but did a double take when I realized there was a crowd of men wearing Defiance colors in the group around Sawyer and Cissie. "Defiance? What're they doing here?"

"I asked Dad and Cannon, they both said it was Sawyer's last-minute idea, since we're making nice with them." Caine rubbed his hand over the back of his head, then he leaned toward my shoulder. "You smell like men's cologne by the way."

I jerked back, thinking he had to be kidding, but when I lifted my shirt and sniffed, sure enough, it smelled like Trent. But I rolled my eyes and brushed Caine off. "I think you're confusing leather for cologne."

I tapped the pack of cigarettes against my palm, tore it open and offered one to Caine, but he shook his head. I turned away to block the wind while I lit up, thinking Caine had accomplished his mission and would return to the party. Instead, he remained in place, shifting his weight from side to side. "Thea hasn't stopped talking about you and Trent."

"Yeah." I waved my hand through the air. "Can we move on to a different subject?"

"Just..." He hesitated, jerking his head in small motions as if trying to figure out what to say. "Be careful."

Then, he headed back inside the bustling banquet hall.

Great advice. Now if I could only figure out how to apply it. I leaned over the railing, trying to collect my thoughts.

When I glanced over my shoulder to make sure no one else was about to destroy my peace, I saw Trent standing next to Cannon. It appeared Cannon was introducing him to someone from the Defiance Club. I pressed my lips together, letting my head fall to the side. I didn't have time for this. Seeing Ruby here reminded me of that. My life— my bruises and years of abuse—was mine. I could handle that. But watching these bikers, and thinking about their kids, the little girls, and the life they'd grow up in meant I didn't have forever.

I'd be ripping families apart, but if that kept one girl from turning out like me, it'd be worth it. Sure, the rules said we respect our own. Don't sleep with a brother's 'Ol Lady—at least not without permission—and never fuck with their kids. But I was living proof those rules could be thrown out the window. And I'd seen the dozens of young girls the men would drag into the bar, get drunk, and have their way with. Maybe I'd only stop one or two lives from being destroyed, but the moment I saw one of those life-wreckers get their due punishment...

My thoughts crashed.

I always thought that's what would make me feel whole again, and then Trent glanced in my direction and smiled. My body petrified where I stood, while inside my head everything exploded in confusion. For a short time that afternoon, I'd let go of all this shit, all the baggage I kept safely nearby to remind me of my objective. Trent claimed he knew what I wanted—revenge. But it was more than revenge.

I flicked the ashes off my cigarette and took a seat on the iron bench that ran along the side of the patio. I watched Trent cross the crowded floor several times, so on the next pass when he got close to the doorway, I yelled, "Prospect."

His lip twisted into the slightest smirk as his head whipped around and he caught my gaze. He stepped around one of the guys, then cut through the group blocking the doorway. Once outside, he took a deep breath as if enjoying the free-moving air. "And what can I do for you?"

"Foot rub." I kicked up my boot-clad foot.

"That, by far, wouldn't be the worst order I've had tonight. Standing on guard duty is highly underrated." He used the collar of his shirt to wipe the sweat from his forehead. "Someone should really check the ventilation in this place."

"We come here every year, and it's always the same."

Trent glanced around, then came closer, but his smirk had faded. His eyes continued to shift, on high alert. "We need to talk."

"Not now," I groaned, pinching the bridge of my nose. Maybe not ever. What we did was good—damn good—but whether he'd gotten cold feet or suddenly wanted something more serious, I wasn't interested.

"It isn't going to wait," he said under his breath.

I took a final drag of my cigarette and crushed it against the concrete with the toe of my boot. "I'm not going to like this, am I?"

We moved off the side of the patio, out of view of

everyone inside, but I could still see the door if anyone stepped out and we had enough distance to ensure that no one inside could hear us over the party.

Trent glanced back just in case. "I heard Gavin talking to a group outside. I don't know what they're planning but it seems a bit suspicious since it involves Defiance, and one those tweakers from the Race Trap is here in Defiance colors."

Oh fuck. My stomach sank. I paced in front of Trent. "Did you mention any of this to Cannon?"

His face twisted. "What am I going to say in the middle of this?" He waved back to the party. "Besides, I didn't figure you wanted me to bring up the Race Trap thing."

"No," I mumbled, but *this*. I didn't know how to deal with this alone. I was supposed to be the one turning the tables, not protecting the club from some other rogue scheme. I rubbed my temples. A cigarette was not effective enough.

The chatter inside suddenly became more punctuated. Yelling. Cracking. The definite sound of knuckles against skin. I took a sidestep and looked inside. At the center of the mess, I saw a group of Defiance brothers surrounded by Devils.

Shit. Damn. Fuck.

So much for a friendly alliance. Bull grabbed one of the Defiance brothers and threw him into a table where four other Devil patches sat. They all then jumped up and joined the brawl. Not that this behavior was uncommon, even without another group present. By the time everyone had their fill of booze and drugs, they always found a new means of entertainment.

"Guess the party is over," I mumbled.

Then I heard someone shout, "Where's Prospect?"

They were out for blood, and they wanted some of it on Trent's hands. I pulled Trent to the edge of the patio and flashed my do not ask questions glare. "I'll meet you in my room."

"Brooke," he hissed, grabbing my arms, but I didn't have time. We didn't have time.

"Go," I said, shoving him back.

His lips pursed while his eyes danced between me and the sound of the erupting party. "Be careful."

I waited until he jumped the railing and disappeared along the path around the building. Then, I dumped the contents of my cigarette pack in the bushes and headed inside. People brushed past me in all directions. Some getting the hell out, and others too distraught to know what they were doing. Like walking through the midst of a mosh pit, I reached the other side of the room battered.

"Where's you little fight-lovin' Prospect now?" Bull called after me.

"I already sent him to grab some cigarettes." I held up my crumpled, empty pack. "But given I can get WWE on pay-per-view from the comfort of my room, I'm out."

Thankfully, Fitch rushed through, shouting at everyone involved.

Yeah, good luck with that, I thought as I slipped out. The tension in my chest faded as I hit the empty lobby, but the wave of relief was cut short when I ran into Damian and two others in the stairwell, standing in a line so I couldn't pass. "You have got to be kidding me."

"Gavin wants to see you," Damian said.

"What else is new?" I tried to shove my way through them. "Tell him to fuck himself, I'm sure he's had a lot of practice."

Damian shoved me backward and I noticed he had an

extra leather slung over his shoulder. He turned slightly, and I saw the Prospect patch. "I don't think you want me to tell him that right now."

I rushed for him, but the other two grabbed my arms before I could reach him.

I'd just sent Trent away from the fight. *What the fuck?*

Gavin must've been outside.

I hadn't taken the time to inventory everyone I saw inside the ballroom.

Footsteps approached behind me, and Bull joined the group. "I take it we're on."

"On?" I took in their hard faces. "On for what?"

"I told you, Gavin wants to see you," Damian said.

"Where's Trent?"

"You mean Prospect?" Damian grinned. "Don't worry, I'm sure he's getting a fitting treatment."

I jerked my arms away from Chester and Dodger, adjusting my cut. "Lead the way."

We exited the lodge though a side door and headed down the hill through the tree line. When the trees cleared, I saw Trent, short torn and head down, on his knees surrounded by Gavin and a dozen others he'd rounded up, for Trent's trial by fists. But this wasn't the typical prospect trial, if it were Sawyer and Cannon would be present, at least. "Gavin, your fight is with me."

"Maybe so, Mama." He kicked Trent in the chest. Trent curled with the blow for an instant, then straightened. His right arm hung limply at his side, but he held the left tensed against his thigh. His forehead twinged with each breath as blood trickled down from cuts on his forehead, lips, and chin. "But it's my duty to test Prospects, isn't it?"

Not in the secret of night away from the other patches. "That's not what this is about."

"Still... well within my duties."

I stood at the final precipice. Gavin had finally found a weakness to hold over me. I stormed over to where he stood, so mighty in his own disgrace. His tongue raked over his crooked and chipped teeth.

"What do you want?" The words ground between my teeth.

He lifted one shoulder casually. His body remained lax, unmoved by any act of violence. "Resign."

Give up everything? Show him how weak I was. No. I looked back toward Trent as Bull raised a thick branch over him, prepared to swing it like a bat.

"Stop," I screamed, lunging to stand between them. If I gave up my patch, I'd resign to their power and whatever they wanted to do with me after. I'd lose my advantage. I'd lose my leverage.

But if I didn't....

"He's had enough," I said.

"That's my call to make, Mama." Gavin snarled. "It's not uncommon for Prospects to never make it through this test. He's weaker than he looks. You're both a weak link. I'm going to prove it."

Only because Trent wasn't fighting. He wasn't supposed to, fighting back now would be the end of it for him either way. And Gavin had the gall to call Trent weak, when he was the weakest among us. Childish. Spoiled. Impudent. I bit back my words, refusing to make this worse.

And what would it say if I let them kill Trent? This was firmly and squarely on me. They'd caused enough damage in the time it took me to get through the party and follow Bull out here. Fucking bastards.

I held my ground between the raised branch and Trent when I heard a twig snap up the hill. Everyone turned as

Cannon, Fitch, and Caine lead the approaching group over the ridge above us.

"What are you doin', Vin?" Cannon called out.

"Weeding out the problems." Gavin stepped forward, holding out his hands. He counted on Sawyer or whatever deal he'd concocted with Defiance to wipe his worthless ass when this was over.

"That's high talk from the biggest weed of all."

Thanks to the bouncing gleam of a flashlight, I noticed the glint of metal in Cannon's hand. Gavin must've too because he whispered over my shoulder, "This isn't over Mama."

"Maybe it's not over, but I've had enough." I stepped back and helped Trent to his feet. "Can you walk?"

"I'll manage."

Cannon gestured for Caine to help with Trent. "Get him upstairs. We'll take care of this."

Just like they'd taken care of everything else going to shit the last couple of decades? "Now you think it's time to do something? Not when I was crawling into Thea's room every night or walking around covered in bruises because none of them will keep their hands off of me. I'm done with this shit."

Cannon stomped in our direction. "Get out of here, Brooke. Now."

"Why? So you can cover all of this up and let Sawyer give Gavin some pat on the back."

Caine hissed my name as he passed by me to take Trent's arm. He took my place, helping Trent back to my room while the others dealt with the mess outside.

"Do you have clothes?" I asked as Caine deposited him on the couch. Trent was covered in leaves, dirt, and blood.

Trent groaned, straightening his body to reach into his

front pocket. The screen on his phone was covered in a web of cracks, and he tossed it aside. "Still with my bike."

"I'll get it while they're all detained." Caine grabbed my ice bucket and headed for the door. "You'll need some ice, too."

"Watch your back," I said.

He mumbled something as the door closed.

"You're gonna need to set my arm," Trent said.

"What?" I spun from staring at the door.

"My shoulder is dislocated." His jaw was tight and pulsing as he spoke. "Adrenaline is a wonderful thing until it starts to wear off."

"I—" I shook my head. I'd dealt with a lot of shit, popping bones back into place on a guy twice my size wasn't one of them.

Trent lay on the couch, kicking his heels up over the arm. "Just keep it parallel to the floor. Stretch it up until it pops into place."

"Trent, I—"

"You're not going to make it hurt any worse than it already does. Just fucking do it."

My instinct wanted to snap, claiming I wasn't afraid of hurting him, but I was in this whole new mess because I couldn't watch him get hurt, or worse. I knelt next to the couch and lifted his arm. I stared at his fingers to avoid seeing the flinch around his eyes.

"Keep it straight," Trent said.

I moved it out, cradling his elbow and wrist as I pushed it over his head. Trent grunted, holding his knuckles to his mouth, and then I felt the pop.

"Ah, fuck," he sighed as the tension in his body gradually released. He wiggled his fingers, tucking the arm against his chest as he sat up. "Gavin caught me as I was coming around the building. Two guys jumped me from behind."

"He had Bull inside. Damian waiting near the other exit. I'm betting they knew I'd direct you away from the fight."

He's a liability. Or am I?

Trent's body sagged now that his arm was set, but he continued to wince with each breath or tiny movement. "I should get cleaned up before I trash your entire room."

I helped him get his shirt off, it was ripped and tattered anyway, so he instructed me to just finish the job. Then, he jumped in the shower while I waited for Caine to return.

I almost didn't move from the couch when I heard the knock, but I rocked myself to my feet, and checked to make sure it was Caine before opening the door. "Thanks."

Rather than just handing me the ice and bag, he stepped inside, tossing Trent's bag onto the couch. "Gavin's up to something. You really going to let him force you out now? After everything?"

"Since when do you care?"

"You chose your method. I chose the one to keep my wife and daughter safe. Your problem is that you're not used to caring about anyone else—not since Dixon died."

I bit the inside of my cheek. "You're really going to lecture me on this tonight?"

"This isn't a lecture, Brooke. Whatever's coming... none of us are going to survive it if we're all fighting different battles. The shit's going to hit the fan. I feel it. This... this isn't the club I grew up in. As soon as everything settles tonight, I'm sending Thea to stay with family. As it looks, she'll take Ruby."

"It doesn't feel much different to me."

"No, I suppose I was blind to a lot of the things you saw.

I should've listened to Dix instead of my Dad." Caine remained stiff, picking at the frayed edge of his front pocket.

Growing impatient at his lingering silence, I asked, "Something else I can do for you?"

"Nah, guess not. Call if you need anything."

When he left, I suspected there was something else, he just couldn't bring himself to say it.

I grabbed Trent's bag and delivered it to the bathroom, pausing as his long silhouette moved in front of the glass door to the shower. He said something, but I couldn't make it out.

"What?" I stepped closer to the shower door.

Again, he mumbled, so I jerked open the shower door. Mistake. He yanked me inside, right under the stream.

"You—" I spit water. "You really think now is the time for this?"

I rubbed the water and mascara from my eyes while Trent chuckled.

"Always seize an opportunity." He leaned his head back and the stream of water traveled down his hair, over his shoulders, and through the divots between his muscles. His torso and thighs were marred with red splotches, scratches, and swollen lumps, particularly down his sides. "Takes my mind off the pain."

"This is my fault. Gavin's using you to get me to step down."

He leaned his head forward and lifted my chin so we were nose to nose. "This is Gavin's fault. Maybe Sawyer's for letting him go. Do you have a plan?"

"No," I whispered. He said he understood my need for revenge, but how deep did that go? "I have to figure out what's in those damn journals. Dix said the answer was there, but I don't even know where to start. Every time he tried to explain his master plan, I cut him off after 'if anything happens to me.'"

Trent winced as he leaned back, rubbing his injured shoulder. "Maybe you're looking for the needle in the haystack when what you really need is hay."

"Fine, but how can I leverage hay if I don't know its purpose?" Time was running out for both of us—all of us.

Chapter Twenty-Four

NO REST FOR THE ADDICTED

Trent

BROOKE'S CLOTHING clung to her curves, and water, darkened by her makeup streaked her cheeks and dripped from her nose.

"You know it's impractical to stand in the shower with all your clothes on."

"You're..." Brooke gave me a flat look, then began stripping off her sopping clothes and tossing them over the metal bar over the back of the shower. "You're lucky I took off my boots."

I hadn't thought about that, but watching her huff, spit, and sputter was well-worth taking the risk. Her forehead was creased with tension, and she drew her shoulders toward her neck. I needed to get her loosened up and talking again, but my efforts in that regard usually led to anything but talking. At first, anyway. But I was trying not to collapse in pain and needed to keep myself occupied as well.

Don't do it, I said to myself. *Don't do it.* Pulling her hips toward me, I leaned into her and nipped at the delicate flesh over her collarbone.

You did it. There was no more room for rational thought.

Brooke nudged me back, but I refused to let go, dunking her right under the full stream of water in the process. She squealed, but as she shoved her hair out of her face. I got a smile, even another laugh.

You did it, I heard in my head again.

It wasn't the biting that was the problem. That I did because I could. The problem was that I fell. I, the Detective, fell for her, the daughter of the Devil.

I swallowed, staring into those fretful brown eyes. Sure, she had her in secrets. She had her own lies and problems, and I had to choose between her and my job. Something I wasn't ready to do. Something I didn't know I would ever be willing to do. And yet that inevitability would sneak up on us both. *You fell, but for fuck's sake don't tell her.*

There were lies between us, lies I couldn't begin to explain. Not now, and I wondered if ever. In the midst of all this, *how can my biggest worry be whether or not one biker would forgive me for being a cop?*

Would it matter? Would she go down with the club? Would she cooperate?

Was there any out from here?

Brooke lifted her fingers to my chest, delicately tracing the twisted thorns that sprawled out from the purple rose tattooed over my heart. I held my breath as her touch moved slightly lower, over the scrawling letters below, *fight*.

"Purple doesn't seem your color," she whispered.

I put my hand over hers, stopping her movements and covering the tattoo. "It's for cystic fibrosis. It's for someone I knew, but she died when we were teenagers."

"Just someone you knew? A tattoo usually means more than a passing acquaintance."

"She was my best friend's little sister. The first girl I ever fell in love with. The only..." my words died away. Until now, she'd been the only person I'd ever felt this gnawing connection to.

I didn't think her face could look that hurt. The doubt in her eyes was so deep in no doubt touched her soul. She'd never tell me what was going on inside that brain, and I had to keep my own wall up as well which meant changing the topic ASAP. "Any idea what Gavin and these Defiance guys are up to?"

"I don't know." Brooke threw her head back and exhaled. "Sawyer thinks he's making a power play with them. Defiance is bad news. Smaller than us, but worse, because they play hard and dirty, especially when it comes to drugs. They also have no qualms dealing in women, and Damian has been pushing to get into the sex business. But I can't imagine they're willing to take orders from Sawyer, so... getting us out of the way would be their best bet."

As I stepped out of the way, she grabbed the bar of soap from the ledge and lathered up, while the cascade of water carried the suds over her curves.

Concentrate, Trent. Upon consideration, getting her naked in the shower wasn't one of my better ideas. I fought to focus on any information that might pull everything together. "I've overheard a couple of people mention someone named Barney."

Brooke pursed her lips and exhaled, blowing away the droplets of water from her lips. "Barney isn't his *name*. He's Sawyer's pet cop, but Sawyer keeps his identity under wraps. I'm guessing he doesn't want anyone else snagging his leverage. I suspect Fitch knows as well, but it's definitely not info anyone is eager to share with me."

She bowed her head, exhausted and broken, as the water battered her skin. "Why are you just fine with all this? Really? You make no sense."

"I wouldn't say I'm just fine with Gavin coming at me every chance he gets." I almost told her the truth. *At this point, would she still freak?* Probably, but time was running out. Whatever this big deal between Defiance and the Devils came to, it wouldn't be good. If we could get in the middle of it, however, turn both sides against one another, that along with Brooke's information could launch a major blow to the entire system.

"Don't tell me you didn't expect that when joining a biker gang." Brooke grabbed the tiny bottle of shampoo and lathered up her matted hair.

"What I didn't expect was you. This whole situation is fucked, but if we're being honest, I'm putting my money on you. They don't see it. They make a living underestimating you, but I'm not dumb enough to make that mistake."

"I'm an object to them. If you were smart, you would've taken the out." Brooke closed her eyes, rubbing the back of her neck as she tipped her head back. "What were you going to tell me outside, before the fight broke out?"

Oh, that... I watched the droplets run over her skin, down her chest and over her breasts. "I don't exactly remember."

"Because you're staring at my boobs, don't exert yourself." She rolled her eyes, turning her back to me.

"Nope, still don't remember." And now I had her ass, but as I drew my gaze higher, I saw the details of the webbed wings stretching around her rib cage. "I saw Gavin meeting with Defiance, they handed over something for

Sawyer, and one of them was from The Race Trap. They were angry Gavin hadn't been with you at The Race Trap."

"What?" Brooke looked over her shoulder. "Gavin knew about that? He was in on it?"

"Seemed that way." Oh, and there was that little detail about the group discussing all of this with a cop present, but this Trent wouldn't have reviewed the employee files for the district to know that. We were all playing a dangerous lies and secrets game. Alone, none of us had the information needed to bring down the club, and that was the point. How much longer could I hold back?

"That makes no sense. Were they setting me up?"

Now that she mentioned it, I hadn't had much time to think on that earlier. If Sawyer had put Gavin and Defiance up to the stunt, he wouldn't have given in so easily when Brooke requested to take me along instead. He would've had no problem putting his foot down. Unless he didn't expect me to be a threat to their plan.

The other alternative was that Gavin planned to double-cross Sawyer somehow.

"You really don't belong here, Trent. You should get out while you still can."

Taking her by the hips, I pulled her back against me. "You've been saying I don't belong here a long time."

"Well, it's true." She leaned her head back against my non-injured shoulder. "We need to get some ice on that shoulder."

I feigned shock. "Almost sounds like you care."

She flipped off the water and swung open the door. "Don't push it, Prospect."

Oh, she cared. And somehow the bravado she used to cover it up was sexy as hell. Every battle intoxicating. But soon, that'd be all over.

I REACHED ACROSS THE BED, there was still a warm spot beneath the blankets, but no Brooke beside me. I groaned as I moved into a half-sitting position. The shoulder may have been the worst of it, but my entire right side ached. I suspected a few bruised ribs and contusions. My left hip was also stiff from taking a boot. It would have been easier to inventory the body parts that didn't ache... possibly my left pinky toe. The rest muddled into a blur. I squinted at the bright red display of the clock, 3:37 am.

Something was off. I could feel it. I checked my phone again, hoping I'd remembered wrong, but it was busted to oblivion.

"Brooke?" I checked the next rooms, but the entire suite was empty, and when I flipped on the light in the living room, I noticed her bag was gone. I should have known she'd been too resolved after the shower. Too quiet.

Screw it, I thought. I hadn't come here to pace in a hotel room. I had to find her and a way to update James. I threw on my jeans much faster than my body would have liked, ignoring the splitting pain from my shoulder, ribs, and face. Every motion reminded me of a different punch, kick, or slap. Just as I fastened my jeans, someone knocked. I caw Caine through the peephole and opened the door.

"Brooke just took off," he said.

"You let her go alone?"

Caine rolled his shoulders back, giving me a questioning glare. "It's Brooke. What was I going to do, lie down in front of her bike?"

He had a point.

"I figured while she was getting a head start, convinced that no one noticed, I'd wake you." He handed me the leather that one of Gavin's men had yanked off in the brawl that had led to my dislocated shoulder. "To make matters worse, Gavin and his crew headed out about thirty minutes ago. I considered following them, but I was more concerned with getting Thea on the road and away from all this for a while. I highly doubt Brooke took the time to notice their missing bikes beforehand."

"Sounds like you're planning for this to go to hell real quick. Anyone else know?" I tossed the jacket on the couch, so I could attempt to pull on a shirt.

"No." He squinted at me. "Are you going to be able to ride?"

My shoulder had stiffened up in the last couple of hours and needed a few weeks to rest, so I wasn't quite sure about that myself. "I'll manage."

Once dressed, I laced up my boots, with more pain than I wanted to admit, and grabbed my bag.

Almost thirty miles from the lodge, Caine pulled ahead, then off the road into an empty lot. "I figured your shoulder could use a break."

While true, we didn't have time for that. Brooke could be walking right into the middle of a disaster and I had no way to report any of it since my phone was busted. Regardless, Caine climbed off his bike and resumed the fidgeting he was famous for as he lit a cigarette. "Also, we're away from the others and"—he handed me his phone—"you should be able to get a signal here."

Huh? I squinted at the phone, wondering who he expected me to call. Brooke? If that were the case, he could have done that himself.

"I know who you are. Or, should I say, what you are. I've suspected since you showed up. You're not exactly what I imagined they'd send, so I kept quiet. I couldn't risk putting

Thea or Cori in danger. I've seen enough of what they do to people who dare to question the brotherhood." He waved the phone at me until I took it. "I'm the one who tipped off the police."

I tipped back in my seat. *Caine*? I had wondered why he was always slipping off.

"You and Brooke though," he shook his head, blowing out a cloud of smoke. "If you're gambling on her having answers, that's a problem. Far as Sawyer's concerned, she's an outsider. He started feeling the same way toward Dixon and he ended up dead. Sawyer let Brooke become Trea-surer to shut her up, make her think she had room to dig right where he could actually keep a close eye on her."

"Why are you telling me all of this now?"

"I've been trying to watch Gavin and his gang. They and Sawyer are circling like a plan is about to come together, but I doubt their goals are the same. And with Defiance showing up back there, it's only a matter of time before things get ugly. I heard Gavin talking about fentanyl a while back when he had a cop on his trail."

"He raped that girl from Ashville."

Caine snorted. "He brought her to The Pit. He wasn't the only one, but I doubt she remembers much of that night. She wouldn't be the first. She wasn't the last. Instead of doing anything smart, he slipped her fentanyl. The detective picked it up without realizing it."

She was fifteen. Winsor had been stuck by a needle hidden by her thigh.

"The cops were already sniffing around, but even those who suspected what Gavin did wouldn't have talked no matter what. They had nothing to link the fentanyl to us, thanks to Brooke and Cannon. They don't let that shit fly, but that only pissed off Gavin, which in turn irritated

Sawyer. The club is falling apart. Sawyer and Gavin want it to conform to their twisted fantasies. Cannon, he doesn't have the worst intentions, but his dedication to the brotherhood blinds him."

As Caine talked, I dialed James's number.

"Hello?" He sounded hesitant.

"It's Trent. My phone got busted last night. I'm heading back to the Point after Brooke. Gavin and his crew are on the move." I looked to Caine. "Any idea where they might be headed?"

Caine stared off for a minute and grimaced. "I don't know for sure, but I managed to tail Gavin out to a warehouse while everyone was dealing with his little stunt that put the garage out of commission. East end of eleventh street, near the old shoe factory. I slipped into a carryout across the street to watch, but I don't know exactly what's going on there."

"You get that?" I asked James.

"Yeah, I'll let Ainsley know and we'll get everything in place."

"There's one more thing, I spotted a cop plotting with Gavin and his crew at the resort last night. I remember his face from my cram session, but not the name. Caucasian, mid-forties, bulky build, dark hair, overgrown goatee, about five-ten, I'd guess."

"Got it. Try not to get yourself killed shot we get there."

I handed Caine's phone back and he tucked it inside his coat. "Does Brooke know you're a cop?"

I stared up at the dark sky, unpolluted by the lights of town but covered by a dreary haze that muted all but the moon. "What do you think?"

Caine swung his leg over his bike and started the engine. "Oh, that's going to blow up."

Chapter Twenty-Five

DEVIL'S OWN LUCK

Trent

WE HEARD tires squeal as we approached The Pit. The front doors of the bar were wide open, swaying on the wind that still carried the fragrance of burning rubber. I barely took time to put the kickstand down on the bike before running inside.

Light spilled across the floor of the dark space from Brooke's office door, and just to the left of it, Brooke's twisted body lay in a puddle of blood.

"Brooke." I moved her head enough to check for a pulse and felt the faint indication of breath on my arm. A trail of blood outlined her right cheek from a cut on her temple. Carefully, I rolled her to her back, discovering the main source of the blood—a large gash across her left thigh which had likely nicked an artery.

"Grab some rags," I yelled. "We're going to need an ambulance."

"Fuck." Caine dialed his phone as he dashed behind the bar.

"Don't you dare tap out now, Brooke." I pressed both palms against the bleeding gash on her leg, trying to stave off some of the bleeding until Caine returned with a stack of folded bar rags.

"Looks like someone else had the same idea she did." He crouched opposite me as I pressed the pile of rags to her thigh, tying them tightly over the wound.

I checked Brooke's pockets. Her keys were gone, and if they'd reached her apartment, they'd hit a jackpot. "We need to make sure they didn't get Dixon's files. They were in her apartment. Check there first and lay low. I'll handle the police."

Caine nodded and headed through the back of the bar to get to Brooke's apartment. Five minutes later, he peeked through the door again, then took off across the bar. "Still locked. There's a secret way out of Sawyer's office if I need it."

As he charged up the stairs, I finally heard the sirens.

"Please, Brooke, stay with me," I whispered, brushing the only non-blood-covered part of my hand against her cheek. Her right hand moved slowly, and I noticed something black next to her hip. The sirens wailed outside the door, so I grabbed the piece of fabric and tucked it in my pocket before the paramedics rushed in.

As they loaded her up, I noticed a cop hanging by the door. He intercepted me as soon as the paramedics rolled Brooke toward the door. He'd been the hooded man chatting with Gavin and the Defiance member at the resort, but I tried not to smirk when he spoke.

"What happened here?" With his hands on his hips, he scanned the bloody floor and my hands.

"Don't know. Just found her and called an ambulance."

He pointed to the front of the building. "Who does the other bike—"

Before he could finish, two men in suits stepped through the doorway. "Officer Dorsey?" James said.

"Excuse me." Dorsey turned on his heel.

"Detective Carter." James flashed his badge, the pointed to Ryan at his side. "And Officer Coriell, Captain Ainsley has agreed to give us jurisdiction—"

Dorsey sputtered, slashing his hand through the air. "You have to be kidding me."

"You're welcome to speak with the Captain—"

Scowling, Dorsey stepped aside to make the call, then huffed. I watched as he paced in front of the door.

"Barney," I mouthed to James.

He nodded. "Yep. Ainsley's on it."

When Dorsey stormed out, James told Ryan to watch the door and I pulled the wad of fabric from my pocket and flattened it out. DEFIANCE. "I think Brooke got this off of whoever attacked her."

I collapsed against the bar.

"Ainsley already has a team in place near the warehouse. Whoever you got your info from was correct. There was already movement inside the building when they set up, and three more guys showed up just a few minutes ago. They're waiting to see if anyone else shows up or tries to leave."

Something slammed upstairs, from the direction of Sawyer's balcony. James and Ryan, both reached for their holsters.

Caine stood at the balcony with his hands up. "I'm assuming based on the chatter they're with you."

"Informant," I said, heading toward the stairs with James in tow. The wooden door at the top was shattered, and Caine hadn't made enough noise for it to be his doing. The room was trashed, drawers destroyed and strewn about the room, bookcases toppled over, papers littered the floor. "Looks like they already turned this rock over."

"Yeah." He gestured toward the busted up back wall. "And they knew exactly where to look. There's a hidden panel in that wall—this building has a lot of those, but they decimated his safe. How's Brooke?"

I shook my head, trying not to think about it. "They didn't really say."

"You two didn't see anyone else here?" James asked.

"We heard them burning rubber as we approached. I'm guessing Brooke caught them downstairs while they were making off with the records." Leaning against an open space in the wall, I rubbed at my aching shoulder. The ride hadn't helped, but for a time the vibrations seemed to numb it a bit. Now that everything had settled, an unrelenting throb set in.

James raised his eyebrows, probably noting every time I flinched. "And what exactly happened to you?"

"There was a bit of a scuffle at the resort last night."

Caine snorted, rubbing the side of his finger over his lips, but before he could comment, Ryan stepped over the debris in the doorway. "Just got off the phone with Libby. Brooke's being diverted straight to Ashville General. Rose is going to meet her there. We also got reports of a small caravan headed toward the point from the East. Two transport vans, an SUV, and four men on bikes wearing Defiance colors. Chief Lewis has everyone ready to move in, and we have eyes on Dorsey. Looks like he's headed in that direction as well."

———

WE MET Captain Ainsley and Chief Lewis near the warehouse on the east end where they had a mobile head-quarters set up to intercept and relay information. Behind the abandoned shoe factory, we remained out of sight to most in the darkened parking lot, while Caine and Ryan waited off to the side with the other officers. Ainsley had a van stationed out front, sitting on the warehouse Caine had indicated.

After greeting James, the captain and chief both looked me over. I'd cleaned off as much blood as possible, but still wore my Devils Leather. Chief Lewis offered me a nod. "Well, you certainly look the part. We have a perimeter set up, out of sight, but we're monitoring activity inside of the building. There are four doors to cover, but they're mainly using the front portion of the building right now."

Ainsley waved for us to join them inside the van, where an officer wearing a headset stared at a series of screens.

"SWAT is ready to go," Ainsley said. "We're trying to get someone into position so we can get ears on the inside as well. There are several busted windows along the west side of the building, so Michaels is moving in to see if he can get a mic set up. If we're successful, we can wait until Defiance shows up and nail them while making the deal. Eyes on the road says we should expect two vans each with a driver and passenger, and three men on bikes in twenty minutes."

From what I'd gathered, Sawyer was offering enough weapons to arm Defiance, and if they were housing them here, they had enough firepower to hold up for a while if it came down to it. If we were lucky, the guns were packed up which would delay easy access, but we had to take them out before they had a chance to put those weapons to use. "Any IDs on the men inside?"

"Four men wearing Devil cuts and two in Defiance, but

we ran the plates on the vehicles outside." Ainsley handed me a list of names, that included Gavin, Damian, and a Sandy Cutter out of Defiance. I assumed she was a relative of the man I'd encountered at Fitch's place when they were haggling over guns.

I pulled the patch from my pocket and tossed it onto the desk. "There's a chance the men who attacked Brooke are here."

"Skid marks in front of the bar would be consistent with a four-wheel vehicle like the SUV," James said.

Chief Lewis tapped the data analyst on the shoulder. "Bring up Lawson's footage from the van."

The screen flickered, and I saw the raw footage of the men, standing near a corner, chatting away without a worry.

I studied the shadowed faces of the men inside, distorted by the old warehouse glass. "We got Gavin, Bull, Damian, and Dodger. The guy on the far left was at the resort last night, he also attacked me and Brooke at The Race Trap Bar last week, trying to get the info Sawyer sent us after. I sent James pictures of the contents. I'm thinking Gavin arranged the attack, he was supposed to be with Brooke and likely intended to let them get away with it, but I was suspicious and changed out the contents of the enve-lope before they made a move on us."

"That how you got endeared to the Treasurer?" Ainsley asked.

"Something like that," I mumbled.

"Chief." The analyst's voice pinched. "We got someone moving in from the north side of the building."

He brought up an image that looked to be from one of the nearby roofs, and I recognized that familiar arrogant gait. "Fuck. That's Sawyer. Any other reports of movement?"

"No," Ainsley said. "Highway Patrol hasn't reported any bikes coming through that way since you reported leaving this morning."

"He must've slipped out during the chaos last night." I tried to remember the last time I'd seen him at the resort. He hadn't been with Cannon or the others when they'd broken up Gavin's little party, but I'd passed him a few times earlier in the night.

"We have ears," the analyst said, flicking a switch.

"This isn't good." I rocked back on my heels, rubbing my hand over the rough stubble on my chin. *Why would he walk in there alone if he isn't with them?* "If Gavin is double crossing him, this is gonna blow up and we're gonna lose Defiance."

"These guys are our main concern," Ainsley said, making a pointed gesture toward the screens.

James leaned forward, studying the images. "How long do we have before Defiance arrives?"

"Fifteen minutes tops. We're ready to move in, but for now we wait for something solid."

I agreed, but I could feel it in my gut. Sawyer had no idea what he was walking into. Gavin waited near the window we monitored from the van, but the other men dispersed away from the windows.

"This better be good, Vinny," Sawyer's muffled voice crackled over the speakers.

Gavin smoothed back his hair. "Oh, it's good all right. Time for me to take my rightful place."

"What—" Before Sawyer could speak the other men came up behind him, guns drawn. A broad-shouldered figure who looked like Bull jerked up Sawyer's jacket and grabbed the gun.

"I'm doing exactly a real Covey would have the balls to do." Gavin had his own gun in his hand now, pacing in front of the windows, tapping it to his temple as he spoke. "See, I've been doing my own digging since you decided it was time to go to bed with Defiance. Giving them something they needed... right. A second charter, maybe. As if they'd ever really bow down to you."

"Ten minutes to Defiance," the analyst said, while the rest of us concentrated on the audio from the warehouse.

"I've been trying to get rid of that bitch of yours. Not like she was ever worth anything, and it just so happened that she ran into us while we were picking up the last of this."

He picked up a journal and waved it in Sawyer's direction. "Interesting read here. Also interesting that you had my father's records... well the man you paid to clean up your mess, because you were too busy dealing with your wife's affairs." Gavin chuckled, a dry and humorless laugh. "So, I'm assuming you knew Brooke wasn't yours when you told us to wreck her, because if not, that would be a little fucked up, even for me."

"Put your fuckin' guns away." Even with the weapons pointed in his direction, Sawyer admonished them like children he had no time for.

Gavin clocked him in the jaw. "She should have walked away when she had the chance, but I don't think she'll be giving us any more problems. I'm just wondering why you didn't just deal with her right along with Hutch."

Sawyer waved his hands in the air. "What the hell are you going to do with all this? What do you think it's going to get you?"

"My own charter with Defiance. I'm taking this fucking town, and anyone who doesn't want to follow is either getting a bullet or a needle."

I couldn't stand still or pay attention to the screen any longer. Sweat beaded down my back, and I felt locked in that tiny space with too many men around me. James bumped my sore arm and I winced.

"Get out of that jacket and put on a vest," Ainsley said.

That was easier said than done, but I wasn't giving them the opportunity to talk me out of this. Unless the men in that building put holes in each other's heads first.

We cleared out of the van and another officer handed me a vest. I threw my jacket on the trunk of a nearby car. "Ainsley must have been on the phone since the moment I called in."

"That was over an hour ago," James said. "He'd already had a preliminary plan in place, although we didn't have a time or location until this morning. He and Lewis might be flying by the seats of their pants, but this has been a long time in the making."

James watched as I wired up my earpiece and tightened the straps on the vest. "You sure you're up for this?"

I gritted my teeth and nodded. "Yeah. I still have one good arm. I'm not like you and taking a bullet at the last minute."

James raised his eyebrows. "This isn't over yet, but SWAT is taking them down. We're cleaning up the mess."

"*I get Gavin.*"

"I'll try to remember that." He slaps me in the good arm, as Ainsley climbs out of the van with an update.

"They've restrained Sawyer. They're keeping him in the back, which splits them up for the raid. The SWAT team is ready to cover every door as soon as Defiance walks in. We need to recover those records and as many live bodies as possible. Leverage to get them to roll later. Then, we'll pluck up anyone else we can before the news hits." Ainsley beckoned me closer. "Brooke Covey is in stable condition, thanks to your quick work. Now, let's put this to bed."

James and I headed inside on the heels of the SWAT units when they gave us the all-clear. Shattered cases of guns littered the floor behind the vans where the men had worked to load up their bounty. Men sat on their knees or were pinned to the ground while officers tightened their cuffs. At the front of the room, I came face-to-face with Sawyer and Gavin.

"Good news," I said as they balked and spattered. "Brooke's going to be fine, you all, however, are under arrest."

I jerked Gavin's arm behind his back and fastened the cuffs. "You have the right to remain silent."

Chapter Twenty-Six

PAPER DEVILS

Brooke

I FOUND *Dixon sitting over the files in my living room. Or his living room. The details were muddled, bending time over on itself.*

For a moment, I was relieved. They didn't get the files. They didn't make it to my apartment.

But why is Dixon here?

Dixon lifted his head. "It's time to get out."

"Then help me." I knelt by the table, but the words and symbols were even more illegible than before, changing as I skimmed from line to line.

I pressed my fingers to my aching temple. I'm so tired. Where's the pain coming from? "I want to stay with you. Please let me stay with you."

Dixon crouched next to me. "Not this time. He still needs you."

As he stood, he disappeared into the light from the window, leaving me all alone in the darkness.

No. No. I don't want to stay. I want the pain to end.

The pain in my head yanked me back like a metal hook

rammed in my temple, dragging me along behind a tow truck. When I opened my eyes, the lights above me added searing pain to the dull pulse.

A brunette woman stood next to me. "Hey, you're okay. It's okay."

"Light." I squeezed my eyes closed. "Fuck."

She pulled the curtains over the window. "That's about as good as I can do. My name is Rose. I'm..." She hesitated. "I'm a victim's advocate with—"

That was enough for me. "You're in the wrong room."

She smiled. "Yeah, I thought you might say that, but I'm pretty sure this is where I'm supposed to be. You were brought in this morning with a gash on your leg and a concussion."

But I'd been alone when I got back to the Point and saw lights in the bar. Well, relatively speaking. As soon as I went in to check my office, three men attacked me. I shook my head. "How did they find me?"

"Trent was with you when the ambulance picked you up."

He followed me? I tried to sit up, but the pain was too much, and I sank back into the pillow. *I really need to kick this hospital habit.*

"Do you remember what happened?" Rose asked.

I lifted my eyebrows and rolled away from her. She's just a useless pawn for the cops, and I had no interest in her information game. I heard the door handle click, followed by the clickity-clack of dress shoes. "If I could get out of this bed, I would rip those fuck—"

When I peeked toward the door, a female with long hair, pulled up in a ponytail, stood over the foot of my bed in a tailored pant suit with a badge hanging from a silver chain around her neck.

"Oh, it just keeps getting better and better."

"I'm Captain Elizabeth Thorne from the Ashville PD."

I'm in hell. And not only had I earned the attention of a cop, but their friggin captain. As bad as that was, I worried I'd find myself in a deeper circle of torment if anyone found those documents in my apartment. "I need to go."

"You have about twenty stitches in your leg," Rose said. "Not to mention muscle damage, and a concussion. Even if you could walk out of this room, how the hell do you think you're getting anywhere else?"

Even the captain looked at her with wide eyes.

I looked her up and down, wondering if she really was who she claimed to be. "For a victim's advocate, you've got some bedside manner."

She cocked her head. "You're not a victim, right?"

Oh, this one might be a worthy advisory. I could admit to a miniscule spark of appreciation at her candor. At least she wasn't standing there pretending to be my long-lost best friend.

"Give us a few minutes," the captain said, gesturing for Rose to step out.

I groaned, unable to escape. I didn't anticipate this run-in to be as easy to handle as those two officers who stopped by The Pit. "Do we really need to do this? I don't have anything to tell you."

"Then, I'll tell you what I know." She crossed her arms and approached the right side of my bed. "You're the Treasurer for the Devils of Ashville Motorcycle Club. A club that's led by your father Sawyer Covey. You lost your brother three years ago after he was kicked out of the club."

"Impressive," I said dryly.

"Last night, you left the Nauvoo Hills Resort and rode back to the Point alone. You were attacked at The Pit by two members of Defiance MC and a member of DOAMC by the name of Damian Garnet."

My arms tingled. I remembered seeing Damian raise the flashlight over his head just before everything went black.

"It appears they had broken in to get Sawyer's records, and probably yours, to offer Defiance MC as part of a deal with their president after Gavin McKee made a bargain under the table to turn Sawyer over to Defiance in exchange for a new charter of his own. We currently have Gavin, Sawyer, three other members of the Devils and ten members of Defiance in custody. The game is over."

No. The tingling across my skin tuned into a sickening burn just below the surface.

"I understand you might have information that might lead to further charges."

"Fuck off." *Where is Trent? How did it all fall without me?*

"Brooke—" She reached for the railing of my bed.

"I said fuck off. I don't have anything to say to you." My eyes burned, so I squeezed them closed, turning away from her. I wanted to go back to the dream. I wanted to see my brother again.

I heard her fancy shoes retreat, and when the door closed, I thought I was alone, but a warm hand squeezed mine. Trent stood over me in a dark T-shirt with his left arm strapped up in a blue sling.

My chest shook, but my mind spun in circles trying to make sense of it all. "You're okay?"

"Mostly." He twisted his left arm toward me. "How are you feeling?"

"Confused. What happened? Did you talk?"

"Caine and I followed you back. He knew where to find Gavin." He closed his eyes, and his right hand went to the pocket of his jeans. I saw the flash of something metallic. "We ambushed them during the deal. We got Sawyer's records. They also had Vernon McKee's records."

We? Who does he mean by we?

He held up his hand, revealing the badge he'd pulled from his pocket. "I'm a cop."

The air rushed from my lungs, and I couldn't seem to get another breath. Cool tears streamed down my face. "You used me. You—" I used all my strength, aiming for the injured shoulder. I would have jumped across the bed and tore his face off if my head didn't feel like a helium balloon. "Get out."

I should have listened to that stone-cold skeptical voice that kept telling me he had an ulterior motive. That's all it had ever been. I'd led him straight to everything, left him alone with my records how many times while I slept? Everything he'd done had been a deception.

He backed away from the bed, but only far enough to lean against the corner near the bathroom.

"You often use sex to get the evidence you need?"

He looked over his shoulder toward the door and seemed a shade paler when he looked back to me and shook his head. "No, it wasn't about that. I'm sorry I had to lie to you but—"

"But now you want something more?" Every word I screamed left the sensation of a crowbar piercing my brain, but I didn't care about the physical pain anymore.

Trent closed his eyes, leaned his head into the wall and drew in a slow breath. "I didn't intend to get close to you or develop feelings for you. You have every reason to be pissed, but once we found you at The Pit, we had to get you in an ambulance and head off Gavin's deal before he handed over an artillery to Defiance to rise up against the Devils."

I caught myself before asking for more details on that. I didn't want to give him the satisfaction of thinking I cared about his little story. But I had so many questions. The Captain mentioned he'd been with Caine, how much did he know? Did Gavin plan to wipe us out? And most of all, what the hell else could he possibly want from me?

Wincing, Trent twisted so that his back was against the wall. "We overheard a few things you should know. I convinced Libby to let me tell you before it comes out down the line."

I lifted my eyebrow, keeping my lips pinched together and folding my arms over my chest. If he expected any of this to buy him a pass, he needed to have his head examined.

"Gavin dug up evidence in one of the journals they stole, and confronted Sawyer about it while we were listening in, so my partner took a look while I was down-stairs getting checked out." He blew out a puff of air, adjusting on his feet again. "It appears that Sawyer and Vernon McKee conspired to set Marcus Hutchinson up for the fall of the BOW after Sawyer learned that he and your mother were having an affair and making plans to disappear with their unborn child. When BOW failed to take Hutchinson out, Sawyer and McKee took matters into their own hands, leaving plenty of evidence behind pointing to the BOW if anyone got suspicious. Sawyer isn't your father."

A piercing ring drilled through my head, and I clamped my hand over my mouth. Suddenly it was obvious why he never treated me as a daughter, but why then, hadn't he gotten rid of me as well?

Trent kicked off the wall, starting in my direction before

I glared, warning him to keep his distance. This little secret didn't make us even.

"Caine is talking to the DA now," Trent said. "Turns out he was the one who filed the anonymous report that got me sent undercover in the first place."

"So why does everyone seem intent on getting me to talk? Sounds like between him and all the journals, you can make a good case against us." I used "us" on purpose, drawing a clear line of demarcation between Trent and myself. I was part of the group. One of the criminals.

"Because I convinced them that you could help make a stronger case. You can make sure all the people who hurt you get exactly what they deserve."

I snorted. "And what exactly are you getting, *Trent?* 'Cause from where I'm lying, you're the biggest piece of shit I see. You made me believe you cared, and that is so much worse than the enemies I knew before."

He dropped his head, rubbing the back of his neck. "My name is Trent Davis, and I know you're not going to believe this, but I do care. I've gone to war with myself every time I'm around you because the last thing I wanted to do was hurt you. I knew I would. I knew I should have stayed away. If you can't forgive me for that, I don't blame you, but please, take the opportunity they're offering you. Get your revenge by making sure everyone one of their sins sees the light of day. Start fresh with a second chance and don't let them take any more of your life than they already have."

He didn't wait around for my reaction or response. As much as I'd thought I wanted him gone, the empty room became more imposing, leaving me alone with my thoughts, questions, memories, and regrets.

UNABLE TO SLEEP for more than a few hours at a time, each day in the hospital blended with the next in a stream of endless visits from nurses, doctors, deliveries of stale food, the clang of custodians emptying the trash, beeping machines, and most irritating, the cops. Every time the door opened, I dug my fingers into the course bedsheets as the rising tension caused my jaw to tick.

coarse

I'm going to lose what's left of my mind before I get out of here. I clicked the TV off again. Second only to the irritation of all the question was the monotonous boredom.

I heard the familiar two knocks, to introduce a visitor who wouldn't listen if I told them to stay out anyway. Then, the police captain peeked around the corner. "I wore quiet shoes, just for you."

"I already gave my statement." I leaned back, staring up at the ceiling as I counted away the seconds until she'd leave.

"I know, and I realize the last few days must have been—"

"Don't." A pulsing pain begins behind my eyes as my eyebrows draw together. "Save your fake pity and whatever means you're intending to use to gain my trust. Trent already fucked what was left of that."

The captain makes a sound in her throat. "And yet, he's still fighting for you. He must see something because he's one of the best judges of character I know. We've worked together for years, and I've never seen him quite like this. He's always claimed he's incapable of falling for anyone, that his ability to love died with Stephanie. But every day, I watch the way he fights for you. He knows you don't want to see him, but he's here checking on you at least once a day."

My eyes burned, but I told myself it was from the budding tension headache. Nothing to do with the traitor. "Did he send you in here to make his case? Do you expect me to open up and spill my guts? Play the victim? Tell you how to decode all of Dixon's notes?"

She presses her lips together. "No. I understand you have no reason to trust me or any of us, but the club is going down with or without your help. But"—she shrugs, pacing toward the window—"maybe Trent's wrong about you. Maybe you don't deserve redemption."

Fuck the reverse psychology card. By now, everyone should have known the answer to that, so I go for my own dirty tactics. "You know, the way you talk about Trent sounds like a lot more than a boss-employee relationship."

Holding my gaze, the captain gives me a tight nod. "Used to be. Before I met my current fiancé and got promoted. Which is why I know there has to be a damn good reason he's fighting for you."

"He's an idiot," I mumbled.

The captain's lips pinched together, and she spun toward the window. "Okay. How many people have you killed? Raped? Drugged?"

I gritted my teeth, wondering if he told her about the whole incident when I laced his beer with drugs. "I was in charge of the money for all those crimes."

She tapped the back of one hand against the palm of her other. "And why'd you do it?"

Because the alternative was worse. The alternative was shacking up with Gavin or some other disgusting creature that belonged in a gutter. Or death. All while Sawyer and the deviants carried merrily onward. I refused to answer.

"According to the reports we have so far, you used your control over the club's money to delay or even stop some of the club's plans. Caine claimed you stepped in and tried to protect some of the girls Gavin brought in."

And received a beating so bad, I couldn't leave my apartment for days. My shoulder blades pulled inward as my back tensed. "A lot of good that did."

"For one girl against an entire club, you seemed to have held your own. And I'm guessing that's because you held leverage over not only their money, but a few of their secrets as well."

I stared off in silence as her words seep deeper into my head.

"Whether you want to admit it, or not, you were a victim as well, and you can make sure they pay for everything they've done. The DA has offered deals to people far less deserving than you, but that offer won't stay on the table forever. Don't let them win by taking you down with them."

Still, I didn't move. I didn't react. The anger building inside of me was paralyzing until once again, I was left alone in the room.

Dix always said my stubborn streak would be my downfall, but it was also the only thing that kept me alive. I grabbed the bedside table next to me and thrust it across the room so it landed against the chair with a resounding clatter. Then, I reached back, shoving everything off the nightstand as well.

Piece by piece everything around me thudded against the floor and walls until a parade of nurses charged into the room. With one syringe, the room blurred and went dark.

I STIRRED IN MY BED, trying to shake the hazy, foggy feeling left in my head from the drugs that locked my brain into an endless repeat of Dixon's warnings. I grabbed the bed railing, pulling myself up. I couldn't handle sliding back into the darkness again.

A shadowed woman in the window closed the book in her lap. "Heard you had some party. You ripped out a few stitches in your leg as well."

I tried to speak or swallow, but my throat was drier than an old tire left in the sun too long.

Rose poured a cup of water and braced it while I took a few sips to cool and soothe my throat. "You here to interrogate me while I'm high?"

"I'm your advocate, not a cop, and either way, I'm not technically on the clock."

"Then why the fuck are you here?"

"I heard you had a rough afternoon and it's not a horrible place to get some studying done." She twisted her fingers together in front of her. "And after you wrecked the room earlier, they were worried you'd be a danger to yourself. I agreed to sit with you because I figured if you were anything like me, you wouldn't appreciate regular sedatives or waking up in restraints."

"The last one was enough." Still fighting to keep my eyes open, I raised the head of the bed, hoping that would force me to stay awake. "But I'm really not in the mood for company."

"I can just go back to studying for my National Counselor Examination, and you can pretend I'm not here." She pushed the table closer so I could reach the water glass and returned to her corner of the room, flipping through a thick textbook and jotting down notes.

He still needs you. In my dream, those had been Dixon's parting words. *What a ridiculous thought.*

My fingers curled into my palms. "Can I borrow some paper and something to write with?"

"Sure." Rose dug through her back, then handed me a notebook and blue pen.

I flipped it open in my lap, staring at the blank page.

Trent,

The pen stopped at the bottom of the comma and refused to move again. I wanted to tell him to fuck off and go to hell, remind him of the bastard he was and how much I hated him, but the words wouldn't come.

I ripped the page out of the notebook, crumpled it up and tossed it in the trash. Then, I started writing anything that came to mind, mostly every one of the symbols I could remember from the code Dix and I came up with and their corresponding words or letters.

I told myself it was something to keep me occupied that would end up wadded in the trash just like the failed letter. As I filled the third page, Rose closed her books and slid them into her bag. "My fiancé will be home soon, so I should head out. You can keep the notebook, if you want."

"Can you do me a favor?" I ripped out the three pages, folded them neatly into a tight square, and wrote Trent's name on the outside. "I mean, you do work for the police, so you'll see Trent, right?"

Chapter Twenty-Seven

DEVIL'S DUES

Brooke

6 weeks later

I CURLED up on the hard cot. Ironic how I skipped prison for all the things I'd done as a Devil and here I sat in a jail cell for something I hadn't done.

Maybe fate did exist. Karma. Whatever you want to call it.

I heard the door open at the far end of the hall, but I didn't move. I was too pissed. Too exhausted. And my stomach was fucking killing me.

But when the man stopped in front of my cell, my feet dropped to the floor and I sat straight up, face-to-face with the man I'd been avoiding. "How'd you know?"

Trent's stoic expression didn't change. "Cops talk, and some like to brag. I got a heads up that you were in holding after an incident at the grocery store."

"Surprise. Surprise." I threw up my hands. "I didn't ask for your help."

He scoffed. "You really want to stay in here?"

"I can handle it." I crossed my arms over my chest and kicked my legs back on the cot.

"Are you really so stubborn you're willing to go down for something you didn't do just to avoid asking for help?" His tone and words knock me back a few paces. It didn't sound like him, but then, I never knew *him*. "Attacking Cissie in the parking lot and going shopping is not your M.O. I came to make sure they thoroughly looked at everything before jumping the gun just because of your history."

I stood and approached the steel bars between us. "And what do you get out of it?"

He sighed but didn't answer. I wondered if it was the light that made him look older. Not a month older, but years. Hair shorter. Eyes darker. None of that sarcastic, quippy, asshole I put up with.

"You want to tell me what happened?" he asked.

"I really have no fucking idea. I was shopping. The cops confronted me and escorted me out where I saw Cissie sniffling near the back of a cruiser. I hadn't even seen her and sure as hell didn't throw her face first into a wall, although the facial did her some good, really."

"Brooke." His admonishing tone hadn't really changed much.

The heavy door down the hall slammed and the officer who'd thrown me in the cage stalked toward us, unlocked and threw open the door. "You're free to go, Miss Covey."

I gritted my teeth. Even though most of the charges associated with my Devil's deeds had been wiped clean with my deal, it hadn't wiped away my name and its inherent connection to Sawyer. "That's it? I thought I was the prize you were going to mount on a wall somewhere."

"Brooke," Trent barked even deeper.

"We will be pursuing false police report charges on the woman who accused you of attacking her, but..." He side-eyed Trent and grumbled. "It was brought to our attention that a camera across the street would have likely captured the incident and after review, we found that she drove her own face into the wall before calling for help."

"Classic," I mumbled.

Trent tugged on my arm. "I'll take you home."

"I seriously didn't ask for your help," I growled, yanking free from his grasp. I still couldn't bear being near him, let alone having his hand on my arm. His touch, the one I wanted and the one that made my stomach turn.

He gave me a look, then turned away, silently heading toward the front of the building. We stopped by the front and picked up my belongings, and he led me out to his car. There was something about his unnerving silence that bothered me even more than his quips and snaps.

We stopped at a blue sedan and the lights flashed.

"That's a cop's car if I ever saw one. Compete downgrade from the hog."

Trent ran his fingers through his hair, shaking his head as he opened the driver's side door. When I didn't move from my spot, he leaned over the roof. "Please, just get in the car. It's too late to catch a bus, and I'm too tired to argue."

Even after all of this. Even after everything I'd said to him in the hospital, all those weeks without a word, he was still looking out for me. He didn't have to. He was under no obligation and getting nothing out of it, except my crass. I stepped toward the car and reached for the door

256

handle. "If you had any sense, you'd stay far away from me."

"And why is that? Because you're stubborn? And infuriating? Because you're in pain, and lashing out is the only way you know how to deal with it? I knew you needed time, so I stayed away, just like you wanted. And maybe you'll never let me in again, but I can't stop caring about you just because you tell me to."

I pulled open the door and slide into the seat, slumping over and burying my face in my palms. I didn't understand him. He could have anyone, yet he continued to pursue the woman who hated him. "Am I just some challenge to you?"

"You are challenging. You're not like anyone else. But you've been hurt far more than most people could ever bear, and I'm sorry that I played a part in that pain. But along the way, I caught a glimpse of this beautiful woman under that tough exterior, and I..." His words died away and I heard him swallow. "All I know is that if I walk away from you without trying, I'll regret it for the rest of my life."

I watched his movements in silence as he reached up to start the car as if watching a stranger. After all, I'd been convinced that's what he was, but it hadn't truly seemed so strange until now. Even at the worst, there'd always been something in the way he looked at me, like I was more than an object. I'd been crushed to figure out his true intentions. To discover he had the darkest ulterior motive of us all, but did he?

I bit at my lower lip, staring down at my twisted fingers in my lap. "I almost got you killed."

"No, you didn't. I went undercover in a biker gang. With what Gavin was plotting, he would've come at me either way."

"He came at you because he knew—" My voice broke

into quiet sob. "For the first time, I had a weakness he could exploit. If Cannon and the others hadn't shown up...."

Trent squeezed my knee, and I sank against the door. "Look, I'm not good at this. I'm not good at any of this. Club life, hiding, hating everyone. My quest for revenge kept me going. I didn't plan for any of this. I woke up in the hospital and everything was different. I blamed you. I hated you because I didn't have anyone else left to hate or blame. I, um, I'm..."

He squinted at me, slowly looking me up and down. "You're gonna give yourself an aneurysm."

I almost whimpered when I tried to swallow, and then I glanced over to see the barely-there traces of that smirk on Trent's face.

As we pulled up to my apartment I wanted to climb out and pretend tonight never happened. "I was angry. Still am." *Get out before the tears come. Run for it.* I licked my lips, resting my fingers on the door handle. "You should go home and get some sleep."

Trent squeezed my thigh. "If you need an excuse to escape, don't use me. I stayed up longer than this when you were in the hospital."

Which time?

"Thank you," I whispered.

Just when I thought I'd make it out of the car, Trent's usual smirk spread into a full grin. "You're welcome."

"You know, once upon a time, I wanted to rip your tongue out and scrub that look off your face."

We both laughed, but it didn't relieve that pang in my chest. "Seriously, what do you see in me?"

"A complete smart-ass." His tongue swept over his teeth, and his eyes sparkled in the glow of the overhead light. "I didn't think I'd ever fall for anyone again, and I certainly didn't expect so much trouble for it. You make the most bull-headed person I've ever met look agreeable. You're strong, determined, and you have a nice ass."

I'd tried to forget what it was like to go around with him. How impossible he made it to hate him, but then, hating him wasn't my true problem. I wanted it to be, that would've made things much simpler. "I'm not the only smart aleck in this car, and I'm sure you've complimented the ass of every woman you've slept with. Your boss, perhaps?"

Trent exhaled, lowering his head. "She wasn't my boss at the time. I won't deny I have a long history of mean-ingless hookups. I enjoy sex, and I'm not ashamed of that."

"You're barking up the wrong tree for that."

"Brooke." Trent twisted in his seat, leaning over the console. He brushed the hair away from my face and took my hand between his. "That's not why I'm here. I haven't been able to think about anyone else since you." A quiet grunt escapes his throat. "I think you broke me, and I'm not complaining."

I raised my gaze as far as his lips, not daring to make it to his eyes. Then, I collapsed against him. He put his arm around my shoulders, resting his chin on the crown of my head. "I know you won't forgive me overnight, but I'm here anytime you need me."

———

THE NEXT EVENING, I went straight home after work, even though what I really needed to finish the shopping I'd started before getting arrested and hauled out of the store. But after that, I wasn't setting foot in there again, which meant I needed to find an alternate I could viably reach with public transportation.

Post-criminal life sucked.

I leaned into the corner of the couch and stared at my phone for the dozenth time since getting off work. Trent's number still taunted me from the cardboard box next to me that doubled as an end table. I hadn't wanted anything to do with the damn emotions he stirred up inside of me. And yet, he'd come for me when I was in trouble.

I wondered if the police would have figured the whole thing out without his intervention. Would they have even tried to find the recordings? All they seemed to see was a person who should've been in prison anyhow. Trent saw something far different.

I squeezed my knees tighter against my chest. Now, I was even less interested in leaving my apartment, not just because of the incident, because I felt like shit. I put Trent's number in my phone, then let my thumb dance over the call button. *He's probably at work anyway. Probably doing pretty much anything that'd be better than talking to cranky me.*

My finger twitched, and the screen went black. For a second, I thought it had gone into standby mode again, but then it lit up.

Calling.

Shit.

I could have backed out, but I held the phone to my ear. *Remember, he's off doing other things and other people.* This would be my confirmation that he had no time for me.

He answered in a stern, clipped tone. "Davis."

He didn't know it was me. Of course, because he'd put it in my hands, giving me his number without asking for mine.

I let out the breath I'd been holding, but my voice abandoned me.

There was a pause, then another. "Hello?"

"It's me."

"Hey, you," he said in a much lighter tone.

"I mean Brooke."

"I know who you are." His lilt sounded teasing. Tempting. This was a bad idea.

"I just..." I didn't know what to say, but he cut off my thoughts.

"Can you hold on a minute?"

Other obligations. "Yeah."

I heard a couple of other muffled voices, the crackle of wind cutting across the mic, and then, with a thump, everything went quiet. "Sorry, James and I were wrapping up and I'm about to leave the station."

I didn't know what to say to that. "Cop stuff..."

"Cop stuff," he repeated back with a hint of laughter in his voice.

He's a cop, I reminded myself, as if it needed repeating. *Cop. Criminal. Cops and members—or former members—of outlaw biker clubs do not mix. Cops and me do not mix.*

My stubbornness threatened to cut off any hope of breathing.

"Everything okay?" he asked.

"No," I said automatically. Having just listed all the reasons we shouldn't mix, my mouth ignored my brain. "I'm not in jail, but I need to go to the store, and I don't feel like leaving the couch. I'd like my neighbors to shut up before I throw something through a wall. You know... life as a reformed biker, or some shit."

Trent made a humming sound. "What do you need from the store?"

"It's not important." Yeah, it was, but I didn't want to discuss those details with him. My stomach was killing me, and my supply was dangerously low, as in probably not going to last until tomorrow low. I needed to suck it up. "You don't want to know."

"Then I wouldn't have asked. What do you need?" This time the question was more emphatic.

"Tampons," I snapped.

"Okay. You want to be more specific?"

I pulled the phone away from my ear and grimaced at it as if he'd be able to see me. *What the fuck?* I rattled off the last brand I remember grabbing.

"Anything else?" he asked.

"You're shitting me."

Trent's bellowing laughter filled my ear. "No, B——" the way he cut off and let out a puff of air, I imagined he was about to call me one of those pet names before he caught himself. I wasn't sure if that excited or annoyed me. "I was raised by a single mom and I've been buying this shit since I was twelve. I really don't give a damn. So, do you want to tell me if there's anything else you need, or would you like me to make an educated guess?"

Oh, that would be interesting. "You are a detective, right?"

He made a sound in his throat. "Careful what you ask for."

I can't believe he's willing to do this. Okay, I had grown up with a bunch of chauvinists where the topic was forbidden. Before we hung up, I added, "Hey, can you please not look like a cop walking around here?"

"I'll do what I can."

When Trent showed up at my door almost an hour later, he had a grocery bag hanging off his arm and a pizza balanced on his hand. He still wore the button-down shirt from work, but no tie and he'd unbuttoned the top buttons. I never thought a guy in a dress shirt could look so hot, but the contradiction between that and his tattoos gave me pause.

Stop, Brooke.

"I didn't order that," I pointed to the pizza. My stomach hurt so bad I hadn't through about food all day. Although, I had to admit that once I smelled it, I was hungry.

"Well, you don't have to eat it, but I'm starving." He handed me the grocery bag. He'd gotten the tampons I mentioned, some pain meds for cramps, heat packs, and a bag of chocolate. I lifted the last up and gave him a questioning look.

"I was assured that chocolate fixes anything by a reliable source."

"Well, uh, thank you."

"Don't," Trent grumbled, and I gave him a questioning look. "Stop thanking me, it's out of character and unnerving."

"Okay, what should I do, then."

Trent sat the pizza on the counter and flipped open the lid. "Want some pizza?"

"I have some Pilsner that would probably go well with that."

Trent nodded, shifting the bite around in his mouth—apparently the cheese was hotter than expected, so I popped the tops off a couple of beers, and we gorged out on the couch.

After we devoured the pizza—three-fourths of which Trent easily took care of—the room went awkwardly silent as we sat back. It was one of those rare moments I couldn't hear at least two screaming neighbors. My eyes drifted down him, catching the glint of metal peeking out from the pocket of his trousers—his badge. I must've stared too long because he pulled it out and laid it with his jacket.

"Putting it out of sight doesn't change anything." I said.

"Keeps you from staring at it."

"I'm just trying to wrap my head around it all. You beating the shit out of Lonnie. All those deliveries Cannon sent you on. Gavin almost killing you." I sank back, slipping sideways on the couch and resting the side of my face against the rough material of the sofa. "I drugged a cop. I smoked pot with a cop. I fucked a cop."

"And I seem to recall you enjoyed it."

Sometimes it amazed me he'd managed to go under-cover with the way he seemed to say whatever the hell popped into his head. Then again, it also made him perfect at what he did.

He pulled my thighs across his lap and began pressing his thumb across the ball of my foot. The sensation was so exquisite, I nearly forgot about everything else for an instant. "You really should have your head examined."

Trent chuckled, and after a second thought, I realized he took that as any perverted male would, so I jabbed my heel into his thigh. "You're incorrigible."

"Don't tell me you just figured that out."

Much as I tried to deny it, I still craved his touch. I don't know how to tell him that, or if I should. Pain and tightness radiated toward my chest, carried on a crushing wave of electricity. I wet my lips.

"Trent—" My mouth audibly snapped shut. If not for the ringing in my ears and the pulse in my chest that seemed to shake everything, I'd have sworn the world had stopped. Or that I had died. I couldn't feel anything except that *thud, thud, thud.* "Kiss me."

Giving my leg a tug, he climbed over me, pressing me to

the couch. His eyes dropped to my lips and remained there a few moments. His head dips slightly lower, and his fingers brush up the hem of my shirt, and my breath hitches.

I grabbed him by the neck, pulling him down until our lips crashed together. Just his taste released strain in my body. Unfurled me. Within seconds I panted for more.

He kissed my mouth and neck. We pawed at each other through our clothes, but it wasn't enough. My core ached for more, cramps long forgotten. I couldn't take the PG rating anymore and fumbled at the buttons on Trent's over-shirt. I yanked it open, pushing it down over his shoulders, but he didn't let me get much farther than that.

"Brooke." He stopped and stared at me for a long second.

I knew he had to be as needy as me. His erection strained against his black dress pants, pressing against me through the fabric.

"I'm not down for making a horror movie, but that doesn't mean I can't give you a good time." Not only was I volunteering to suck him off, I was looking forward to it.

He held his hand over mine, and I wondered if he was going to budge, but then he smirked. "You're the boss."

Part of my mind screamed, *damn straight I am*, while freeing his over-shirt from his arms and tugging the white t-shirt underneath over his head. Other parts of my brain weren't so inclined to agree, however.

I didn't feel like the boss.

I didn't feel in control over much of anything anymore. Particularly my life.

And Trent... Not in any stretch of the imagination did I feel in control where Trent was concerned.

I dug my feet into the couch, and grabbed onto the back to pull myself up, forcing Trent back to his own side of the couch where I straddled his lap and traced my fingers over his bare chest.

Trent didn't have to take orders from me. Not in any way. A hundred times he could have forced himself on me.

He's stronger than me. Bigger than me. Bigger than most of the men who'd done just that. He didn't have to take my power to prove something.

I slid back until my feet could touch the floor, then I knelt between his knees, keeping my eyes trained on his as I unbuttoned his pants and inched the zipper lower. He raised his hips as I pulled the fabric lower, freeing his cock from its cage of material. I ran my fingers over the length of it. Pre-cum already beaded at the tip, and when I licked it off, Trent grunted, rocking his hips forward slightly.

I took my time, taking in the salty, bitter taste of pre-cum and his skin as I worked my way along his shaft. Every few seconds, he shifted, and I heard his breath hitch, but I continued my leisurely pace.

I wanted payback. For all the times the motherfucker had made me say *please*.

Fuck, I could have continued all night, but decided not to leave him suffering too long. I took his length into my mouth, my jaw stretching as wide as possible to accommodate him.

His jaw clenched. He wanted more. That was obvious, but he wasn't jamming himself down my throat to get it.

I worked my hand up and down his shaft, while my mouth tended to the tip of his shaft. Sucking, licking, pulling until he stiffened, on the very edge.

Trent's hand jerked in my hair. "Gonna cum."

I stopped, dead. Letting his cock slide out of my mouth. Then I flicked a finger over the tip, just to test how closer he was.

And let's not forget payback.

Trent grunted. The vein over his left temple throbbing.

"If I needed a warning, I'd tell you that." I licked my lips slowly, watching his eyes move to take in every detail.

His Adam's apple bobbed, then his head dropped back. "Want me to say please?"

"No." I licked the tip of his cock again and his entire body stiffened. Then I spit, coating him again and stroking my hand over him.

I'm blowing a cop.

A cop who just moments ago told me that he loved me. Loved.

I needed to stop thinking, so I took him in my throat, swallowing him deeper until I couldn't stand it.

Every sound he made mingled in my senses with his taste and smell, sending an intoxicating pulse down to my already worked up core. I pressed my thighs together, aching to be touched.

Sex had never turned me on... not the idea or the fantasy. Before Trent all I knew of sex was forced upon me. Blow jobs sure as hell never hot and needy. They were a job. A means to an end.

It's not a surprise that Trent would change that too. He's already fucked up the rest of my life.

Trent's fingers brushed against my temple, pushing aside my hair, and drawing my gaze up to his face again. His eyes were trained on me, half hooded, yet intense with lust.

Fuck. I moved my free hand between my own legs, pressing against the burning ache. Watching him come apart under my touch was enough to do the same to me.

I thought it impossible, but I slid my hand down the front of my yoga pants, just enough to feel my burning clit between my fingertips. I moaned around Trent's cock and he bucked under me, sending hot liquid against the back of my throat. One hand twisted in my hair, the other dug into the arm of the couch.

"Goddamn," he shouted. A raw, primal grit to his voice that clenched my core and sent me over the edge as well.

As I licked him clean, trying to cover my own shaking muscles, the full gravity of everything seemed to fall over my bag, like a plastic bag. I couldn't move.

"Brooke?" Trent squeezed my hand that fisted around the waist of his loose pants.

I pulled my hand back and jumped to my feet. But I was unsteady. Wrong. I still couldn't breathe, and I despised the feeling. I wanted to hate Trent for causing it. I wanted to lash out but... I also had to come to terms with the fact that he didn't cause it. "I need a minute."

Chapter Twenty-Eight

THE DEVIL TO LAY

Brooke

I GOT CLEANED up and leaned over the sink, between the torrent of thoughts and the wailing voices in the apartment next door, I couldn't pull myself together. Thread by thread, the restraints snapped around everything. I felt the eruption start in my chest and work its way up my throat. I buried my face in a towel, trying to halt it's exit but the scream I held back turned into a choking sob as the tears broke free.

Thanks to Trent, I felt something. And what was I supposed to do with that? I didn't just feel something. All at once, with a terrifying rip, I felt everything. The agony of finding my mom dead, the terror of Sawyer sneaking into my room at night, the heart-stopping moment he handed me over to Gavin and the members of the club for my sixteenth birthday, burying Dixon.

Every time Gavin beat down my door or grabbed me in the back of the club.

Every advance of every male member.

Every order to fuck or seduce this man or that so Sawyer could have a distraction or blackmail.

I leaned over the counter sobbing as the voices in the next room elevated to screams of ecstasy.

I grabbed the nearest bottle off the counter and chucked it at the wall. "Shut the fuck up!"

I'd had enough of them, the people upstairs, downstairs, the other side, across the hall. Most enough I had enough of the screams in my own head. Tears and pain I'd suppressed for year.

Behind me, the door shook with a gentle knock, and I had to steady myself before I remembered Trent was still here. It wasn't one of *them.*

"Brooke? Are you okay?"

Fuck that question. Fuck it all. I sank to the floor in tears as the wails of agony broke free from my chest.

"Brooke?" Trent called again. Probably numerous times. My perception was fragments as bits of past and present fused together, covered in blood.

Every time I thought I had it under control another storm roared through me, until I sat, curled up, with my knees against my chest, rocking.

I can't do this. I can't break down. I don't fucking break down. Tears are weak.

And yet, I cried like a child, unable to hold it in.

As I sucked it up again, drying my face on the towel I clutched to my chest. I reached up and flicked the doorknob, unlocking it and letting the door open an inch just to stop the incessant calls from the other side. Trent was immediately on the floor next to me, sitting with his back to the wall. Hand on my arm. Hand rubbing my back. He pulled me against him, just as the next storm broke loose. I felt the pain, as if it were all happening over again. Helpless to fight. Revenge gone. Stuck in a foreign reality, shit-hole apartment, lousy job, nothing in my control. I had nothing left to use as a seal to stop the flood.

I threw myself over his legs, shaking with the sobs until I thought I'd vomit, and they receded again.

Trent rubbed my neck, back, arms, with touches both soothing and burning. "Talk to me, Brooke."

"I hate you," I mumbled, using that as my strength to straighten once again. "I hate you. You and your fucking badge and stupid clothes. This world and it's stupid rules."

In my rage, I slammed my arms across the counter, then sent everything flying. I reached for the glass bottle at the corner, intending to throw it through the mirror when Trent grabbed my arm.

"Breathe, Brooke."

"Fuck off." I shoved him back. "Didn't you hear me? I fucking hate you." I screamed in his face, but he didn't flinch or turn away.

Instead, gently taking my hands and pulling me to his chest, he said, "Okay."

"I can't. I can't," I sobbed against him as the next wave hit, crippling me faster than the impact of a leather-clad shoe. "I hurt."

My knees gave, but Trent held me, lowering me to the floor. I twisted away, falling to my hand and knees. "Everything hurts. I can't make it stop."

I smacked the floor with the palm of my hand, hoping the real pain would chase away the imagined. "Mom. And Dix. And Sawyer. And...."

"You're okay, Brooke." Trent sounded so sure and his touch never left me.

I'd never had that. Never had this. Not even enough to

know what this is. Do I hate him? He boils this anger inside of me.

Trent pulled me back to sit on my heels. "You're okay, babe."

My eyes snapped to his. I definitely hated him. I fisted my hands against my stomach. "I can't handle all if this. All at once. From every side, from *inside*."

He held my face between his palms, caressing my cheeks with his thumbs. "You can, Brooke, you already did. And you bottled it all up, stored it all away, using your anger to create a plug to keep it all restrained, but it doesn't make you any weaker to feel it or show it. We all have pain, and you've definitely had more than most, but you're also the strongest person I know. Sometimes you have to feel the pain."

As my breathing slowed, my muscles gave up under the weight of themselves and I sagged against him. "I don't know how to do this. All of this. I have no control over anything, my shitty apartment, the bus I catch to go to work. Even my job was part of an arrangement because who really trusts the woman who's only experience is running a biker hangout and cooking the club books? And then there's you. I don't understand. I don't understand why you're here. Why you're so gentle. Why you don't hate me. I—"

I couldn't even talk anymore. My brain as inundated as every millimeter lit up all at once with flashes of memories. Everything, as far back as I could remember. Caine. Thea. My first bike. The abortion Sawyer forced me to have at fifteen to hide the fact he'd been fucking me.

"Look at me, Brooke." Trent nudged my cheek. "You're going to get through this. It may not feel like it tonight or tomorrow, but you're not fighting alone. I'm not walking away."

He didn't know half the things I'd experienced. "You don't know... all the details."

He squeezed my cheeks a bit harder. "I don't give a shit about the details. You thought you weren't going to make it out of that club alive. I saw it on your face at the resort, but you did. And because of you, most of the people who hurt you will never do it again. I understand you're struggling right now but consider this your fuck you to the universe because you beat the odds. You got this. No one said this would be easy, but you've already overcome the worst."

"Is this your buck up and move on, speech?"

"Not entirely, because you are going to have to face those memories and that pain to get past them."

Another voice yelling from the room above may as well have been an ice pick through my brain. I sighed, rolling my neck back.

Trent's hand landed against my thigh, giving it a squeeze. "How about you pack an overnight bag and come home with me? It's quieter, there's more room, so I can give you space if you need it."

I shook my head. *Why? Why doesn't he hate me just as much?* "I just told you, multiple times, how much I hate you."

"Look," Trent adjusted, taking a seat on the edge of the tub. "If you need to hate me right now, hate me. Doesn't change how I feel. Doesn't change the offer. You can stay as long as you want."

———

WE PARKED IN THE DRIVE, next to the front porch. The front porch was framed with stonework and columns, accenting the house's beige siding. "So, this is what a cop's house looks like..."

Trent gave me a wry look. "I picked it for the garage. The rest had to have a bit of work."

Since I'd stopped crying my head had been pounding out its own version of a heavy metal drum solo, and when the porch light came on, I squinted against the brightness. Trent took me under his arm, carrying my bag as he led me up the stairs.

was

Inside, the house as pretty basic, with an over-sized suede couch and armchairs in the living room surrounding the large TV screen on the far wall. My breath caught in my throat as I remembered paying Trent that surprise visit with the six-pack of beer and the bottle I'd laced just for him. *Why am I here? Why did he bring me?*

He'd always seemed to see past my acts, but that didn't diminish any of the shit I'd done. I couldn't even figure out if I felt guilty for it. For years, I'd detached from everything, and yet, suddenly, that dam collapsed.

"Can I get you anything?" Trent asked. "Something to drink."

I hoped he meant alcohol, but he pulled a couple of sports drinks out of the fridge.

"Can't you at least spike it?"

He gave me a flat look. "I could, but you should really re-hydrate first."

Good grief. I snatched the bottle out of his hand, catching a glimpse of a picture that hung in the hall just outside the kitchen. Trent, probably as a teenager with what looked like a younger version of James and a brunette girl. "Is that the girl you mentioned?"

"Stephanie," he said. "She was James's younger sister. He wasn't so thrilled with us at first, but then, he seemed all for it. We took that picture about three months before she passed."

Do you give someone condolences for that? For something that happened decades ago. I wasn't good at knowing what to say, so I slipped my arm around his waist and leaned against his chest.

"You remind me of her sometimes. That fighting determination in the face of the odds."

I rested my cheek against his shoulder and exhaled. *If only I knew what or how to fight now.* I'd wasted a lot of energy over the last few weeks fighting the past and the memories. Grappling with the hatred that seethed in my chest with no release. It all faded as Trent's warmth consumed me. His hands worked over my back, and heat rushed down my neck as he breathed against me. Normally I found the quiet unsettling, but in this moment, it was drowned out by pulse of emotions through me. I never understood the concept of describing someone's embrace as home. Maybe I wasn't home yet, but something in my mangled spirit found peace in his presence. "I don't hate you."

Trent made a sound in his throat and placed his hand to my cheek. His kiss was gentle at first, like the faint beat of an aching heart, growing in intensity as our tongues collided and he squeezed my body to his. When we finally parted for a breath of air, he gave me that devilish smirk and whispered, "I love you, too."

My shoulders constricted, and Trent smoothed away the wrinkle between my brows.

After a brief tour of the house, we climbed into bed. Trent pulled me against him, our bodies curling together as his chest pressed against my back. I squeezed his arm when he draped it over my middle. "You're probably going to wake up pretty bruised if you insist on sleeping this close."

"Worth it," he muttered into my hair.

Am I really worth it? Although I still doubted it, I wondered if I could find a way to make it true.

———

I WOKE to Trent's groaning as he rolled across the bed and grabbed his phone. Somehow, I hadn't even heard the ringing until just before he silenced it. "Davis... Yeah, I'll be right there."

I tried checking the time on my phone, but the battery had died. The room was still dark, but the dull light of dawn crept in below the curtains.

"Sorry, but I gotta go." Trent stood at the foot of the bed, quickly pulling on a pair of black slacks, and throwing a white button-up shirt on over the T-shirt he'd slept in. "I'll be back as soon as I can, but it'll probably be a few hours."

"What about me?" I forced myself up on one elbow.

Trent gave me a quizzical look as he slipped a thin, black belt through the loops on his pants. "Do you want to go to the police station?"

"No, but—"

"I'll leave a set of keys out for you downstairs." He came around the bed and gave me a quick kiss. "Silver keys go to the house, gold key to the garage. Don't scratch anything."

After he rushed out, I tried to get back to sleep, but curiosity got the better of me, so I changed and went downstairs to find the keys on the narrow table by the landing and headed out to the garage. I fumbled inside the dark building until I found the light switch about two feet inside the door. The overhead lights flickered then brightened. Closest to the door, Trent had a metal frame for a roadster, but then I saw a form on the far end of the building covered with a tarp and gasped.

"He has a motorcycle." I navigated the maze of car parts and tools, almost tipping over some metal contraption that caught on my jeans in the process. Then, I pulled back the tarp to reveal a sleek black Triumph underneath. It was basic, a few years old, but most importantly, it had two wheels and an engine. "Freedom."

I spent the better part of the morning aimlessly driving, just to enjoy the rumble of the engine and wind through my hair. The first time in six weeks I didn't have to rely on public transportation, and I had nowhere to go. By the time I returned to Trent's house and put the motorcycle away, my mind was clear, and my body exhausted, so I crashed on the couch.

———

"BROOKE." Something flicked the tip of my nose and I swatted my arm through the air. Trent caught my wrist, chuckling as he dropped it to push my feet aside and take a seat on the couch.

"I put a few hundred miles on your bike," I mumbled, still trying to wake up.

"Thought you would enjoy that." Trent loosened his tie and tossed it over the arm of the couch. Watching him take it off and undo the top buttons on his shirt stoked a warmth in my stomach.

Moving to my knees, I straddled his lap, running the tips of my thumbs over the rough stubble along his jawline. "Just so you know, I'm not giving it back."

"You thinking of adding grand theft to the record?"

"You gave me the keys, so technically—" I leaned my

head to the side, raising my eyebrows. Something pressed at my thigh, just above my right knee. I shifted to find his badge clipped to his belt and plucked it free.

"You're not going to get weird about that again, are you?" Trent asked, as I stared at the words Ashville Police under his engraved number. I laid it next to his tie and wrapped my arms around his neck.

"I guess if you're willing to put up with me, I'll get used to all the cop shit."

Epilogue

Brooke

TRENT STRETCHED ABOVE ME, stiffening as we both climaxed. Chests heaving, bodies slicked with sweat, we collapsed together. I hadn't realized he'd take up the gauntlet I'd thrown down at the resort when I'd told him I hated sex, but damn, it seemed to be his new mission in life.

"Your friends are going to be here soon," I said, still catching my breath. It was his birthday, mid-June, and apparently the perfect excuse for a huge barbecue. I figured as long as beer was involved, I could tolerate multiple cops for a while.

"They're grown, they can wait a few minutes if necessary." Trent kissed my shoulder and down my arm.

"You really are insatiable sometimes."

As soon as I sat up, he flipped me back onto the bed. "You still haven't told me what you might like to do for *your* birthday."

It was three weeks away, and I'd been avoiding it. I'd

told him I didn't want to celebrate it, or anything that reminded me of the club, Sawyer, or the life I lead, but he insisted this was part of my new start. "Can we just pretend it's like any other day?"

Trent pressed his forehead to mine. "I know you've been looking into changing your name."

That was a sore spot as well, I didn't want to share Sawyer's fucking last name anymore. Especially since learning he wasn't my father in any single way. Not even the sperm donor. *Thank goodness.* "Yeah, and the court won't let me do it as long as I'm on parole, unless you're thinking of some legal finagling."

Trent grinned. "There is one way around it."

My chest buzzed as I stared up at him.

"Marry me."

Huh? I shoved his shoulder back. I couldn't seriously consider that. "What makes you think I want to marry you?"

Trent leaned to his side, propping himself up on one elbow, and shrugging the other shoulder. "Who else do you *not hate?*"

I bit my lips, trying to hide my reaction. That had become our regular thing, his "I love you's" to my "I don't hate you's." No matter how many times I scoffed or rolled my eyes. "Are you serious?"

"Yes. Unless you don't like Brooke Davis."

Mrs. Detective Trent Davis. God, that's so weird. I snorted and rolled toward him, but he didn't laugh. *He is really friggin serious about this.*

The doorbell rang and I jumped up to get dressed, simply because it gave me an out for this argument. I couldn't say yes, but I didn't want to say no.

Trent caught me by the waist. "Not until I get an answer."

"I am not wearing a dress."

"Good, that means I can wear jeans." Brushing my hair aside, he kissed my neck.

Persistent and undeterrable as ever. The doorbell rang again, but he wasn't letting go.

"Why are you so intent on saving me?" I asked.

"Saving you?" He chuckled. "You hit that quota after two trips to the emergency room. I'm done saving you."

He mentioned neither the jail cell nor the complete psychological breakdown.

"I'm just intent on keeping you, so what do you say?"

Downstairs, I heard the front door open and people moving through the house. They'd given up on us and would probably start the barbecue anyway.

I sighed. "Sure."

"I ask you to marry me and get a 'sure?'"

I twisted in his arms, holding my finger up in front of his face. "You technically didn't *ask*. Didn't even drop to you knee."

"I've been on my knees for you plenty," he reminded me with a wry look. It usually involved some impressive tongue action, too. "And, if I had gotten on my knee to ask you, you might've kicked me in the balls, so I figured this was safer."

I had to hand it to him, he knew what he was getting into, but that didn't make him any wiser for plowing on ahead. "You're probably right about that, but now that I've agreed to your insane plot, can we get dressed and head downstairs before someone drinks all the beer?"

By the time we went downstairs his friends were already in the kitchen getting food prepared and helping themselves to the beer. Rose and James stood near the counter prepping burgers and cutting up toppings while Colt and Aubrey sat at the table entertaining three children, their toddler son, Aubrey's six-year-old niece, and James's five-year-old cousin.

I hung back in the doorway, while Trent greeted his friends and passed me a beer. While they chatted, the gravity of our previous conversation settled on my chest. A new name to go along with my new life. I thought my probation officer was going to have a stroke when I moved in with a detective, so I could only imagine his reaction to this.

I felt like I'd just pole-vaulted a hundred miles past my comfort zone, and yet, somehow the calm matched my anxiety stride for stride. The past was gone. The club was gone. My club. Everything I'd ever worked for or against. Most of the Devils would rot in jail until they were far too old to ruin anyone else's lives. Caine's cooperation meant he and Thea were free to get their daughter out of harm's way as well.

For years, I'd imagined my life would end with the Devils, one way or another. I'd accepted it because my situation had convinced me that revenge was the only thing worth fighting for. Then, Trent came along and ruined everything. That rotten jackass. He offered a different kind of revenge.

Maybe I could let the shadows pass.

Colt had survived the transition from crime to hanging out with cops so much that he'd asked Trent to be A.J.'s godfather. He had a family. Seemed perfectly happy. At least I wasn't the only former criminal in the room.

AFTER WE ATE, the kids laughed and played in the grass while everyone sat around chatting and drinking. I steeled myself and walked over to Trent while he was slightly alone, leaning against the porch railing while the others sat in a half circle of lawn chairs, oohing and ahhing over A.J. attempting to walk to Colt.

As I walked toward Trent and his eyes landed on me, his smile widened, and he held out his arm, cradling me by the shoulders beside him. He squeezed me tighter, resting his chin on the top of my head, and I wrapped my drink-free arm around him as well. Then, he kissed my cheek and moved his lips to my ear. "I'm sorry if I pushed you—"

"No," I whispered.

Taking me by the hand, he led me to the steps, where we took a seat, and I looped my arm through his, lying my head against his shoulder. "What if I can't ever say... you know."

I really hoped he could figure out what I referred to, saying as much as I did created an ache, reminding me of the sensation when I'd lost it in the bathroom of my apartment.

"I love you?" The wrinkles around his eyes deepened and his throat pulsed as he swallowed. "You haven't taken my bike and left or found any other opportunity to run off since I invited you here. I know that in itself has been hard as hail for you. I don't need you to say anything."

hell

He always rolled with it. My mood swings, the moments I just needed to be alone, and the times I needed him to just be around in silence. When I snapped at him, he laughed, and as soon as my anger wore off, I always realized how stupid it sounded in the first place. He didn't have to put up with any of that. My wounds weren't healing perfectly, they were ugly, sometimes ripping open for no apparent reason, but he never failed to tend them with patience.

I couldn't feel my fingers. I couldn't feel anything except the strange heat radiating from my chest. He was far more than I ever thought I deserved. "You going to tell your friends about your little plot?"

Trent glanced over at his yard full of people, then back to me. "Nah, I figure we'll wait until after and surprise the hell out of them."

I tried to hold back my laugh as I raised my beer to my lips. "I swear, you're a fucking masochist."

"But...." He leaned into me, pressing his lips to my temple. "You don't hate me."

More from Skye Callahan

The Redline Series

vinci-books.com/skyignition

My desires run darker, deeper. I hunger for raw, unadulterated pain – the kind that sears through flesh and soul.

Vanilla games of dominance, with their safe words and limits, leave me cold. I seek the real thing, the primal truth that lurks beneath our civilized veneer.

Turn the page for a preview…

Ignition: Chapter One

Aubrey

I WRUNG MY HANDS; they were clammy and cold despite the oppressing heat backstage. The music thumped through my body, embedding its rhythm deep into my bone marrow, until it felt like every cell thrummed and vibrated under the invisible assault. The resulting tension was the only thing keeping me upright.

Devlin sauntered up next to me, freshly pressed in his expensive black suit. His naturally tanned skin looked even darker in the dim lighting while his dark brown eyes bore through me as he handed me a mini-bottle of water. I took it with both shaking hands—afraid that with the state of my nerves I might drop it.

Everyone talks about the consequences of making stupid decisions—this wasn't one anyone had ever mentioned to me.

"You're up in fifteen," he said impassively, his warm hand stroking my jaw as I took a long swig of water. To all outward appearances, he was a walking oxymoron—hot and cold rolled into one. His touches perceived as caring, his voice as if he couldn't give two fucks. But there was no dualism about him. His intentions were refined and single-minded—every action was carefully concocted.

I ignored his touch as much as possible, but I'd learned long ago that trying to avoid his passes was futile.

"Try to look like you're enjoying yourself," he said.

Beyond his shoulder, I watched the other girls, gathered along the wall on the opposite side of the stage entrance. A clique that I didn't belong in and never wanted to. I was here for one thing, and then I was gone—utterly convinced that I was not and would not ever be anything like them. Their robes hung open, revealing their tiny and glittery stage costumes underneath. Most of them had already performed, and now they giggled—usually glancing side-ways at me and making crinkled expressions that looked less than amused at my presence.

As if I wanted to be here dressed in this gaudy costume that pinched my boobs, poked at my ribs, and chafed every-where it touched only to barely qualify as decent. I expected a boob to pop out before I even made it halfway across the stage, and I wouldn't be surprised at all if at least one nipple made a premature appearance—not that anyone would complain. To make matters worse, the whole ensemble was brought to a painful close by the tall stilettos that pinched my feet and left me as wobbly as a drunken teenager.

I still wore far more than I would be when I came back off stage after my eight-minute routine. That thought did little to calm my nerves. I wanted to be done with it all, and yet I dreaded the end more than anything. I may have a body appropriate for the stage—as Devlin assured me in his sugary sweet tone—but did I have the confidence, poise, or coordination? Not at all.

This would be my first night on stage, but it wasn't my first night waiting in the wings. The atmosphere was different, comparatively calm and quiet—as if all attention was focused on me, waiting for me to screw up, to break an ankle, or fall on my face. Devlin had given me a week to train with one of the more experienced girls. She refused to refer to me by anything except Sway because I could barely stay upright in the heels they gave me to practice in.

One week. A seven-day orientation into the pit of torture.

That wasn't long enough to master walking in stilettos, let alone to learn to "dance" in them.

And I don't mean wiggle your derriere and toss bits of your costume into the crowd kind of dancing. Half of the moves these girls performed, I would never be able to perfect in flat shoes with months of practice. If anything, I had to give them that.

All I had to do was get through that eight minutes. That was my only goal for the night. One dance at a time.

Pivot. Dip. Twist.

Don't break an ankle.

Smile. Tease.

Not too slow. Not too fast.

I barely remembered a damn thing from my routines.

I should've run, but the time for that had passed long ago—before I realized there was something I should be running from. I spent too long trying to hold my head high and prove I could do things my own way. And in essence, that's what I was still doing. I convinced myself that all I had to do now was put my serious face on, fulfill my end of the bargain, and get out.

I would pay my own dues—shitty as they were. But it wouldn't be that easy. I basically needed a bulldozer just to consider balancing my finances, especially once Devlin stampeded his way into every facet of my life.

I thought I could get ahead. Yet every time, the opportunity slipped away like the first snow spoiled by a warm spell, until I found myself owing more than I could imagine making in a year to a well-dressed, smooth-talking businessman.

A rat.

One with less than auspicious "business" interests and more connections than the mayor.

"Sway," Devlin patted my cheek, and I jumped back, balancing myself against the wall before my ankle rolled out from under me.

I was going to be his first dancer to walk out on stage and kill myself. Especially if my nerves didn't calm.

Hell, even if they did.

Imagine the bill he'd come up with then. Even in death, I'd never escape this man.

I can't do this. But I also couldn't let those words hit my mouth. I owed Devlin, and I'd seen what lengths he'd go to collect, or even worse, what he'd do to punish someone who tried to run. This was my out, and all I had to do was walk out on that stage and do as I was told.

He pressed against me, flattening his hands against the wall on either side of my head. "You remember what you have to do?"

The subtle smell of his expensive cologne and aftershave stung my nose, and his closeness made it hard to breathe or swallow. I had felt the same way the first time I'd seen him. Before I knew who he was and what he was capable of.

He seemed innocuous then. Overwhelming in his

wealth and power, but polite and reserved. I later learned that this was all a shell that he hid behind for the public eye. The real Devlin was far from reserved and only polite when it best served his interest.

I'd fallen hard for his quick glances, subtle smiles, and unerring attention. His gaze could make me quiver and lose sight of reality. Even when I knew it was too good to be true, he captivated me. Promised me things my imagination couldn't comprehend. And I wanted to play along just a little while to see what it was like, but before I knew it, he held my own life in his hands as blackmail.

"Don't screw it up and you have nothing to worry about." His voice was still like a purr that stirred in my stomach—except now that stirring was nausea inducing.

It was tempting to ignore the first part of his statement —to pretend his words were an attempt to be reassuring, not threatening. Then again, that fantasy world that my brain created to cope was probably how I let myself get in so deep in the first place. Positive thoughts, shooting for the stars, and rose-colored glasses only got you so far without a map and a safety net. Now, I was spiraling back down to earth with only one man to catch me—and he was only willing to do that because I was currently worth a lot of money to him.

The music died down, and the burning need to vomit rose in my throat, but I couldn't imagine how much being sick all over Devlin's suit would add to my time in torment.

I felt like I was swimming through time, the world around me distorting and rippling as Devlin stepped back, took the empty water bottle from my hands, and pushed me toward the stage.

The dancer exiting glowered at me as she yanked her robe off a hook and covered her mostly naked form. The chatters and cheers of the large—I assumed mostly male—crowd roared in my ears, overwhelming my senses.

I took a step toward the curtain, waiting for my cue, but I was jerked back.

My robe.

I loosened the sash and felt the material slide down my shoulders, leaving me cold and bare to the onslaught of the club air. An unseen hand pulled the fabric away—Devlin, I assumed. Here to either watch me make a fool of myself or to ensure that I was returning his "investment."

I twisted in my costume—attempting to cover as much of myself as I could—useless as it was.

The music kicked up again. My song. My cue.

I moved toward the curtains, but my movement disconnected from my mind somehow. Bright stage lights flashed and beyond that, I could barely make out the crowd—distant faces, waving hands. Too much movement to take in. Instinct took over, and I just hoped it would serve me well.

I sauntered to the front of the long stage at the mercy of the crowd's gaping mouths and hungry eyes. Whistles and catcalls filled the air under the steady stream of music as I concentrated on keeping my steps in time with the rhythm. My fingers connected with the cold metal of the pole, and I used it to center myself and find balance as I flipped forward, throwing my blonde hair over my face. I twisted and swayed, moving with the music while the club and the reality of the situation faded. I wasn't myself—I was simply a leaf caught on the wind of the melody, losing tiny parts of myself as that breeze yanked and pulled my fragile form.

As the music died, I picked up the last of the cash and made my way backstage. The ground beneath me continued to buck and sway as a new tune overtook the sounds of the rowdy crowd. I braced myself against the wall for an instant, but before I could slip on my robe, Devlin plucked the cash from my hands and shoved me toward his office.

"You call that a strip tease?" he said dryly as he counted the bills. "You know the deal can only work while your tits are still perky, right?" He copped a feel to illustrate his point.

Staring down at the cash, I dragged the robe up my arms and cinched the sash around my waist. It was never enough. It never could be.

"Unless you want me to finance a boob-job next." Devlin stared at my chest and frowned. "It couldn't hurt."

Despite the water, my throat was so dry I was certain it would crack open if I swallowed or spoke, so I shook my head, still feeling like the situation was surreal.

"Well, you're going to figure out how to do better than this." He jerked an apron off a wall and shoved it at me. "Go wait tables."

I hugged my robe around myself. Surely, he meant for me to change first since I was only wearing a tiny bra and G-string.

"Leave your robe in the dressing room."

"But the waitresses wear—"

He hooked his index finger under my chin, hauling me mercilessly forward with just a delicate touch. "They're *my* waitresses, I know what they wear." He smirked. "And you'll wear exactly what you have on—might be your only chance at tips."

He reached into the small fridge near his desk and tossed me another bottle of water. "Stay hydrated. You don't get sympathy points for passing out."

I chugged down the water—focusing on not crying since

I couldn't afford to spend another hour fixing my makeup. Not to mention the flack I'd get from Devlin and the girls.

My only salvation was that by the time I hit the floor, I was too worried about a hundred other things to think about what I was wearing. After all, I had hundreds of customers to avoid tripping over or falling into.

Within ten steps, a broad-shouldered man stopped in my path. He wore a short-sleeved V-neck that revealed muscular arms and a hint of chiseled chest that were from what I could tell covered in detailed tattoos. I raised my eyes as high as his shoulders where his slightly wavy brown hair ended, but shame and insecurity prohibited me from proceeding to his face.

"Excuse me," I began. "I have to—" Actually, I had no idea where I was supposed to begin.

He flicked up a fifty-dollar bill, holding it in front of my face. Excitement ran through me, followed by suspicion and dread. *What the hell would he expect me to do to earn that?*

"I caught your performance." His finger touched my chin, lifting my face, but I jerked back.

Rule number one, no touching—that was the rule, right? Maybe the first rule was no sex, but I was sure touching was in there somewhere. My brain seemed to be doing somersaults in my head as I searched for the answers.

He tilted his head, looking me over with his cool green eyes, then he took a large step to close in on me again, still holding the bill firmly within my reach. "Want this?"

I nodded reluctantly. I couldn't take my eyes off it, as if it were some mirage that would vanish at any moment.

"Take it," he said.

I half expected him to tackle me in the middle of the club or to do something equally threatening. This was too easy. He pulled it back a few inches, and desperation kicked in, so I grabbed it.

He smiled, his gaze raking across my naked skin and making me shiver.

"See that curtain," he said, pointing to a red curtain flanked by mirrors on the side wall. One of the private viewing rooms that lined the long stage. "Pick up two scotches, neat, and bring them into that room."

"Right away, sir." I expected him to ask for something ridiculous given the amount of money, but I wasn't going to argue.

He caught my wrist before I could rush away. "Don't call me sir."

I nodded and slipped away, my skin warmed against the air by sheer embarrassment alone. Walking out on stage and performing was a different beast to being on the same level as the gawking and handsy crowd.

Once I fought my way across the room, I stared at the bar for a moment. I wasn't a server—hadn't been trained as such, and I had no idea where to begin.

The bartender put up his hand and waved me to the empty end of the bar. Like most of Devlin's employees, he kept his hair cut almost to the scalp and wore a white dress shirt that hugged his intimidating, muscular build. "Ya got an order?"

"Uh, yeah. Two scotches, neat." Neat? I didn't even know what that meant. *Why would someone order a drink messy?*

He grunted and walked away while I fingered the stiff bill in my money pouch. The bartender sat the glasses down, but as soon as I reached for them, but he shook his head and waved my hands away with one swift downward motion.

Maybe I was supposed to pay first. I jerked back, and his

mouth flattened. He reached over the bar and pulled a serving tray from a cubby near me, then sat both glasses on napkins, placed them on the tray, and slid it to me.

Lovely. Added to the list of things I hated about this place—being schooled by a silent and grumpy bartender.

Brushing it off, I grabbed the tray and fought my way back through the crowd, feeling intentionally misplaced hands all over my body as I passed. Until finally, the red curtain was a welcome sight, offering a momentary respite from the sea of hot-bodied men.

I hoped he already had company based on the second drink, but when I pushed aside the fabric, he sat alone on a long plush couch. Sprawled back and enjoying the view through the one-way glass, he looked like he didn't have a care in the world.

I glanced around, paying particular attention to the dark corners of the room, suspicious that he had a friend or two lurking.

"Expecting a ghost?" he asked with a lilt of humor.

The question danced around in my brain before triggering an answer. I shook my head both to answer his question and in an attempt to shake away the murky fog that had settled over me.

"You're quiet." He waved me nearer, taking his time to watch and ogle before accepting the glass I offered. He sipped slowly, leaving me standing there awkwardly with the tray balanced on one hand and no tables to sit the second drink on. With the first glass finally empty, he sat back and rolled the glass between his fingers. His eyes never left me, moving up and down until my body felt heated as if I was standing next to a fire. Stinging ripples overtook my skin as it rose to goosebumps, leaving me helpless to the knowledge that he could also see my hardened nipples easily through my thin top.

"You want the second one, right?" I asked, hoping to hurry him along.

He lifted his eyebrows briefly. "I'll get around to it."

"I need to get to *work*." I shifted my weight to relieve the pain in my feet and to keep myself going. No one mentioned the post-dance adrenaline crash could be so intense.

"You are working." He leaned forward, putting his elbows on his thighs. His breath moved against my stomach and up between my breasts as he stared up at me and spoke again. "I believe what you mean is that you need to earn your share. Would you rather be standing there looking tasty or outside rubbing skin with the crowd while doing it?"

He had a fucking point there, but I wasn't fond of being described by a stranger as "tasty" and it didn't make standing under his accessing gaze any more desirable.

His hand grazed my side, and I stepped back. "No touching."

"I touch what I want." Grabbing the pocket on my apron, he pulled me closer and kept me there. "We can call in Devlin to set that straight."

Contest it, my brain shouted, but his expression was unchanging and calm, and all I needed was to piss off Devlin. *Again.*

"You're friends with him?" I asked.

"When it's convenient," he said with a slight scowl darkening his face. It quickly faded as his gaze settled on my face. "And you? How did you get involved with him? Tell me how he convinced you to work in his club."

"I needed the job."

"You needed the *money*—you suck at the job."

I tried not to take the sting of his insult too personally. I knew he was right, but hearing the truth from the mouth of a stranger was a blow to my tenuous grasp on self-confidence.

"You're not like the other girls." He reached to touch my hair, but I swatted his hand away.

"It's just first night jitters."

"Jitters." He made a sound in his throat. "Pick up that glass," he said gesturing to the second glass on my tray. I did as he said, but he didn't move to take it. He simply stared at it, so I instinctively followed his gaze, curious as to what was so interesting. The liquid sat there, steady in my outstretched hand with barely a ripple of movement that was more likely a result of the deep bass of the music rather than a shaky hand. We both stared in silence for a moment —and I wondered if he'd been testing me the whole time.

Why?

"You sure are steady for someone so *'jittery.'*" His hand shot out and grabbed the glass. The quick motion startled me for a second, but I didn't move from my spot. Then, he downed the liquid in one gulp and returned both glasses to the tray before lifting everything from my hand and setting it on the end of the couch.

I felt everything passing around me in a muted haze. Maybe jitters wasn't the right word, but it was something. Anxiety weighed down my senses and made it hard to think straight. I felt hands on my sides again, pulling me closer.

"Stop."

He raised his eyebrows but didn't listen, pulling my knees up so I straddled him on the couch.

Grab your copy...
vinci-books.com/skyignition

About the Author

Skye Callahan is a bestselling author who enjoys writing fiction to explore the darker aspects of human nature and the resiliency needed to survive and overcome difficult situations. She hopes to show that even through the darkest moments and overwhelming circumstances, one can find the inner strength to adapt and eventually heal.

Skye lives in the hills of Appalachia with her husband and their feline overlords: Sassy, Knight, Raith, Dresden, and Crowley, and enjoys hanging out in the yard with all the natural wildlife (except rattlesnakes). When she's not reading or writing, she might be found in the garden, watching horror movies, or playing video games with the hubs. Prior to pursuing writing full-time, Skye earned an M.A. in History and participated in numerous local history projects, including a full-length Civil War documentary for PBS.